'Riveting . . . a polyphonic drama of money and class'
Observer, 10 best debut novelists for 2025

'Deftly tackles dark subject matters'
Sunday Times

'Extraordinary. I think this will be one of the most admired and talked-about books this year'
Irish Times

'The success of *The Benefactors* is the way it treads across familiar fare – sexual assault, the rise of sites like OnlyFans and the associated judgements, the intersections of class and our innate hypocrisies – and tackles them in surprising ways'
Harper's Bazaar, 5 debut female authors to read in 2025

'A truly special author – so special that you want to keep her for yourself . . . with a voice that is crystal clear and a viewpoint that takes in the world's cruelties and joys, Erskine's talent shines in *The Benefactors*'
Irish Independent

'An excellent novel, all those voices so vivid and precise, appropriately startling at times and incredibly smart and timely on class and privilege'
David Nicholls, author of *You Are Here*

'An astonishing novel from a writer at the height of her powers. There's not a sentence I don't believe, or a character I don't feel something for . . . Wendy Erskine is a true artist'
Michael Magee, author of *Close to Home*

'I miss it already. Even when they were being horrible bastards the characters were stirring my heart . . . she's an incredible writer. All these voices so true and so loud in my ear. What a beautiful, hilarious blast of brilliance'
Donal Ryan, author of *Heart, Be at Peace*

'A joy to read sentences like these from a writer as talented as this'
Sinéad Gleeson, author of *Hagstone*

'A truly remarkable novel – *The Benefactors* is both intimate and panoramic, full of clear-eyed compassion and wry wit'
Colin Walsh, author of *Kala*

'You are totally transported into these characters' lives. They are living people and I missed them when I finished'
Sheena Patel, author of *I'm a Fan*

'Wendy Erskine's writing is inimitable – so fresh, so sharp, so wry, so alive; so much contemporary fiction feels flat and fake in comparison'
Lucy Caldwell, author of *These Days*

'We're all better off for being able to read a novel as rich as this'
Jon McGregor, author of *Reservoir 13*

'Wendy Erskine is one of the best writers working in Ireland right now and *The Benefactors* is all her own, astute and full of feeling'
Nicole Flattery, author of *Nothing Special*

'What a voice. What assurance and execution. Wendy Erskine writes like nobody else. *The Benefactors* is a masterful, memorable, electric novel that conveys a community of people and all their dramas pitch-perfectly, seemingly without manipulation, because the craft is deft and the feeling is real as all hell'
Caoilinn Hughes, author of *The Alternatives*

'A profound and memorable novel. Its acuity is matched by the brilliance of its prose'
Adrian Duncan, author of *The Gorgeous Inertia of the Earth*

'*The Benefactors* is an essential novel, and Wendy Erskine an essential novelist. It is an inspired testament to survival – I was incredibly moved by it'
Peter Scalpello, author of *Limbic*

'Even in their darkest moments, Erskine never lets go of her characters, never lets them be anything but alive on the page. I won't soon recover, and don't really want to, from the clarity and cold power of this book'
Ben Pester, author of *Am I in the Right Place?*

'Books are made of words. And sentences. Of stories and sounds and of voices. *The Benefactors* is further proof that Erskine is a true master of all the above'
Keiran Goddard, author of *I See Buildings Fall Like Lightning*

'*The Benefactors* is a novel of trauma that speaks from all of its perspectives simultaneously. In its lack of judgement, and in the redemptive joy and sadness of its telling, it is a profound work of art'
David Keenan, author of *This Is Memorial Device*

Wendy Erskine is the author of two short story collections, *Sweet Home* and *Dance Move*. She was shortlisted for the Edge Hill Prize and the Republic of Consciousness Prize, longlisted for the Gordon Burn Prize and the *Sunday Times* Audible Short Story Award, and she received the Butler Literary Award and the Edge Hill Readers' Choice Award. She edited the art anthology *well I just kind of like it*. A Fellow of the Royal Society of Literature, she is a frequent broadcaster and interviewer, and works as a secondary school teacher in Belfast. *The Benefactors* is her debut novel.

THE BENEFACTORS

Wendy Erskine

Sceptre

First published in Great Britain in 2025 by Sceptre
An imprint of Hodder & Stoughton Limited
An Hachette UK company

1

The authorised representative in the EEA is Hachette Ireland, 8 Castlecourt Centre, Dublin 15, D15 XTP3, Ireland (email: info@hbgi.ie)

Copyright © Wendy Erskine 2025

The right of Wendy Erskine to be identified as the Author of the Work has been asserted by her in accordance with the Copyright, Designs and Patents Act 1988.

All rights reserved. No part of this publication may be reproduced, stored in a retrieval system, or transmitted, in any form or by any means without the prior written permission of the publisher, nor be otherwise circulated in any form of binding or cover other than that in which it is published and without a similar condition being imposed on the subsequent purchaser.

All characters in this publication are fictitious and any resemblance to real persons, living or dead, is purely coincidental.

A CIP catalogue record for this title is available from the British Library

Hardback ISBN 9781399741668
Trade Paperback ISBN 9781399741675
ebook ISBN 9781399741682

Typeset in Sabon MT by Hewer Text UK Ltd, Edinburgh
Printed and bound in Great Britain by Clays Ltd, Elcograf S.p.A.

Hodder & Stoughton policy is to use papers that are natural, renewable and recyclable products and made from wood grown in sustainable forests. The logging and manufacturing processes are expected to conform to the environmental regulations of the country of origin.

Hodder & Stoughton Limited
Carmelite House
50 Victoria Embankment
London EC4Y 0DZ

www.sceptrebooks.co.uk

For Rosemary Erskine and Matilda Reid

I don't know if you think this is really weird but when there's something on the news or Belfast Live or, say, I just hear talk about stuff that's gone down – a murder or an attack or a fight – I always *immediately* look up online the people involved. I suppose it's to see if we have any mutuals, but it's also to find out what they look like. It makes me feel more involved with it all, if I can picture it, picture *them*. Like, say some random guy's got stabbed in the town, you're just, oh, some random guy's got stabbed in the town. But then, if you've got five mutuals, and if you see the pics of him with his wee baby girl at the park, the little cutie giving him a kiss, you are like, oh my god that is so, so tragic. She's going to grow up without her daddy. When I heard them talking the other week in the shop, about that girl Misty and those three rich guys, to be fair I didn't know what to think, I mean, Bennyz and all that, but when I checked her out online she was nowhere near as slutty looking as I thought she'd be. Like, nowhere fucking near. She actually looked friendly and somebody that wouldn't be a real bitch, so that made me think that there was no way she could be lying or have wanted that to happen. A while ago there was this seventeen-year-old guy who was killed by the cops. They were chasing him because he was in a stolen car. I looked him up. His name was Senan. We had only one mutual, a girl I hardly know, but he liked loads of the same films as me, and the same stuff on TV. We even liked the exact same restaurant in the town. I watched all the YouTube clips he'd shared and I could see we had the total identical sense of humour. We would've got on brilliant, if we'd known each other. In fact, I really regret that we never met. And I'm so sorry that he died. He wasn't a bad boy. We could've been good. But yeah, Misty looked friendly. Those were not good guys.

The weeping cherry is, to my mind, the most elegant tree. Its double blossoms are magnificent, the masses of deep pink flowers concealing branches which, come winter, possess a bare and spectral beauty. There is one in the neighbouring front garden. Sad to say, in that house some boys are meant to have taken advantage of a young girl. But a tree of such grace, the weeping cherry.

Frankie drives to the gym, already having done fifty lengths in the warm gloom of her own pool. Early summer, but the sky is still charcoal. Frankie doesn't acknowledge the young man in reception who quickly hides the energy drink he's just opened. When his cheery good morning goes unanswered, he sets to polishing the marble panel behind him. Mrs Levine never usually says hello anyway.

The beautiful Levine home could be described as 'California Modern' even though the location is Ladyhill, six miles outside Belfast. Its clean lines and huge windows differentiate it from the other big houses, with their turrets and crow-stepped gables, their Scottish baronial style. Twenty years ago, Neil Levine saw the plans for this place and he snapped it up. The Levine house has ample room for its own gym, but Frankie prefers to come here. Her hair's still damp when she starts her rotation of the weights machines. She chews gum as she pushes on the leg press, her knees now almost level with her cheekbones, her movements smooth and fluid, black Lycra tight on firm skin. A personal trainer and his client, a man in his seventies who made his money in pharmaceuticals, silently watch Frankie as she does her pull-ups on the bar. The old man shakes his head. Wow. She moves to the free weights.

Afterwards, Frankie showers in the changing rooms. She has a personal locker, number 7, the same as her room at Jackie Boyce Residence. Of course she was going to choose number 7. It's always there, in her codes, in her pin numbers. Each changing cubicle has a stack of fluffy white towels, a little lamp and a wooden seat. Frankie sits there for a minute, her eyes closed, before she starts to apply the body cream to her legs and stomach, her breasts. She still hasn't quite got used to the new weight of them; it still surprises her when she leans forward a certain way. But the surgeon had been pleased and she is too. She scoops one and then the other into the satin of her bra. Frankie looks at the little metal fitting on the door. It's always the same in communal changing rooms, communal toilets, communal living, wherever you are.

The Levine place is on a private road, pocked with potholes; a rapid, late brake will send up a fountain of loose gravel. The residents could afford to resurface the road every season but they choose not to bother. It adds a certain colour and insouciance. This fucking road! they like to say, shaking their heads. This fucking road! It kills me!

Neil has already left when Frankie returns, his coffee cup and plate on the kitchen table. He's gone to the States on business: Santa Clara and then San Francisco. Babes, Frankie had said, when he told her about the trip. She'd been eating a banana. She'd set it down and tried to look a little plaintive. Neil wasn't sure how long he'd be away: if the initial meeting was positive, then he might be there a week. If not, he'd be back more quickly. Neil didn't really need to work or go anywhere but he was keen to remain investment- and project-focused. It's just the way I am, he said. There's no dopamine hit turning over a steak on a barbecue. That said, it made no difference to anything whether these ventures were flops or successes. His early '90s innovation in compression software had seen to that. Babes, Frankie said. I'll miss you.

Chris isn't awake yet; he doesn't need to be at his job in the hotel restaurant until the evening. He was out late last night: Frankie heard him come in at about two in the morning. Nina is still asleep too.

Frankie has a dressing room, zoned into categories. The specially crafted wooden racks store the stiletto heels that Neil likes her to wear, and her trainers, her running shoes. Boots – ankle, calf, thigh – are in another section. Frankie doesn't adore clothes in the way some people seem to, as though they're a type of art. Expensive or cheap, they all get sweaty and dirty. They end up in a pile on the floor. But she likes the ordering and unboxing, the glances of envy when she's wearing something that others couldn't possibly ever get or afford. Fuck them.

Mostly she buys what she wants online. Occasionally she goes with Neil; he loves to sit and watch her come out from the changing room. Oh babes. She thought he'd grow tired of that, but it hasn't happened. The first year after she'd moved to Ladyhill and become Mrs Frankie Levine she went back home to London, to a shop where she'd actually worked for a few months before she got into the private airline. No one in the shop knew her or could remember her, apart from this one girl called Celia. Frankie looked with disdain at everything on the rails then purchased one small item, a wisp of a one-shouldered top. It was, proportionate to size, probably the single most expensive thing there. As Celia folded it, in awed respect for its preciousness, Frankie drummed her fingers on the counter. She stared hard at Celia's gel manicure, starting to peel on two fingers.

On the clean pavement outside, Frankie said under her breath, cocksuckers cocksuckers cocksuckers cocksuckers, as she passed the man and woman getting out of their chauffeured car, that woman in the hijab and her husband, going into the flagship store where the new season window was bondage luxe. That trip she also went back to see her old primary school. There were a few wizened sunflowers in the playground where they'd tried to cheer the place up. She remembered her coat hook in the hallway with a picture of a snail above it, and the words Brittany Hendricks. She never knew who Brittany Hendricks was. And Frankie never wore that flimsy top. She shoved it in the bin in the hotel bathroom and then went down to the bar and had a half-bottle of champagne. That Celia, she'd never been one of the worst anyway. Pity one of the bosses hadn't been about.

Later, at ten, Frankie takes Nina to her tennis lesson. She's had one every Saturday for the last month, and there's the same group of girls on the adjacent court having a communal session while Nina has her individual one. The coach is a smiling, rangy guy who says 'beautiful play' a lot, even though it's not. Every time Nina misses a shot, which is frequently, she dissolves into giggles and looks over to the other court to see if any of the others are looking. But they never are. Frankie sees them twirling their racquets around and around, giving each other dainty pushes when their coach's back is turned. Although it's bright, it's chilly. The girls shiver and perform little dance steps to keep warm. Nina looks like a child compared to them.

As usual, when the lesson is over, they go to a café.

'You should pay more attention,' Frankie says. 'If you want to get any better.'

'But I don't want to get any better.'

'Well, if you don't want to get any better, then fine. Continue to pay no attention.'

'See that girl over there with the red hoodie? That's Megan Pearce.'

'Oh yeah, who's she?'

'Megan Pearce. I told you the other day. She called me a boring bitch.'

'OK,' Frankie says. 'Ignore it.'

'Well actually, listen to this, Frankie. If being a bitch means . . . if being a bitch means that I am setting healthy boundaries with toxic people, then I am so glad I am a bitch!'

She looks at Frankie expectantly.

'That's not what she said. She said you were a *boring bitch*.'

'You're meant to be on my side.' Nina's eyes go glassy. 'You are meant to be on my side.'

'But I am,' Frankie says. 'I was just pointing out what she actually said.'

Frankie hadn't always been sure of the kids. When she met them, Chris was thirteen and Nina eight. They had lost their mother only a few months previously. Neil brought them over to London and they stayed in a beautiful place in Richmond, with a river view. It belonged to a friend of his. They all played snakes and ladders on the floor: those kids, their dad and the woman with whom he'd been having an affair while their mother was in the hospice. Whenever Frankie landed on a ladder, she miscounted and moved to the next square. That was being like a parent, yeah? That's the kind of thing you did? Later, Neil took Chris to Stamford Bridge and Nina went with Frankie to Hamleys. She held the kid's hand. It felt so easily crushed, the bones like jelly.

When Frankie was her age, she had one more year before ending up in Steinex House, and then Armfield, and then

Jackie Boyce Residence. It was too far away to travel to the secondary school from Armfield. She had to go to a different one but they never did manage to get her the right uniform. Her shoes were fabric pumps! Skinny back then and her hair was red, her face a mass of freckles. A scribble of a person. A couple of people in Armfield were fine, but others not so. The ones in charge, big Mal and the other one, made two of the boys fight in the rec room, taking bets on who would win.

But Jackie Boyce Residence. Good old Jackie Boyce. Jackie Boyce before she died had laid down a lot of rules about how she wanted kids to be treated. Dignity, privacy, community, and so on and so on and so on, so you got your own room and even your own key to the front door. When Frankie saw her new room, the walls were covered in yellow Sellotape from the girl who had been there before. When she lay on the bed she saw that the girl had carved a heart into the wall with a knife. Later on, Frankie got a knife from the kitchen and put an arrow through it.

Michelle was across the corridor. Even now, in the café, Frankie gives a brief smile, thinking of that room of hers, which smelled beautiful. Michelle had perfume bottles lined up along the windowsill. She saw Frankie looking at them and said, 'Don't even think about touching any of my stuff, you hear?'

'I don't want to touch your stuff. But know what, it's not a crime to look.'

'Did I even say you could look? I didn't. I didn't even say you could look.'

'Then why do you have the door of your room open if you don't want people to see anything?'

'Because I feel like it. Anyway, what's it to you, fucker?'

'Nothing. But I looked in because you had your door open. *Fucker.*'

As Frankie went to go, Michelle said, 'You can try one of the perfumes if you want but not the one on the end because that's special. Also, the Thierry Mugler's Angel's empty. It's just there for display.'

Michelle lit a cigarette and stood up to lean out of the window. 'Thierry Mugler's Angel smells of things rotting in bins, like them bins I can see. Right. Down. There. Some of them perfumes are worth a fortune and you can't just get them in any old shop, you know.'

Michelle moved away from the window. 'Well sit down,' she said. 'Don't just stand there like a sad sack. Jesus. You're putting me on fucking edge just hanging around like that.' She patted a spot on the bed.

'So you're the new arrival we heard about called Frances,' Michelle said.

'Frankie.'

'Well, Frankie, please let me tell you something. Please let me tell you that I do not want to know your back story. I do not want to know it at all, so please don't fucking bore me with it.'

'What you mean?'

'What I mean is that I don't want to know your back story. I don't want to know how you ended up here or who couldn't look after you or your bruises or the time you were left in the cold all night. Everything that you have ever said or done up to this point, this point right now! Right now!' She pointed with one of the bottles. 'That's back story! See the moment you walked in? Gone. This moment right now? Gone. Whoosh – away – that's it, that's all done sad sack sad day and I am not interested in back story sobstory gobstory. I do not give a fuck about it, so please' – and she puffed herself with one of her bottles – 'so please don't bother me with it. Just don't bother.'

So no need to say anything about her mum's arms, or how sleep looked like death, how death looked like sleep.

'That look you got,' Michelle said, 'Like, what are you aiming for, with that look?'

'I ain't got a look.'

'Course you do. It's impossible to not have a look, even if that look is shit.'

'Well,' said Frankie, tucking her hair behind her ear, 'maybe you could help give me a better look then.'

'Oh yeah? You think so? You think I don't have better things to do with my time?'

'Where did you get all them perfumes?' Frankie said.

'Where you think?'

'I don't know, do I? If I knew I wouldn't be asking.'

Michelle laughed. 'Well, let me show you this. I got this yesterday.' She brought out of the wardrobe a bag with elegant writing on a pink background. She tipped something out onto the bed.

'What is it?' Frankie asked.

'It's a basque with attached shorts,' said Michelle. 'A guy I've been seeing bought me that. People have bought me other stuff. This basque with attached shorts, it's not my favourite thing I have, but I still like it. I mean, it's pretty nice. Alright, let's see what we are going to do with you, Miss Frankie Frank Franks. Come over here so I can look at your face. Come over here close!'

Frankie knows that even in this café eyes slide over her, approvingly, disapprovingly, looking for the gift of a rounded stomach or the insinuation of veins on a calf. They'll not find them. When she first arrived in Ladyhill, it wasn't always pleasant. For sure, she could have apologetically sloped around, in baggy clothes and no make-up, hair scraped back in a ponytail. But no, she returned the stares, insolent, naked under leather. When she and Neil went out for dinner, she would arch her back as she gazed at the menu, wind a strand of hair around her finger as she looked at the wine list. She would reach across the table to kiss him and he was in a constant state of excitement. That woman, a tank in a blue dress, approached Frankie in the restaurant toilets one time. Frankie was doing her make-up at the mirror and saw the bulky reflection. The woman's voice trembled a little as she spoke. 'I'd just like you to know that I find you and your behaviour absolutely reprehensible.'

'Yeah?' said Frankie as she got her perfume from her bag.

'I do,' she replied. 'Barbara was a very great friend of mine.'

Frankie sprayed her left wrist, her right wrist, rubbed them together and then left the bathroom.

'What shall we drink?' Neil said, when she returned.

'Something special,' Frankie replied.

The way Michelle made her over, Frankie hardly recognised herself. She kept looking at her legs in the heels that she had given her to wear.

'Keep your face fresh looking!' Michelle said. 'Because that is your thing. That's your look. I know about these things. You look really young and fresh, like one of those little gymnasts. Romanians or something. Russians. Doing the splits. But not too young though, because we need you to get in!'

'I can do the splits,' Frankie said.

'Well, I bet you can and aren't the guys just going to love you, Frankie Franks.'

That evening they went to a club, Frankie's first time somewhere like that.

The taxi there was pre-paid and the driver, a West Ham supporter, talked to Michelle the whole time about football. When they got out, they were joined by Amrita and Coggy. Coggy's voice was low and clear, like she should have been on the news, telling people about an earthquake somewhere, or a massacre. That old Coggy style, a man's suit jacket with nothing on underneath. There was a huge queue. Michelle gave the bouncer a playful punch on the arm. 'Alright, Clem, you beaten anyone up this week? Only kidding!' and she blew him a kiss.

'What age is this one?' he said, pointing at Frankie.

'Why, do you fancy her?' Michelle asked, laughing.

He held up his left hand with its gold ring. 'No, I don't think so,' he said. 'Alright, girls, in you go.'

The drinks in the place were nice, easy to sip, free. 'Don't go fucking overboard, you hear me?' Michelle said. 'Because I am not carting you back if you get sick.'

Frankie sat for a while, watching Coggy's slow dancing. Then she moved to the toilets, jumped up to sit on the bank of sinks, her back against the mirror, as the people went in and out. Two women talked about a man who was meant to come next week, or was it the week after? They couldn't decide. Complicated life he has, one of them said and the other nodded. Complicated life. The strip lighting made their faces pinched and white, but later, on the dance floor, weren't they beautiful with those cheekbones? The owner, a guy called Tosh, arrived and he ordered them all champagne. He sat up on a high bar stool with his hand resting on Amrita's thigh, his spread fingers dimpling her flesh. At the end of the night, they found a café, miraculously open, and had mugs of tea, the chips shared between them in the middle of the table.

'Tired?' Coggy said to Frankie. 'You'll be in bed soon, little sweetheart.' And she pulled her over, so that Frankie's head rested on her shoulder.

Michelle was rubbing her arm where she said someone had elbowed her on the dance floor. 'I don't know about that place,' she declared. 'We should be going somewhere with more class.'

'Is Tosh Amrita's boyfriend?' Frankie had asked as they tiptoed up the stairs of Jackie Boyce Residence.

Michelle laughed. 'Yeah. On a Tuesday.'

Good times. Good times. Oh yeah. A couple of nights a week and free entry, free drink and, later, free drugs. Michelle took Frankie to a friend who cut her hair into a pixie crop and bleached it blonde. School, never a priority, retreated into dim insignificance. On one of the last days a teacher, dopey cow, gave out a worksheet and it said on the front, The Future is Yours, with the Yours in massive letters. That seemed strange because it wasn't just hers: it was everyone's. The worksheet then asked her to list her strengths and how she was going to maximise these aspects of herself.

Frankie asked Michelle about it. What were her strengths and how was she maximising them?

'Well,' Michelle said, 'anybody asked about their strengths needs to think, have I got good tits, a good ass or good legs?'

'That's not what it means.'

'So if you know what it means then why are you asking me? Maximise yourself now by getting me a Coke from the fridge. If anyone has touched my Cokes I am going to kill them.'

Over time they moved to different parties. Five-star hotels along the same drag, penthouse suites, houses in the country. On one occasion, in a massive function room in a hotel in Park Lane, a crowd of guys arrived from some country, she couldn't remember the name of it. There was a man in a shirt and tie and glasses, like a little professor, and he came into the room where they all were, them and some other girls, and said, 'Is everyone happy with anal?' She and Michelle looked at each other and burst out laughing. They said it, like a catchphrase, on many later occasions. Having a cup of tea in the morning, taking a seat on a bus. Is everyone happy with anal? One of those non-disclosure parties was the most boring she had ever been at, full of politicians. She was wearing an expensive dress that night, with a flippy little cream skirt, but when she looked down at her nails she could see a crescent of black dirt where the white met the pink. They hardly ever went to a café afterwards.

Nina can't eat all of the pancakes and decorative berries. She dips the little branch of redcurrants in the icing sugar that was dusted everywhere, makes white prints on the black plate. 'I just don't really see the point of tennis,' she says.

'Winning,' Frankie says.

'Yeah, but I don't really see the point of winning.'

'Be a loser then.'

'Not everything's winners and losers,' says Nina. 'It's taking part that counts.'

'In a game you don't see the point of.' Frankie blows a bubble with her chewing gum and bursts it with a little smack. 'OK, let's go.'

At the counter, Megan Pearce's mother is also waiting to pay. Her face is friendly and flushed. She says hello with a nod of recognition. But Frankie looks at the girl behind the counter who has just asked who's next.

'Oh, you go first,' Megan Pearce's mother says to Frankie, even though it's clear that she herself has been waiting longer. Frankie points to where they were sitting and then she pays. As they leave, Nina turns around to see Megan Pearce and her mum getting their receipt.

When they get back to the house, Chris is in the kitchen.

'Oh, look who it is,' Nina says. 'Chris Piss.'

He ignores her and gets a two-litre bottle of milk from the fridge, starts drinking from it.

'You should put that in a glass,' Nina says.

'Put what in a glass?' And he drinks again.

'The milk.'

'Well, I'm finished with it now.'

And he puts the bottle back in the fridge.

Mate, let me tell you, I got to the stage of life where, if it's not about love to some degree, then I don't want to know. I just don't. Bands, films, TV, what have you, I'm done with people shouting about disaffection or alienation or exploitation or angst or whatever. I don't want to fucking hear about it anymore. That's not to say I'm looking for some Hollywood feelgood bullshit. I'm talking something harder. Love.

Summer, so Boogie gets behind the wheel of the taxi early. He usually comes back on Saturdays to make Gen and Misty a bit of breakfast. He's never enjoyed driving, per se. Means to an end. Some of the drivers reminisce about the wonderful day they got a fare to West Cork, a round trip of over sixteen hours. Fuck that. Horrible prospect. Plus, he hates the countryside, fields. They make him nervous. Boogie's going to bring the girls their breakfast in bed on their trays: Gen's has hot air balloons and Misty's looks like denim.

Car's like a confessional, so he hears a lot. They don't see his face other than maybe a curve of cheek. He passes no judgement. You kidding? If someone wants to tell him about how he is picking them up from the house of the guy they are illicitly banging, then so what? It's all the same to him. Pay your money, cheerio, close the door. Secret trysts, feuds, the trips down memory lane of murderers, up to them. The only thing he doesn't like are a couple of addresses where people go to get what they need while he waits outside, or when he has to deliver a package from one of those addresses to somewhere else. That said, it's a fare like any other. He's not doing anything wrong, personally.

But yeah, there's been all sorts. One time, late in a dirty old day, this guy, seventies, got in from one of those droopy old men's pubs. Said nothing the whole journey, not a word, and when he was being taken up O'Neill Road between the two big graveyards, fella started getting twitchy, looking to one side and then to the other. Lot of people dead and gone, Boogie said, trying to make conversation. Grim Reaper comes to us all. But the man was silent. They were turning into his road, funny little spot on the side of the hill, when the man said, you know what he was a bit of a mouth and so no one really liked him but in his locker there was the lunch he never got to eat, a tangerine, a bap and biscuits wrapped in cling film. Sat there, just sat there for months after he'd gone, tangerine all shrunk and the bread green. The man couldn't stand it any longer, so he took the stuff and threw it in the river that ran along the back of the factory. He had been the one to leave the gate unlocked, like they told him, so the guy could be killed. I was the one who let them in, he said again, as he handed over his money. Long time ago now, mate, Boogie murmured. Long time ago now.

True to say there's been a lot of funny things as well. One particular guy, and it is no word of a lie, actually got his dick out and was preparing to have a wank. I mean, come on! Jeez, is that not a step too far? He said, and his voice was polite, very civilised, and his tone extremely reasonable, he said, do you mind at all if I just work away here? And Boogie said, well actually, pal, I do fucking mind. I very much mind. And so he had stopped the car there and then and asked the man to get out, which of course he did in a perfectly co-operative manner. The man said sorry as he zipped up his trousers on that bleak stretch of car showrooms.

That's the world in which kids have to exist. Disturbing sometimes to think about it. Although, of course, teenagers can be frightening too. All the kids in the back and their friend's head tipped back, mouth lolled open. Wooahh!

Check her out! She's gone! Nadia! Nadia! That drug they are always taking nowadays. Should I be driving to the hospital? Boogie asked. And he makes a turn in the direction of the Royal, but the next thing it is Nadia asking what time it is. No, mate, she's grand but can you stop at the shop there because I need something? Will only be a minute.

Sometimes though nothing's said at all and there's a sadness, nothing made explicit but it's there, a crazy ass melancholy that stays when they get out which means that sometimes, even in the rain, he needs to open a window to let it disappear.

His fares might comment on the photos that hang from the rear-view mirror, alongside the air fresheners in the shape of jellybeans, trees and boxing gloves. It's the two girls in red pyjamas, Christmas time, beaming. Those your kids? they'll say. Sometimes, if the person who is asking has a paedo vibe for some reason, he'll just give a curt yup. Other occasions, he might be more expansive. Yup, my two, drive me demented.

Boogie never planned on having them. What a surprise when they appeared that afternoon all that time ago. He'd been lying in bed after a night at Marko McFerran's. McFerran's flat had art on the walls from his travels. He'd been talking that evening about this kick-boxing championship he'd been to in Bangkok and how a guy's face basically just split, clean split, and Marko McFerran said that at that moment he had a moment of realisation that we are just bags of muscle, bone and blood, that our skin is just an envelope. We're just envelopes. Boogie was lying in bed, staring at the ceiling, thinking about us all being bags for meat to be held in when Jay started shouting for him to get up. Jay was banging on the door. 'Boogie, there's people here!'

A kid was sitting on the sofa and blocking the TV there was a buggy and a baby. Misty and Geneva.

'Some woman,' Jay said, 'came in, left them, fucked off.'

'It was our mummy,' Misty said.

'Did this mummy of yours say when she was coming back?'

'Look what I can do!' Misty said, arching back into a crab's bend before kicking her legs and standing on her feet again.

'Misty, that's very good. But did your mummy say when she was coming back?'

The baby, Geneva, watched him with big, serious eyes. Misty looked kind of chipped. He hadn't seen her in over two years. Her fringe was cut all wonky and although half of her baby teeth were missing the big ones hadn't come through yet. When she grinned, it was like a Hallowe'en pumpkin. She saw him looking at the scratches on her legs.

'There's this big house, see, and they close the way we used to get into it, the easy way, because that way you just climbed over the gate but now we've got to go in this other way through the bushes and all of these big brambles and that's where I got sliced.'

The baby continued to stare at him.

'What there is in this old house,' Misty said, 'is that there's all of these old cups and saucers and sometimes, do you know what we do, we smash them against the wall, throw them real hard and then we try to put them back together like jigsaws.' She danced a little jig. 'Like jigsaws,' she said.

'Well, don't be smashing that now, Misty,' said Boogie, pointing at a mug on the floor with its inch of cold tea. 'No smashing allowed. I'm going to see if I can get in contact with your mummy and see what's happening.'

He looked again at the baby in the buggy. He had seen pictures of it online but it was older now. He had zoomed in on one of the newborn ones, made it fill the whole screen to see if he felt something like recognition or pride, if not love. But there was nothing because it looked like every other baby he'd ever seen, plus they'd put it in an Arsenal top and he was a Spurs supporter. He wondered if Leigh had done this deliberately, to annoy him, but he reckoned not and that her new guy probably just supported Arsenal. He read once how you might think that there are all of these Machiavellis running around, strategising, plotting, putting babies in Arsenal tops, but in reality most people are stupid and do stuff without too much consideration or forethought. He still thinks that today. Read too deeply into individuals' actions and you end up crediting them with too much intelligence. Way too much intelligence.

Boogie met Leigh in Glasgow. He was over with a crowd of lads, eighteen years old, and she was with her cousin who lived there. They didn't even wait until they got back to one of the hotels. They did it around the back of a Malaysian restaurant and that seemed just so brilliant, so unusual. There wasn't a single Malaysian restaurant in Northern Ireland. He knew because he checked. She was twelve years older than him. It was wonderful for about two weeks. She had this little saying that if you couldn't accept her at her worst then you didn't deserve her at her best.

'I get ya,' Boogie said one time. 'Who was it said that first? Was it Marilyn Monroe?'

'I did,' said Leigh. 'I came up with it.'

'No you didn't. Somebody else did. It's been about for years.'

'You're denying how I feel and you are making light of it.'

'No I'm not, what you on about? I'm saying that every second bird out there who can be a bit of pain at times has got that on their timeline or status update.'

'You're not taking my mental health seriously.'

'Who the fuck mentioned mental health?'

'Exactly. That's exactly my point.'

'Then you should go to the doctor. Get tablets.'

'I been taking the tablets since I was twelve years of age,' she said.

When the kids joke about Boogie getting a girlfriend, he says that maybe one of these days he might just surprise them. But he doesn't have the time. Plus, he doesn't want the disruption. His own mother had a procession of guys. After one leaving, there would be a little paradise for a few months of the two of them watching the TV together, folding the washing together. And then, new arrival, coming down in the morning in greasy boxers, scratching his balls, leaning against the back door for a smoke. Be nice! his mum would say. It's not difficult! Well yeah, it actually fucking was. He ended up moving out and living with Nan D, his dead dad's mother when he was fourteen. Jeez, he was a terrible one back then for the five-finger discount, but not stuff for himself all of the time, he got things for Nan D as well, stuff she liked – bottles of perfume. His mother got married again when Boogie was eighteen and moved to Warrington with her new husband. He goes to visit them at Easter every year. Nan D looks after the kids and he comes back with the same two Easter eggs. He would be very disappointed now if either of the girls shoplifted.

I love you baby I love you more than anyone ever I would kill anyone who ever did anything bad to you. I would die for you. If you left me I would kill myself. This was Leigh. There was always a lot of talk about killing which, depending on how you looked at it, could be sexy and intense, or else very depressing. After they slept together, she would cry: loud, shuddering sobs. In a way it was like living life at full velocity, big time, like moments in movies where they play opera. But then he would look around at the wet clothes drying over radiators and think, well, not really. And there was always the kid in the other room, Leigh's seven-year-old, Misty. Leigh locked her door sometimes and Misty would be banging on it.

'Never worry, she's got lots of stimulation in there,' Leigh said. 'The room is chocka with toys. She's fine.'

When Leigh said she was pregnant, he was neither pleased nor horrified, although Nan D was appalled. 'In the name of god, what were you doing? You fucking fool. You fucking dope. You are going to be tied to that shambles for the next eighteen years. That's if it's even your baby and I wouldn't be convinced at all that it is.'

Nan D had not thought much of Leigh on the occasion when he brought her to her house.

'What you got to remember,' Boogie said afterwards, 'is that a lot has happened to her in her life.'

'Nobody gets a bye-ball on acting like a cunt because they have had a lot happening to them in their life,' said Nan D. 'That's the point of life. That a lot happens.'

'You're harsh,' said Boogie.

Nan D took a sip of her tea.

'Not really,' she said.

They split up when she was four months pregnant. She said she was moving to Glasgow to stay with her cousin.

She would hold out, she said, for a guy who really wanted her and who would appreciate her worth. He had to agree, secretly, that he didn't really want her and that her worth was something he would have some difficulty locating. But she didn't have to hold out too long, because within a month the new guy came along.

His jobs this morning will probably be quite small: a few trips into town or to the airport. He has a little book where he writes down all of his fares and jobs. Everything is automated, but even so, he likes to keep his own records. He used to drive for another firm who let him dress how he pleased, but now it's a shirt and tie. They gave him a complimentary fleece with the name of the firm and its phone number embossed on it, same as the sign on the roof of the car. When he went to the parents' event at Gen's school, she told him to make sure he took down the sign.

'Why?' said Misty. 'Do you not want your little grammar school friends to know that your daddy drives a taxi? You embarrassed? You ashamed?'

'No,' Gen said. 'I just don't want them knowing all of our business.'

Boogie made sure that he took it down. He stopped some distance away from the big, symmetrical white building with its gate lodge, and put the roof sign in the boot.

Of all of the things, that day, when Leigh left the kids with him, what he decided to do was take them to the zoo. He thought that seemed a reasonable activity for someone who had to look after children. It was a sweltering afternoon when they got out of the flat. All the colours were looking hard. He managed to get Jay to come with him. When they tried to get on the bus, the driver said they were above their quota of buggies already. 'You what?' Boogie said.

'Can you fold it up?' the bus driver asked.

'No, don't know how to do that, mate.' So they had to wait for the next bus.

The zoo, positioned on the side of the Cave Hill, involved a steep walk. Misty was in front of them and walked backwards as she talked. 'We could imagine that we are climbing Mount Everest!' she said. Boogie's head was pounding and his back sore from pushing the buggy, something Jay refused to do. 'People are already going to think we are a couple of gay boys with our kids,' he said. 'Boogie, who are these wee girls?'

'That one,' he said, 'is Leigh's kid. And then that baby,' and he whispered it so Misty couldn't hear, 'is probably, actually mine. I mean, fuck's sake.'

'Shit, no way.'

'The ma is a nut.'

'She's still the mother of your kid. She's a mother at the end of the day.'

'So what?' said Boogie. 'What's this about? Are mothers fucking sacred all of a sudden?'

'Well, I don't think, all of a sudden. That's why it is not a good thing to say motherfucker, you know? People don't like it cos you are meant to have respect for mothers.'

'That's like saying cocksucker is offensive because you are meant to have respect for cocks. Anyway, we shouldn't be talking like this around kids.'

It was incredible what the zoo charged to get in. 'But they're little kids!' Boogie said. 'That one's a fucking baby!'

'That's why they pay child rates,' the woman said. 'I take it you don't spend much time going out and about with these youngsters otherwise you'd know the price of things.'

And once they were in, he regretted ever coming. Why hadn't they gone to a park somewhere, or a place with a free bouncy castle? The animals, regardless of species, had cool, bored stares and he didn't like the pinkness of their mouths, or the weaselly creatures with bushy tails that they let out of an enclosure to run down a winding path. Misty chased after them, trying to catch one. The din of the café, sound and colour bouncing off the walls, people sucking straws, twisting in their seats, dirty dishes stacked on every table. They all had cartons of orange juice, even Jay.

'Geneva's hungry,' Misty said. 'And so am I.'

'We'll get an ice cream when we get out,' Boogie replied. 'There's a van at the entrance.'

A message came through on his phone from Leigh to say that the kids would be with him for a week because everything had got too much for her. Her relationship had ended and there were other issues. She was sure he'd understand.

Boogie makes them tea. Gen takes milk and Misty doesn't. They each have a bowl of cereal and some toast cut into triangles. He carries Gen's hot air balloon tray first of all, puts it on her bedside table. 'Hey,' he says. 'Breakfast.' Mid-morning breakfast. And then he brings up Misty's. She was working last night in the hotel and she'll be there this evening too. Geneva and Misty Johnston. They've got Leigh's surname, obviously.

In the late afternoon, when I visit Alex's care home, I find him sitting in thin yellow light from the high windows. It's always warm, airless. On rare occasions, Alex recognises me, albeit fleetingly, but I now find such moments of lucidity disconcerting, and even unwelcome. I would prefer not to be reminded of what has been lost. We've been married for over fifty years. Our children are well into their forties. The care home is in Histon, only a short drive from our house.

Alex was known as A. D. J. Shelley. His name was often prefaced with the words, the Marxist anthropological philosopher. The Marxist anthropological philosopher, A. D. J. Shelley. His big work was *Concepts of Human Essence*, published in 1984, but he considered his later book, *Aristotelian Marxism*, more stringent in its analysis. We met when he had just completed his doctorate at Cambridge.

In 1995, we spent some time in Prague. Alex took up a position for two terms at Charles University. A prominent member of the new Czech government had been a student of Alex's and so, in addition to his academic role, he worked with a government department in an advisory capacity. The only other period when he left Cambridge was in the late 1970s, when he took a year's post with the Transport and General Workers' Union as a union historian and education officer. In truth, Alex's interest in 'the worker' was rather more, shall we say, *theoretical* than this job necessitated and, thus, it was not a particularly enjoyable time for him. Analogous to this, I suppose, is my own attempt at working with deprived children in Belfast in the late 1960s during an ill-advised and, thankfully, short-lived religious phase. At one point, I was hit by a stone.

When I go to see him, I like to bring a piece of fruit, a pear, say. I take care that it is the nicest I can find, the ripest, the most unblemished. I take a knife and sit, in that still, warm room, paring slices, handing them to him, one by one, until all that is left is the core. I don't know what he thinks when he eats.

I was surprised to hear any of what went on because as far as I'm concerned it was a brilliant evening. I talked to Ellie for the first time. We ended up in that dopey wee kitchen at some point. We got chatting and she said that she had never been to the Mournes before. How the fuck could you have lived here all your life and never been to the Mourne mountains? I mean, that just defies belief. I said, you should go. Do you want to go? And she said, yes, sure, that would be good. When? And I said what about tomorrow? And she said, yes. And so that's what we did. It was great. An amazing day. So still up there. And beautiful. But we talked a lot, too.

The mannequins' semi-abstract faces, their suggestions of eyes, are moulded from softly speckled plastic. The bodies are more defined and the grey quads look tense and powerful. Miriam has run a finger down a bicep in Sports JPX, where the plastic meets the edge of a garment with its dangling price tag. She'll go there after she leaves this restaurant. Sports JPX. Who would ever have anticipated she'd yearn to be in a sports shop?

Before arriving, she picked up Haady's birthday cake for tomorrow and it sits in its box on the table, the words Abdel Salam written in blue biro. The 'e' was originally a 'u' – Abdul. Someone must initially have misspelt it in the bakery and then made a correction. Miriam gets a pen from her bag and writes Mrs M. in front of the name. Mrs M. Abdel Salam.

A friend from work was meant to join her for an early lunch, but he called this morning to cancel. Miriam, on bereavement leave and not having seen him in months, was looking forward to it – he always has amusing, if embellished stories – but she's also relieved not to have to answer any of the questions he might have asked after the second glass of wine. And now she can have a whole bottle to herself.

She's brought a book. It's full of young women's non-problems. After every page, her overriding response is, so what? I hear what you say, but so what? From the cover,

Miriam had expected a kind of cool and expansive perspicacity, but this is juvenile solipsism. 'Is someone else joining you today?' the waiter asks.

'Nope,' she says.

The wine is beautifully cold and Miriam puts the book back in her bag. She looks out of the big windows at the people passing. From where she sits she can see only their disembodied heads, bobbing along the cobbled street. The doors to the kitchen open and close. She takes out her phone. She recently changed the photo from Kahlil to her and the boys. They are on a beach, on holiday, and everyone is smiling. But obviously Kahlil took the photo, so no escaping.

Nothing on the menu is appealing, not even the burger. What makes your soul sing? A burger. Miriam could have anything or nothing from what's on offer. It's all the same to her. She's got sharp cheekbones now and every skirt hangs loose. Her hands are veined in a way she can't ever remember. But she cooks the same as usual for Haady and Rami; she makes them their favourite dishes in a methodical, precise way, then washes up while they eat.

When she was a kid, her parents had done mission work overseas. One time at a fellowship meeting everyone had to write down what made their soul sing. The declarations were randomly read out. God's love! Christ the Redeemer in the hearts of all! Her sister Martha had written something sensible. What makes your soul sing? Miriam had written a burger, with lots of toppings. They'd made her sit for a morning in the room with the slit window, with only water, a bible and time for reflection.

She'd never wanted to be in any of those hot countries. Miriam used to think of a heavy winter coat and how, if she turned her head to the side, all she would see was the dark lining of the hood. Her mother's hair was cropped short for the mission work, but Miriam and Martha were permitted to have theirs long on the condition that it would always be tightly plaited. They would poke sticks or pencils into their braids, trying to ease the tug at their pink scalps.

Miriam looks around the restaurant. It's funny how everyone in the room who has blonde hair has it more or less the same colour. Ash, honey, golden, beach blonde: basically everyone, after a few washes, has the same colour. Her own hair, dirty blonde, is dyed black so that it matches the boys'. It's been that way since they were little. The waiter returns and asks her if she wants to order.

'Sure,' she says.

And she points at the first item on the menu.

Miriam's glad that Haady is so confident. If you said to Haady, I know you are only thirteen but this evening I need you to fly halfway around the world and perform this task, he would do it. He'd love it. Haady is like Kahlil – never intimidated. He even looks like him. Kahlil could never understand how Rami was sometimes so nervous. Rami would stare at the blank pages of his homework, reluctant to make a mark on the page. In primary school, the teacher would say that he was on his own at lunchtime, drifting around. She didn't tell Kahlil because she knew it would annoy him. But she spoke to Rami. Why don't you play games, she said, with the other kids? I just like the wet days better, he said, when everyone has to stay inside. When he went to the secondary school, the teacher said that he was quite well integrated.

'Really?' Miriam said.

'Well, kind of,' the teacher replied.

'What can I say, there's a lot of big personalities in that particular class. Chris. Line-up. A few others. I am just not one of the in-crowd,' Rami said simply, when Miriam asked him.

'Well, the in-crowd suck,' Miriam said, 'and they always have done, since time immemorial.'

'That's the kind of thing a mum says,' Rami replied.

He seems to like working in Die Halle. He likes the discount he gets on all those expensive clothes. Rami will come into his own when he leaves for university. That's what Miriam thinks.

But anyway, what's so unusual about being quiet? That's how she was as a teenager, the odd missionary-family kid. She kept her opinions to herself and stuck pictures of animals on the front of her ring binder. She listened to the others in the class talking about their parties and said nothing. She was hardworking. But here's the thing. Why, when people are quiet, do others assume that constitutes agreement? Why, when you don't talk much, should that be interpreted as interest in another's conversation, rather than boredom? Miriam kept quiet because she was waiting for something. She didn't know what it was, but she knew what it wasn't. She had mostly contempt for her classmates' moderate attempts at hedonism.

The waiter brings her a tiny salad. 'Thank you,' she says.

'Can I get you anything else? Some bread maybe?'

'No thanks.'

'More water?'

'No, really, all good.'

'There's nothing else I can do for you just at present?'

'No, nothing else you can do for me.'

In fact, yes, she wants to call him back to say. Yes, there is something that this young man, this stranger can do. He can sit down opposite her, in that empty chair, take a seat, remove that black apron and listen, listen while she tells the story of how she met her husband. That's what he can do for her. She pours herself a final large glass of wine. Religious upbringing, studious, dissatisfied, unhappy. But waiting.

So, let me tell you, stranger. I'd been working in the library and was waiting for a bus. Spring rain on tarmac. Maybe there was that. The bus was late. I got a book from my bag. Sudden screech of brakes when a van pulled up and a guy in a black and yellow shirt got out, doors opening and slamming. He went into a takeaway, came out, went to the van, carried in sacks, cardboard boxes. Then drums of oil and balanced on top of them a white bag, which slipped off onto the pavement. A woman took a dainty little side step to avoid it. Do you know, I heaved it over my shoulder, took it into the takeaway. The woman behind the counter was laughing at something the guy was saying. The guy was Kahlil, you know? You understand that? The woman was laughing, shaking her head. The print of the shirt was conch shells, swirling yellow, threaded through with chains. I just stared at this shirt, following the patterns, waiting for him to turn around, see the bag, see me. When he did, he said, thank you! And I went out, sat at the bus stop once more. I watched him come out, lock the doors of the van, leap in and drive off.

So that's Kahlil, right? And that's how we met.

How nice it is to remember. Let me tell it to you all over again she says silently to the waiter who comes to ask if she wants anything else.

'A cocktail?'

'Would you like to see the list?'

'No, why don't you pick one? I don't care. Anything so long as it isn't sweet.'

* * *

The way he banged the doors, the oil drums, the woman's face as she laughed, Miriam turned it over like coins in her pocket all the next week. She could not see anything looping – a computer lead, a piece of string – without thinking about the sinuous swirls of that shirt. When she worked in the library, the text had danced around; it didn't want to be read, because even it knew the weight of a white bag, or the sound of a van's brakes was more important. Miriam waited again the next week at the same bus stop, at the same time. No show. He didn't appear the week after that either. Well then, simple. She would go into the takeaway, no subterfuge, say, Who's your supplier? Can you tell me?

The woman, a different one, said that she didn't have his number but if she waited until Eamonn came in, he could give it to her. Think Kahlil has some place on the Donegall Road, the woman remembered. Above a barber's shop. But you'd be better hanging around for Eamonn if you want the number.

The next day she skipped class to go to the Donegall Road. Even the graffiti seemed beguiling. There was more than one barber's. She stared at a shop with a red sign and a photo of a motorbike in the window – but there was no upstairs. From another one a child looked down from a bedroom window. He was holding a toy plane. She waved up to him and he closed the curtain. But she kept looking up and he reappeared, gave Miriam a little wave.

There was another place, shabby, where they were pulling down the metal shuttering early. She said, the name new, nice on her tongue, I'm looking for Kahlil. To sound the syllables was a thrill. And the guy pointed to a door wedged open with a brick. She went up the narrow, rickety staircase, carpeted like it had once been someone's home. Up the stairs, slowly, to the top. She stood on the landing, an open door, a room in front of her, the windows obscured by boxes. He was there, crouched down, looking at papers that were spread out on the floor. He got up to check some detail on one of the boxes. But are these details relevant? Miriam wants to say to this young man, if he could sit down across the table from her. Do you want to know instead about the gold necklace against his skin? Or what his shoulders looked like? Do you? Kahlil turned round when Miriam said hi. She came into the room to stand in the small space that wasn't taken up with takeaway supplies.

The waiter returns with the cocktail.

'It's whiskey-based,' he says. 'Not too sweet. It's made with—'

'Fine,' Miriam replies. 'Thank you.'

First she took off her skirt which was blue and long. And then Miriam reached up to remove her grey jumper. She felt bare floorboards when she took off her shoes. What you doing? he said. But he seemed more amused than alarmed. What you doing? She took off her bra, feeling a fleeting embarrassment when it was warm and soft in her hand. She dropped it to the ground and looked at him. She can't say what he saw. But he came over and kissed her, ran his hands over her gently, then pulled her pants to one side. Before this, she'd never kissed a guy.

So yes, she wants to say to the waiter, sitting opposite. What do you make of that?

You sure went for it! he says, laughing. She did. She was already in love. It wasn't complicated like people made it out to be. Proof of compatibility, unspoken negotiations, aeons of getting to know people over the course of various benign activities. It was all unnecessary when you could simply have sex above a barber's shop, surrounded by boxes destined for takeaways all over the city. It was as simple and fantastic as that.

While she was dressing, Kahlil asked what her name was and she told him. She couldn't find her jumper and he pointed to where it was, underneath some plastic wrap.

'What you got in your bag, Miriam?' he said.

'Just my books and my notes.'

'Notes?'

'Law. I do law.'

He laughed and shook his head. She asked him, when she was leaving, if he could remember their first meeting. He said no, he hadn't a clue. She lifted a sack and handed it to him.

'Botanic,' she said. 'You had that shirt on. The yellow and black one.'

He said that was one of his favourites. He seemed to think it was entirely unsurprising and reasonable that someone would see him doing his deliveries, in his favourite shirt, and dedicate themselves to tracking him down.

'I was in my best shirt,' he said. 'What can I say? I'm a handsome guy. I'm a business owner.' And he gave her a kiss.

He didn't want her to see where he lived. 'It's a guy flat,' he said, for him and four, sometimes five or six others. It wouldn't be long before he had himself sorted out and she could come to his own place. In the meantime, they met in a hotel where Kahlil knew the manager. They always got the disabled access room, which often wasn't booked. From the bed, all you could see were trees, their branches shaking on even a sunny day. He undressed slowly, folding his clothes and laying them over the chair.

It's busier now in the restaurant. The walls are white, apart from a huge abstract painting. She looks at its muddied colours, where the oil paint is raised and clotted. The chatter and laughing seems to be rising in pitch. A peal comes from a nearby table, two teenage girls and their parents. The mum tosses her head back. The younger girl has olive skin, long hair. She is wearing a little yellow vest top that says FIRENZE on it. Miriam and Kahlil went to Florence one time. They went to Rome too, on that trip. She remembers the place they stayed that overlooked a white courtyard. Kahlil loved the shops. He spent a fortune in Roberto Cavalli, oh my god. There was a beggar lying flat out on the pavement outside the Louis Vuitton shop – not someone who was homeless or a bit down on their luck, but a beggar wrapped in a black blanket, like something from the Middle Ages, right outside the Louis Vuitton shop. The older sister sees Miriam looking and stares back at her, full of pretty contempt, it seems, for the woman sitting alone. Miriam returns her stare, mouths, fuck you. The girl, surprised, looks away and laughs extravagantly at something her mother has just said. That painting, full of its significance as the only one on the wall, yields nothing of its meaning, if it has one.

When Miriam leaves the restaurant she realises as she reaches the end of the street that she has left the box, the one which bears her name in biro and contains the birthday cake for Haady, which she had ordered specially. But Miriam is already on her way to Sports JPX. She looks down the cobbled street to where she can just see the restaurant's sign. No, she won't go back now. She needs to get to Sports JPX, its mannequins so like Kahlil. No one will steal a birthday cake. She'll go back afterwards to pick it up.

Strange work some people might think, but I've got used to it. It's nights. It's a small room and there are six monitors showing what's happening in six particular security locations. I'm looking for anything unusual: people, movement, activity. I can watch them all at once and I've become attuned to the small changes that might be of interest or concern. Then there's a number I have to ring. At the beginning, I used to want to see something suspicious so that would trigger some action, but now I'm more receptive to the vibe of seeing nothing. The time passes and sometimes I'm surprised how quickly it's gone. I like the multiple monitors. At times, when I'm in the flat, looking at my single screen, I feel it's a bit limited.

At Victorian Day in school, there were all kinds of activities. You could make peg dolls or roll a hoop in the playground, stitch samplers or play with spinning tops. At one table, you were able to make a silhouette of a person, by cutting out a shape on black paper. Then you would stick it on a white background. The logo for Bennyz is like that. It's a man in a top hat and, although you cannot see, it feels like he's smiling. Bennyz is short for Benefactors.

Misty takes a sip of the tea that Boogie brought, takes a bite of toast. A delivery update appears on her phone. The ring light is due to arrive today. Cool! She doesn't use her real name for Bennyz. No way. Unless you want to end up with a bunch of old sleazes you shouldn't call yourself Becki-Lee, Heidi-Kym, Layla, Lacey – or Misty. Right from the beginning, she has just wanted a few people who are nice and kind of classy. People who are sort of sophisticated, like older versions of Chris, maybe. She calls herself Elizabeth. Elizabeth Barrett Browning. She remembered that name from a poster of a woman, outside one of the English rooms in school. Elizabeth Barrett Browning looked like she had just got a really good curly blow dry, except someone had flattened it on top. Back then, they had different styles. In the picture, she was wearing a black coat over a lacy white blouse. The name's a good one for the vibe she wants to create.

In terms of the Bennyz levels, she mainly goes for primary or secondary. One of her regulars, Mike in

Wyoming, just wants to talk and that's primary factor. He sometimes chats about how his day at work has gone, whether customers were cranky or not. Secondary factor is more dirty talk. Misty doesn't feel she really has the voice for it. Secondary factor is not her thing! A Belfast accent isn't ideal and it's difficult to keep from laughing at some of the things they say. For example, this dude in a brilliant house with a colossal fireplace wanted her to say, I love touching your silky cock. And so she did. She added in a 'just', because that seemed to make it sound more enthusiastic somehow. I just love touching your silky cock. But he kept saying *cock! cock!* You are saying *cack*. I want you to say *cock*. Cock. Not cack. She pursed her lips together so her voice sounded more English like his. But, waste of time, because the man with the silky cack and the fireplace didn't continue his *beneficence* to Elizabeth Barrett Browning. That is what they call payment. Beneficence. Sounds so fancy.

Tertiary factor is access to exclusive content, dictated by the beneficiary. Misty is prepared to take off most of her clothes – but not her pants – and then strike a few poses on and off her bed. She's only done it a couple of times. She made sure that she moved her old cuddly toy off the bed, the one with the zip where she can put her pyjamas. Because, sad to say, that would attract the wrong crowd. There are so many wrong crowds, of one type or another. She also ensures that she closes the curtains so that no one sees the bus going past or all the roofs of the opposite houses. Her curtains have spaceships on them but they're so faded no paedos would be able to make them out. They've been there since they moved into this house after the poky wee flat.

Elite factor is a subscription level when the benefactor can ask for whatever they want. He can be, as they say, *master of the script*. They illustrate this on the website with a silhouette image of an ink pot and a quill. There's so many girls on the site and a lot of them are really beautiful. She's not that, but it takes all sorts. And, she thinks, as she takes another bite of toast, the ring light is going to be good. It's going to give her skin that luminous quality. Well hopefully, with the money she paid for it.

She's got a Bennyz outfit that she wears. She wanted something different to the other girls who are in booty shorts and bra tops. She tried to pimp up Elizabeth Barrett Browning in the picture. So she wears a white blouse with a lace collar. It's real old-fashioned looking. And then she has this little piece of black satin ribbon that she ties in a bow. She wears a tight black velvet skirt. She keeps her make-up what's called 'soft glam', apart from her eyebrows which she likes to have really defined. She gathers up her hair in a ponytail, but loose so that strands fall down around her face. She's not going to copy Elizabeth Barrett Browning's actual hairstyle. No. She's hoping to make at least a little bit of cash. Boogie doesn't know about her involvement in this. She nearly always does it when he is out at work. Geneva's listened at the bedroom door and she sometimes threatens to tout. But she won't.

Misty looks at her hand where she'd been testing lipsticks earlier. So many reds. Last year she thought that maybe she could have a career in stage and special effects make-up. Oxygenated blood is bright red. Like MAC Ruby Woo. Old blood is the colour of dark chocolate. Scabs are a mix of aubergine and lemon and green. She puts her tray on the floor and sinks back down into her warm bed. She doesn't need to be in work until the afternoon. The hotel is better than the previous place, the shop when she was always on homeware, which translated into folding towels over and over. Why did people keep lifting the towels out, holding them up as if they'd just had a shower? Everybody knows the shape of a towel. What were they expecting to see? Jesus's face on it? Misty witnessed people stealing stuff all of the time in that place, even the towels. A woman once took five and shoved them into a holdall. She saw Misty watching, and held her finger to her mouth to go *Sshhhh!* Funny how even though she worked in the place and was dressed in the uniform, the woman expected that Misty would be on her side. The bosses of the hotel have visited once. They own hotels all over, even in the States. After they had gone, the layout of the reception area changed because they said so. Misty never said anything about the towels, of course not.

Most of the people who work in the hotel are pretty friendly, although not all of them. Vanessa who works behind the bar part-time has a smile that drops after half a second. Misty has practised doing it but she can't get her mouth rearranged to neutral so swiftly. But then people can be not nice everywhere. Some of the Bennyz men are terrible; they feel they can say whatever they want. Move one hand here and one hand there and arch your back, bend over now. Now! She had laughed and said, It's actually not possible to do all of those things at once. Shut up, I didn't ask you to speak. Do what Daddy tells you. She laughed again and then his yellow room was replaced with the Bennyz logo. Alright, cheerio.

Mike is nice though. His wife left him a few years ago, but he says that she was a good woman. He works in some place that sells farm equipment. He showed her a picture of his son, who was killed in the military in Afghanistan. That's him, Mike said. And there's not an hour of the day goes by, Elizabeth, when I don't think of him. What a fucking stupid world this is when I'm sitting here and he's in a box. He showed her another picture of his son, this time holding a giant fish he had caught. Mike had said on the first session that he liked *Braveheart*. He thought it was a real good film. You're Scottish, right? he said. No I'm not Scottish, Misty replied, I'm from Northern Ireland, I'm from Belfast. Mike said that he had never paid for sex in his life and he never would. He said that there was something very, very sad about a guy like him talking to a young girl half a world away in Belfast, Northern Ireland. Are you getting a good education? he asked. I hope you are getting a good education.

Only one person has ever seen her totally naked and that was Sam. She's not counting Robbie Coleman from school because she didn't even take off her trousers and her top stayed on. Every time Misty went to Sam's house, the washing machine was on, churning away. The whole house smelled of the scented granules called Spring Awakening. Sam was always warm, even when they were sitting outside in the dark of night. His cheek and his neck were soft and perfumed like Spring Awakening. And then one time he just said that that was it, he didn't think they should see each other anymore. But why? she asked, panicked, horrified. Is there somebody else that you want to be with? No, Sam said, it was just that he wanted to spend more time with his guys, doing stuff. The group of lads that he hung round with. But why, she said, because you aren't even yourself whenever you are with them! You hardly say anything! The way you act! The way you speak! Well, that is just the way it is, he said. That's how I feel. She messaged him at two in the morning to say that she hated him. And then at half past three she sent another message to say she loved him. She attached a picture of herself naked. He didn't reply either time. She got Boogie to buy Spring Awakening.

Martine is one of the girls in work. Martine always tucks her hotel trousers into black boots so she looks like a farmer just in from the field. She takes home any extra food from the kitchen and her mother has multiple sclerosis. She gets annoyed because other people don't care enough about Yemen. She freaked about it in the staff area one night. 'I wanted to ask you,' Martine said when they were cleaning tables one time, 'if you've got a Bennyz account.'

'No,' said Misty. 'Who said I did?'

'Didn't think you would have one. That kind of thing is really only for the very stupid.'

'Who said I did?'

'Maybe Vanessa or Chris or one of those other twats. I think I heard them talking about it.'

'They're friends of mine,' Misty said. 'They're friends of mine actually.'

'Are they? Seriously?'

'Yeah.'

She's been to Chris's house on a few occasions. The last time they were in Line-up's car and on the way they picked up a girl called Maddie Lynch, or Lynchie, as they called her. Line-up used to work in the hotel but he got fired because he was always late. Lynchie always looks as if she's thrown on a bunch of shapeless clothes in ten seconds flat. But maybe the guys like her because the clothes look as though they could be pulled off in ten seconds flat. When they went up Chris's drive, the men working in the garden stood up as the car went past, then resumed working again.

They went to the top of the house, where Chris has a kind of mini flat with a bedroom, bathroom and living room. 'OK, Misty,' Line-up said, 'let's see what you got.' It was maybe the third or fourth time she'd got them weed, although not much of it. Line-up gave her a few notes and without looking she put them in her bag. She trusted him. 'Thanks,' she said.

Misty was sitting on one of the big leather sofas. Line-up, standing, opened a can of beer and poured a little of it over her head. It trickled down the side of her face. 'Hey!' she said. 'Don't you do that!'

'Why are you laughing?' Lynchie asked.

'Because it's funny,' Misty said.

'No it's not.' Lynchie's voice is always loud and slow, like she's the lead in the school play. 'All I can say,' Lynchie said, 'is that you guys better not even think of pouring any beer over me because, let me assure you, I won't be giggling about it.'

'We won't,' Line-up said.

Chris has decks. White shelves run the length of the room.

'Wow,' Misty said, exactly as she did the last time that she was there. 'You've got so many records. Where do you get them all?'

Lynchie blew out her smoke. 'My dad's new girlfriend is from Montenegro,' she said. 'That's near Croatia, isn't it?'

'Yeah,' said Chris, opening the doors that lead out onto the balcony that looks onto the big back garden. 'Borders Bosnia, Serbia, Albania.'

'God, I want to get so wasted,' Lynchie said, 'but tonight I can't because tomorrow I need to work on something and this friend of my dad's is coming round to help me. It's this fucking behavioural economics course I'm doing online.

It's just so random. Well actually,' she said, 'it's not. It'll look good when I apply for college in the States.' She took a tin of balm from her bag. 'Jesus, my lips are so fucking dry. Put on some music, Chrissy.'

He played a slow, lolloping beat. No one had offered Misty a beer, so she got up and, holding a can in the air, asked, 'Is it alright if I take this?'

Chris was nodding his head to the music.

As she moved back to the sofa, Misty half danced, dipping and swinging her hips a little, one arm in the air.

'The auditions for *Britain's Got Talent* were last month,' Lynchie said.

'Oh no, I think that Misty should definitely just continue doing that,' Line-up said. 'Can you throw in a few more moves?'

'Why don't *you* throw in a few moves?' said Lynchie. 'You could do a couple of slut drops, Line-up, and try to get a bit more svelte.'

'So cruel!' Line-up said. 'So unkind!' He punched his stomach and then his arm. 'This is pure muscle.'

Misty did a wine movement, tried to be slinky. She looked to see if Chris was watching but he was changing a record.

'Nice,' said Line-up.

'Oh, for god's sake,' said Lynchie.

When Misty went to the bathroom, she didn't use Chris's ensuite. She wanted to see the little sister's room with its candy-coloured canopies, or his parents' room with its huge square bed. She tiptoed in for a peek. Big windows everywhere in this place, square views of sea! Lying on the floor was a sort of silky black top with thin straps. There were doors to a big bathroom and two wardrobe rooms. The woman's was the size of a small shop. Misty ran her hand along the rail of hangers. Some of the clothes still had their tags on them! Then she slipped out, back to the others. Chris's mum is called Frankie, except she's his stepmother. Misty has seen the little sister, Nina, hanging around, watching.

'What about your actual mum?' she had asked Chris.

'She's dead.'

'Boogie is my stepdad,' she offered. 'And I don't really see my mum.'

Chris didn't ask anything further. Chris's face was so handsome.

For years after they were with Boogie, their mum never made much contact. Some parents, when they split up, wanted to blot out the other person, squirrelling away the letters that were sent, or never slipping under the tree the present that had arrived two weeks before, wrapped up with a tag saying, 'I love you, I miss you.' But Boogie, Misty knows, would've handed the presents over, had their mum ever sent any.

Then suddenly, one time, kaboom, their mum invited them to spend a few days with her in Scotland. It would be a special holiday. Boogie gave them some spending money and marked the day of their return with a big red circle on the calendar. He flew over with them and it should have been fun because Misty and Gen hadn't been on a plane before – but they were frightened, too, of this person they couldn't have identified in a line-up. Once, in an argument with Boogie, about leaving her room in a mess, Misty had said, well, I will just go and live with my mum then! That's what I'll do! She might as well have said that she was going to live with the old woman in the shoe, or a pterodactyl. And so now it was strange to be going on a plane to see her. When they landed in Glasgow, Boogie gave her a phone. 'Put that in your bag,' he said, 'and don't let anybody see it. That's your burner. The only number in it is mine and so in case of emergency, like, if you don't like it, give me a ring.' He was staying with a pal. 'You going to spy on us?' Misty asked. 'Going to be spying to make sure you are on your best behaviour,' he said. When she was there, she would turn her head quickly, to see if she could catch him in some shady corner.

Their mum looked like she had arrived at a party when she came through the doors at the airport.

'Would you look at the face on him?' she said to the girls. 'Big grumpy lugs. What's wrong with you?'

She stuck out her tongue at Boogie and the girls gave a little laugh.

'Let me give all of yous the biggest hug yous have ever had in your lives.'

And she flung her arms around each of them in turn.

'Boogie!' she said. 'You smell nice. Is that Armani?'

'No it's not,' he said. 'Be good, girls. I'll see you in a few days.' He kissed them and gave Misty a wink.

On the bus from the airport, their mum kept talking about their hair and how they needed something done to it. She didn't mean nit treatment, which was good, because Misty hated that oily, sticky lotion which suffocated them. No, their mum said she didn't know what Boogie was at, letting them have those dowdy as fuck haircuts. When they got back to her flat, which was up three flights of stairs, her friend Heather was there.

'All that hair hanging like droopy wee dogs,' their mother said. 'They need something that is going to liven them up, Heather.' Misty could even get a colour if she wanted. 'Misty, do you want a colour?'

Their mum's friend cut Gen's hair into a lopsided bob. Misty's was lightened to the shade of a banana. Their mum got blow-dried ringlets, crispy to the touch. A surprise when they got back was the other little kid there, who turned out to be their brother. Ewan always wanted to clamber onto their mum's knee and sometimes she would scoop him up and pretend that he was a little jockey, galloping faster and faster as she bounced her leg. She would throw in some jumps and give a commentary. But sometimes she would push him away. Go play with your toys. Well, you are doing a kid no favours by making them act all clingy! she would say. When he was annoyed, Ewan didn't cry. He made a long, single-note whine.

Being with their mum felt like when you were doing your work at a table at school, but the legs weren't all the same length, so suddenly it tipped to one side when you weren't expecting it. Well, with the table, that was easily sorted out because you could just fold up a bit of paper and wedge it under the leg. Their mum had a pair of shoes worth over four hundred quid and she would let them put them on as long as they only walked on the carpet with them.

One day they went to a kind of office. In the waiting room, there was a fake plant in a silver tub and Misty coloured its leaves in blue with a felt tip that some other kid had left lying on the floor. Their mum had an argument with a woman who was meant to be next in the queue.

'I've been here longer but I had to go to the toilet,' the woman said.

'Well, you shouldn't have moved then, should you?'

'What do you think I should've done, pished myself all over the floor just in case some cheeky bastard tried to take my place?'

'Oh shut it and get to fuck.'

Misty liked her mum's face. She had a scar, when you looked up close, at the edge of her right eyebrow and it ran into her hairline. 'What happened to you, Mummy?' she asked.

'A ring,' she said, 'when I was a little kid.'

'How come?'

'I got hit and the hand had a ring on it.'

'Oh,' Misty said.

She lay in bed thinking about it. Maybe it was a big bulging ruby, or a signet ring. An icy, hard diamond meeting thin skin. A skinny little kid could be knocked across the room, getting hit like that. She eventually went to sleep, the burner phone under her pillow.

A couple of Christmases ago her mum rang Boogie from the ferry terminal and said that she had nowhere to go. He picked her up and she slept on their sofa.

'What's Ewan getting for his presents?' Misty asked. 'Does the same lady still do your hair?'

Her mum looked as though she couldn't remember who these people were. On Christmas Day, she brought out of her holdall a little bag in the shape of a Santa hat filled with strange presents: a small bowl for Boogie, the kind of thing that would have a serving of baby boiled potatoes in it in a restaurant. For Misty and Gen there were detective books, which looked like somebody had already read them. When she spoke, she kept putting her hand over her mouth because she had lost two teeth. She had been out with friends and had fallen down a stairwell in the dark, she said. They were halfway through their dessert, which was a Christmas cheesecake and not all that nice, when their mum started crying. Gen and Misty sat either side of her saying, 'What's wrong? Don't worry!' Nan D and Boogie stayed where they were.

* * *

When Misty was talking to Martine about that crowd being friends of hers, she could have told her about the night she got a taxi with Line-up, Chris and this other guy, Rami Abdel Salam, and yeah, also Eugene Cleary. They were in the taxi with Line-up and Eugene facing her. Chris started to kiss her, which she had not been expecting at all. I mean, it was Chris Levine! Then she felt hands on her knees, pushing them apart and suddenly she was looking at Rami, who's always so serious. And nervous. But the hands on her knees belonged to Line-up.

'Hey!' she said. 'You stop that.'

'You're no fun,' he said.

The taxi stopped to let out Eugene Cleary. He had on a baseball cap with an ice-cream cone on the front. Then it was Misty.

'See you!' she shouted and they all waved goodbye.

Line-up said that Martine was vile, a real dog. She reminded him of some politician or other but he couldn't remember her name. 'The fat one,' he said.

'Is your main problem with Martine the fact that you don't find her attractive?' Lynchie asked. 'Not everyone's reason for existence is for you to find them hot.'

'I like all sorts of people,' Line-up said. 'They don't need to be hot, Lynchie. I just don't like Martine. I like Misty for example even though she's FSM.'

'What's that?' Lynchie asked.

'Free school meals.'

'I never in all my life had free school meals!' Misty said. It was true. She loved the lunches Boogie made.

'I would have thought, Line-up,' Lynchie said, 'that coming from a background like yours, you might be a bit more – egalitarian – in your attitudes.'

'Eagle what?'

'That with Bronagh being such a champion of the proletariat you might have had more enlightened attitudes.'

'Oh I get you. My mum and her steeks.'

'Does she ever bring any of them home?'

'What do *you* think? Chris, have you got any more beers?'

'I'm going to a festival in the first week of September with my cousins,' Lynchie said. 'The ones from the south. It's in Sweden. Oh god, my lips are still so dry.'

Misty takes the last sip of her tea and puts the cup on the windowsill. Does she need to wash her hair or can she get another day out of it? Chris will probably be working tonight. She rubs the back of her head. There's some dry shampoo in the bathroom and a spray of that will be fine.

Post smack habit, I worked on the Dublin to Belfast train as a conductor. The two-and-a-half-hour journey, which I sometimes made four times a day, dispensed with any sense of fixity or trajectory, while still providing incessant movement. It suited me. I liked the juddering space between carriages. One time, on the last train from Belfast, I came across a woman, in her forties I would say, alone, and very drunk. She couldn't find her ticket. She dipped her hands repeatedly into a big black leather bag but retrieved nothing. I walked on, but thought, as I clipped the tickets of the others on the train, of her white face.

When the train pulled in to Dublin Connolly, I saw her stagger down the steps, almost losing her footing. She stood on the platform as the other passengers wove by. I approached her and asked if she needed help to get somewhere. When she started crying, I took her arm and managed to walk with her to a nearby hotel – cheap – on Amiens Street. I paid for a room and we went up to it in a tiny lift where I had to lean her against the side to keep her upright. The room was white and square. Old-fashioned. I took off her coat, put it on the chair, and then pulled back the covers of the bed. She lay down and I slipped off her shoes. Then I pulled the covers over her. Her hands lay white on them. She wore a wedding ring. I switched off the light and left.

Aren't railway stations always suffused with romance? Even poor old Connolly, Stáisiún Uí Chonghaile, named after the socialist revolutionary who was tied to a chair to be shot by the British. All that night I dreamed of her, or lay awake thinking about her, standing under the high roof of the station, sleeping in that antiquated little room.

I went back the next morning, nervous, excited. I still had the key. You were high on being the saviour, my friend said, when I told her about it, years later, after a long drinking session in a bar in Dingle. I know you! I know what you were hoping for!

I went up again in the lift, walked the corridor to the room. When I went in, she wasn't there. The bed was neatly made and what hung in the air was alcohol and something softer, like irises. I felt a ridiculous sadness, as if I had missed a great love. There was no trace of her, apart from a scrap of paper lying over near the door, a receipt for three euro. Here. I still have it.

Bronagh Farrell, along with Patience Johnson and Fatima Bazzi, has been running through the arrangements with tech support for the last twenty minutes. The event's been billed as a 'Kids' Breakfast'. That doesn't mean Choco Loops floating in milk and abandoned crusts. The attendees will be offered a selection of delights unloaded early this morning from the van of an excellent Bronx-based caterer. The screen is positioned to the left of a five-metre-square vertical garden. Invitees have started to arrive, taking seats at the clusters of walnut tables. The Kids' Breakfast shouldn't be a place for the meretricious. Most people are discreetly dressed, in stealth cuts appreciated by those who recognise the detailing of an engraved button made of horn – Celine – or the certain narrowness of a collar. That's as it should be at a fundraising event for children's services. The compere, in a brown pants-suit, is checking her notes, running her hand through her mop of honey hair. The three participants are shown to a room off the main area where there are two grey leather couches. They are here to talk about children in Monrovia, Beirut, Belfast.

Bronagh is from 411. The project takes its name from the number of the old house where it used to be, a big, draughty place with buckets to catch the water that dripped through the leaky roof, and bells in each room for the long dead servants. But now there's a purpose-built centre with pitches, two gyms, music rooms, medical suites. There's therapies, a short-term education unit. Kids can get legal advice. The project is passionate about the arts. And sport. Occasionally famous people drop by when their schedules allow it. Over the years, Bronagh has welcomed footballers, musicians, actors, entrepreneurs to the 411 centre. Last year one celebrity invited her to a big Christmas party in Killiney. What a view! But Donal said he hadn't enjoyed it. If he had wanted to talk to a property developer, then he could just have gone to one of those wine bars on the Lisburn Road rather than driving a four-hour round trip down south in the rain to talk to some self-satisfied Dub boasting about his finances.

Bronagh's flight got in last night. She made all the arrangements herself. She answers the phone in reception sometimes. People are surprised to see her there, but it's important that there are as few hierarchical structures as possible: that's always been her ideology. Bronagh, like everyone else, takes her turn cleaning the place down at the end of the night. Someone took a photo of her doing it, in her overalls, face flushed as she wielded a dustpan and brush. That image has sometimes been used as her head-shot in newspapers or other publicity materials, rather than the one taken for that purpose by the professional photographer, the one where she is gazing beatifically at some object stage right. The dustpan one serves her better.

Patience Johnson asks where she is staying and when Bronagh mentions the name of the hotel she says immediately she hasn't heard of it. Bronagh asks Patience where she is staying. With friends in Staten Island, she says. Fatima Bazzi says, no way, that's where she is too. She is staying with her partner's cousin. Bronagh opens one of the bottles of water sitting on the table between the sofas. Patience says that she feels nervous; she hasn't done anything like this before. She has only just got this job with the charity. Before that she was working in a university.

'No need to be nervous,' Bronagh says. 'It's not a hostile audience. Everyone wants to help. So much anyway,' Bronagh continues, 'is actually to do with what happens later. When we go to meet the real cabal at Mary Donovan-Leitner's place. We'll meet the serious players there. I've been here before and that's how it works.'

'Sounds kinda scary,' Patience says.

'Yeah,' says Fatima. 'Eeek!'

It's not a competition of course, because the people at the Kids' Breakfast can afford to fund all manner of multiple projects, but in all likelihood they'll just choose one. They'll prefer to focus, get to know the cause, engage, respond. That's the aspiration anyway. If they are thinking purely in terms of need, well, Bronagh knows that 411 is at the bottom of the pile. Yes of course she can talk about the high suicide rates of young men, transgenerational trauma, paramilitary control, substance abuse – hell, she can even go for broke and chuck her grandfather, murdered by loyalist paramilitaries, into the mix – but, day to day, objectively, the kids' lives in Northern Ireland are undoubtedly more secure than those in Lebanon and Liberia. Should we only bother with someone if they're in mortal jeopardy or their final death throes? Let this pair do what they can to get the cash for their kids, and she will match, or better, them. When Patience was flicking through her presentation, it looked like she had no pictures, no photos. Well, that's a mistake right from the start.

There is a knock at the door and the compere comes in to introduce herself more formally. She says that the tech help has told her the running order is Patience, Fatima, Bronagh. Is that alright? A young man comes to fit them with little clip-on mics. Bronagh has worn a jumpsuit with patch pockets that can easily accommodate the transmitter. She smiles as Patience looks for a place to clip it on her tight blue jersey dress. 'I'll just hold it!' Patience says. Bronagh checks her make-up in the mirror behind the sofa, smooths her hair. The tech help sticks his head in the door. 'Alright, guys, about five minutes to show-time!' he says.

When they walk out, they're greeted by warm applause. The room is saturated with yellow light and Bronagh looks up at that vertical garden which seems almost to be growing, the leaves unfurling and elongating. She could take clippers to it. The compere gives complicated and extravagant thanks to people who are there, and people who can't be. She says *we* a lot to stress that they are a group with a shared set of values, although Bronagh hardly thinks the compere is one of *them*. She saw earlier the price on the sole of the shoes she is wearing, when the woman put one foot behind her ankle as she talked to the sound guy. Bronagh couldn't see the exact figure but it was two digits, followed by a decimal, followed by another two digits. Someone in black courts that cheap is hardly going to turn things around for Liberian kids.

A message comes through on Bronagh's phone.

u seen my white polo shirt shirt????

Patience speaks first in a low, clear voice. She has fed her transmitter down her dress so it sits like a carbuncle halfway down her back. That said, Bronagh can see some members of the audience taking in her soft curves. She can see the eyes wander from Patience's face to her breasts, stretching the fabric. She is explaining about civil war. It's detailed and there is even one man who has taken out a notebook and is jotting down the salient points of what she is saying. He pauses every so often before writing again.

They don't need to know this. They don't want to know this. There is only so much context that these people will want to be told. How far back is Patience going? Decades. She needs to keep the focus on specific individuals, preferably young kids, and ideally ones that have had good photos taken of them.

Bronagh will be focusing on a story almost perfect in its dreadful asymmetry. She has told it many times over, but she knows how to make it seem just a little under-rehearsed. She knows the point where it is endearing to get slightly flustered or lose her place. The Anderson story is powerful. On the way from the airport, she saw a billboard with Finn Anderson positioned behind the three main characters in that new franchise. He could always do accents. He was always a great mimic. Johnny was too. There was a year between them, but they might as well have been twins with those crew cuts and pointed, strong little teeth. Finn's had those fixed. He has an even line of white now.

do YOU know where my shirt IS????? ANSWER Mum ffs.

She puts her arm around her phone, the way she did when she was a kid and didn't want someone to copy her work. Blue ironing basket, she types back to Lyness.

Finn and Johnny Anderson were the usual wannabe hoods, who still drank milkshakes. They'd moved from another part of the city after both being excluded from their original school. That was eight years ago. After a few stand-offs in the centre, they established themselves as top dogs. It helped that there were the two of them. The rules then, as now, were that to be involved in that particular programme, it was mandatory to attend the centre at least four nights a week, plus four hours at the weekends. But the Andersons didn't keep to that. When the other kids were asked the brothers' whereabouts, their faces were studiously blank. If participants turned up late, it was the centre's policy that they would be turned away. Other kids would remonstrate or beg – but the brothers would shrug and walk off. Cheerio, I don't give a fuck, Finn might say. On a good day, Johnny could be a bit more co-operative. One time they needed lots of old equipment shifted out and into a van. He took pride in lifting more precarious stacks of boxes than anyone else, making twice as many journeys. You could get a job in a removals firm, Johnny, she remembered saying. He gave her a look to show what a ridiculous prospect he considered that to be.

It's never been her particular forte, banter with the kids. Banter, or whatever you wanted to call it: badinage, mega laughs, repartee. Why should it be? It isn't what she's there for. Still, it's annoying when there are those quick little looks that they sometimes share: the kids, the other members of the team. How's everybody's favourite removals guy? Mick McConnell said to Johnny a few days later. And they had exchanged glances. She has occasionally taken Mick to task. Privately, quietly, of course. One time it was after there had been a photo for a group of kids who had just done a ten-kilometre run. They were all there in the 411 tracksuits with Bronagh in the centre and the photographer had said for everyone to move in closer. (One of those tracksuit tops, it had appeared in a video for a Moldovan hip hop group. Unfortunately, it featured many references to AK47s, but still, there it was, their tracksuit!) When the guy wanted everyone to get tighter in the shot, she had said, 'Move in, Aaron, would you? Yes, that's better.'

'Barry you mean,' Mick McConnell had said. 'Barry, skoosh in a bit, would you?'

Bronagh said afterwards, Mick McConnell on the other side of her desk, that she did not appreciate that kind of comment.

'What kind of comment?' he said, laughing. 'Giving a kid his right name?'

'You know what I mean.'

'Actually, I don't know what you mean.'

'Yes you do.'

'Alright. I'll be honest, whether they are kids or not, whoever they are, they should be given the courtesy of the right name. I don't think that's a big deal.'

'But not in front of the photographer. There was no need for a comment like that in front of the photographer.'

'Well I doubt he either heard or cared,' Mick McConnell said. 'But alright, I am really very sorry because I thought I was being helpful.'

'You weren't at all.'

'I'm sorry then, Bronagh.'

She wasn't sure if he was or he wasn't.

'That's all,' she said. 'That's all, Mick. You can head on now.'

And so he went back to the gym or wherever it was that he had come from. It is impossible for her to know everyone's name, of course it is. But since then, she has always been more careful. She uses the phrase 'my friend' a lot. Thank you, my friend, she says to a boy at the centre who holds open a door for her. Well, hello, my friend, she begins her conversation with the person who has been sent to her for not following the rules again. Aaron, or a boy like him, will be projected during her presentation onto that big wall next to the vertical garden. Aaron in grey Nike, his hood up.

* * *

It's not in that basket, comes the message from Lyness.

Mum ffs I'm going out.

If it's not in the basket, then she doesn't know where it is. Amy, who comes in to do the cleaning and some general housekeeping once a week, could possibly have put it in Donal's cupboard in error. Lyness will get a shock come September when he will have to take care of himself.

'The trouble is, we've spoilt him,' Donal says.

'No we haven't,' Bronagh replies. 'He's just typical of all young people.'

'We've spoilt him and he knows the value of nothing.'

'Like you when you were his age. You lived in one of the biggest houses in the town.'

'Yeah, and I had a job working on a farm from when I was fourteen years old.'

'Well, Lyness had a job! In the restaurant! In the hotel!'

'Lyness *had* a job. And he lost it. A couple of shifts a week. I don't think it was exactly hard graft.'

A message comes back.

Mum I need £££ to go out tonite. Any chance?

Patience is still talking. The man has stopped making notes. Outside she can see the azure sky. Glassy. It's great to be in New York. She always loves coming here. It's a little personal triumph. New York was the first and only place she was ever sacked. Erika, Anita, Steven, Sarge Bond, she knows exactly what everyone in the band is doing right now. Erika is a yoga instructor and reiki healer in Hastings. Her studio is above an estate agent's. She's not one of these lithe and limber women. She looks fragile, with thinning hair. Anita did a bit of modelling but now works in payroll software. She advertised a scratch card and a vitamin supplement around 2010. Sarge is a lecturer in Level 2 popular music at a college in Wakefield. And then Steven is bald, the peroxide bowl cut all gone. He sells his art online and sometimes he has his daughter, a little girl with plaits, hold the pictures. 'Maisie's favourite!' the text says. Might they know about her? Possibly. Objectively, she is a success whether they have or haven't looked her up.

Bronagh's always been a great organiser. The level of chaos into which she was born rendered it essential, unless she was to proceed, for the rest of her life, lurching from one shambles to the next. Her parents, both doctors, never had any toilet roll. Bronagh insists that now the cupboard under their stairs is full of luxury toilet tissue. The white shelves of the fridge always sat serenely empty. Life and death was their business, and then there was everything else, which wasn't. Bronagh knew that if she wanted order she would need to provide it herself. She asked for an alarm clock for her birthday. She broke everything down into a series of functions and lists. It was that easy. There was nothing that could not be reduced to a series of steps.

This ability made her a pretty invaluable presence. At a teenage party she could work out how everyone would get there: public transport, lifts, taxis. She would sort out the carryout, letting everyone know how much they had to pay. At a house party, she would have a system for picking up the glasses and bottles. Within twenty minutes, total transformation. She was invited to lots of things because of her flair for organisation all through college. When she finished, she worked in an arts centre where again her skills made her invaluable. And then along came Steven. She knew him because he and his band had caused a fire at the centre. At a climactic moment during their most epic song, he tried to set fire to a bunch of roses, but they weren't dry enough. Bronagh could have pointed that out, had she known he was going to do that. She could have found some better suited to the purpose. But the cellophane that was wrapped around the flowers did catch quite spectacularly and then torched a dangling paper streamer. She thought when she saw him loitering in the arts centre foyer that he was there to apologise, but instead it was to talk to her about the band.

'Our new album,' he said, 'is influenced by Emil Cioran.'
'Who's he?' Bronagh asked.
'A nihilist philosopher.'
'I see.'
'But do you?' he asked. 'I wonder if you do. Anyway, he's an anti-natalist, Bronagh. And I am too. I mean, let's just be generally revolutionary. Put them all up against the wall. Glock 43. Boom boom boom. But really what we need is someone to take us to the next level, and that someone could possibly be you.'

She took charge and then before she knew it she was sorting schedules, rehearsal times, press releases, interviews. They got a deal, their album took off, they went to the States. They finished in New York. She remembers the message from Steven to ask that they would all meet in a particular diner. They'd played a great show the night before. The mood would be celebratory, congratulatory. Amazingly they had all arrived before she had. Well, that was strange because usually she had to get them up, particularly the girls. She was for ever trying to renegotiate check-out times with front desks because they were all unable to drag their carcasses out of bed. But there they all sat, Erika and Anita in the gauzy slip dresses and knee boots they'd both got the day before. Erika stretched languidly, tucking her legs underneath her on the plastic red diner seat.

Steven began. 'We're all here because, well, there's no other way of putting it, but we are going to have to let you go.'

Bronagh looked from one face to another.

'Go where?' she said.

'In common parlance,' Steven said, 'I think it is known as—'

'Getting the fucking sack,' Sarge said. 'Sorry.'

'Yeah, sorry.' Erica made a little girl sad face.

But why? The reason, it transpired, was that they had found someone more simpatico to their music. She just wasn't really their type of person.

'I mean, Bronagh,' Sarge said, 'what music do you even listen to?'

In the diner that morning, she couldn't think.

When she went back to the hotel, she put all of their boarding passes in a plastic folder and left it at reception. She picked up the dry cleaning from the shop. She wanted to spit on it but instead she folded the garments carefully and told the receptionist which rooms they were for. She phoned the record company to let them know the news and then finally left a message for Sarge, reminding him of the interview he was doing with a drum magazine later that day. Then she checked herself in to another, cheaper hotel.

She lay in the hotel room for the day, staring at the broken surround of the light fitting, listening to the building works outside, the pneumatic drill. There was silence for a few hours before a different sound began, emanating from somewhere below. It was karaoke. She gave her hair a quick brush, cleaned her teeth and went down. Men who had taken off their ties and put them in their pockets, who had undone their top buttons, were standing on chairs. She took a seat beside a woman who said that her husband was sitting there.

Oh sorry, Bronagh mouthed, but then the husband arrived and squeezed onto the banquette beside them. They were college professors in education from Alabama, in town for a conference with three post-grad students. They indicated a table where two women and one guy sat. Later, Bronagh went with the college professors for an all-you-can-eat buffet, where the woman talked about how she had worked in education for years and loved it. She felt good about it every day of her life. There was nothing more rewarding than working with kids. Kids with challenges. She regretted that, as she'd progressed, she had ended up with less contact time. Her husband agreed. They asked what she did and she said that until recently she'd been in the music business, but that she too wanted to work with kids.

It took a while, it took years of study, but she managed it. She'll probably allude to this Damascene experience this morning, since she is here, in the city where she first decided to follow the path that led eventually to the centre. It will necessarily be a different version, one which will involve greater agency and conscious choice. Sacking won't be mentioned. But it will use the New York locale. The version of the Andersons that she tells will be one that is uncomplicated and binary, with no competing perspectives. That's the problem with Patience's account. She's lost them now. No matter what she does, any retrieval will be difficult after all of this complicated political nuance. And then Ebola into the mix! Her main point is about child labour, right? So why all of this?

The way Finn tells it, and therefore the way she tells it, is that the centre saved his life. It got him into acting and if that hadn't happened, he would have gone the same way as his brother. How it started: somebody contacted the centre to ask if there was anyone who wanted to be an extra in a crowd scene of a movie. This isn't unusual. They often contact the centre. It's not a strange occurrence for one of the girls to take off leggings and a crop top and emerge as a teenage medieval peasant. There was a lot of talk one time about the hanging some of the boys saw in a jail courtyard. The kids get good money for these filming gigs, so there's always plenty of volunteers. And of course everyone likes the association with 411. The Andersons and a crowd of others were there as waifs and strays in some version of old London town that was constructed in the paint hall in the Titanic Quarter. Whatever transpired, Finn came to the attention of the director. He said afterwards it was the way Finn moved. And, as a result, he was given a couple of lines to say, even though that wasn't meant to happen. The director remembered him and, six months later, flew him to Slovenia where he was given a tiny part in a chaotic film that didn't do well. After that, it was the one about the boxing club, the one that was the surprise hit. His face. He just looked like a person you'd known all your life.

Finn was off, doing the boxing film, and Johnny slid into hanging around with another group of people. His mother threw him out of the house after the second drugs raid. He stayed with friends for a bit, slept on sofas and then ended up for a couple of nights in a hostel when the last set of friends fell out with him over money. A fight broke out one night at the hostel and he was cut on the leg with a broken bottle, but he was too wrecked to realise how serious it was. He bled out in his room on his own.

My brother, Finn says, was just as talented as me, and better looking for sure. But he didn't have the same level of support and so things worked out very different. The centre helped me find out what I was good at, made me a better version of myself. While I was at movie events and working with some of the people I admired most in the world, my brother was alone.

It's all only partially true. Because Johnny was still attending the centre when he died, albeit sporadically. Johnny continued there when Finn was suspended for a period, post the paint hall film, for dealing drugs in 411's toilets. Also, Johnny had been an extra that day too. Did he walk so incredibly differently to Finn? Was his face less likeable? Maybe Finn just happened to be standing in closer proximity to the director when they were having a break. Maybe Finn just happened to speak more loudly when he was telling some story to the other guys.

Finn has a partner now, a Canadian actor, Brodie Shaq, who has just brought out her own line of glow products: highlighters and ampoules. He continues to make sizeable donations to the centre and, in memory of his brother, there's the Johnny Anderson Gym, or, as the kids call it, the Junkie Anderson gym, or just the junkie. 'I've been doing half an hour of dead lifts in the junkie.' That wasn't fair because Johnny wasn't ever a junkie. Finn is coming back to the centre in September and everyone will flock to see him. She remembers a time when Johnny brought her a cup of tea from the machine. She never asked him to do that but she must have looked like she needed it. He brought it in, set it on her desk, said, There you go, boss. Another time he gave her a hug. Come here, he said, and he gave her a hug, patted his hand on her back. There was a fraction of a second when she felt he wanted to hold on to her, but then he dropped his hands. See you next week, boss, he said.

Mum 50 quid any chance!

It was the time when she was happiest, the four years before Lyness went to school. They'd tried for a baby for so long. She had been working back then on health education for teens, doing her hormone injections in the toilets before talking to fourteen-year-olds who got pregnant the first time they had sex round the back of the local shops. But then there was Lyness, two months premature and all the more precious as a result. When they eventually got him home, she never wanted to take him outside. Why had they ever painted the walls those zingy yellows, why was that expensive wallpaper so acidic? She wanted a cave for them, a warm and cocooning gloom. She resigned from her job and dedicated her time to Lyness, although Donal queried if that was necessary. People said motherhood was so boring, that they didn't feel fulfilled. Seriously? Lyness was glorious and all that she wanted.

She was pleased when he didn't take well to primary school, fought at the door with the teacher, kicked the classroom assistant. They said that he needed a more phased induction. It wasn't until December that he was able to manage the same hours as the rest of the other children. She wore that as a badge of pride. And then, after that, he was integrated into the system. Not so very long until he was querying and questioning her.

Patience has gone on longer than the impeccably polite email advised. Fleetingly, in order to illustrate a point, there is an image of an exhausted, thin little girl. But her face can't be seen properly, so what a mistake. Bronagh looks at the vertical garden, at the shimmering, soaring buildings outside, the trays from the caterers, and she thinks of the gratitude that she and the others will be required to show.

There is applause and Patience sits down. Fatima nods in her direction, mouths well done. And so Bronagh does the same. When Fatima Bazzi gets up to talk about her project, Bronagh takes a sip of water. Fatima is talking about a school where children with special needs are taught. It was badly damaged by a bomb blast and they have been trying to rebuild it ever since. She is angry, though. Bronagh hears it in her voice, the impatience with people who have consistently let the children down. But the audience won't appreciate it, Bronagh knows that. There's a mode that it's necessary to adopt. Resilient, stoic, sunny. Everything is possible. Getting annoyed makes them feel uneasy, because ultimately maybe you are angry at them, sitting there, listening to all of this before going back to their beautiful apartments where the doorman greets them with a cheery smile and the delivery from that new deli has just arrived. By virtue of their affluence, they are automatically the problem. Getting angry will be taken personally. A slight note of frustration, however, is fine.

Bronagh has spoken in so many places. Not so long ago she was at an event in London, held by a sociology department, to do with education in non-standard institutions. She met another delegate, Sydney, who taught in prisons. Well, she did one day a fortnight. She taught literature to small groups of guys who were interested in a pre-access university course. Sydney had trained as a ballet dancer, so even when she walked across to get a coffee, her movement seemed to be telling a story. Bronagh suggested they go for a drink at the end of the session to a bar she knew in Bloomsbury. On the way, they both bought a lipstick in the same colour. It seemed simultaneously frivolous and indicative of how well they got on, even though it had only been a couple of hours. They also drank the same cocktails, quite a few of them, and then Sydney told her how she had just finished having an affair.

'Oh my god, not with one of the prisoners?' Bronagh asked.

'No, I'm not that much of a cliché,' Sydney replied.

It was a man called Martin. She didn't elaborate much beyond that. And then, because of what had been revealed, Bronagh felt that she should share something too. She said that she'd had an affair too, with a guy called Mick McConnell.

'Lemme guess,' Sydney said. 'Great sex. Off the scale sex.'

Bronagh nodded sheepishly and took a gulp of brandy sour.

She and Sydney hadn't stayed in contact.

Mum!!!! come on!!!!

A week after they bought Lyness a car, he had a crash and it was a total write-off. It was extreme good luck that no one was injured. The police said that he had been driving very carelessly. Bronagh spoke to Donal about this, and said wasn't it par for the course with young men Lyness's age? Donal had said that when he was fourteen, he had taken his mother's car and driven it around late one night. He had put it back in the exact same spot and she'd never known. But, he said, that was in a one-horse town in the middle of nowhere. I didn't meet another car.

Three of the boys in the car had to be hospitalised, two overnight, although Lyness was discharged when they established there was essentially nothing wrong with him. All the parents were at the hospital together. They stood holding coffees. That one woman, her polystyrene cup crimped with teeth marks, said, 'So Lyness just gets to go?'

'Yes,' Bronagh said, 'because there isn't any reason for him to stay in overnight. We've got the leaflet about what we need to do. You know, re concussion.'

'It's alright for some,' she said.

Her husband nudged her arm.

'Well, I don't care! None of this would have happened if your son hadn't been driving.'

'Nobody forced your son to get in the car with my boy,' Donal said.

'Have the police breathalysed him, I wonder?' the woman said. 'Or done any other tests?'

'As far as I know there's no issue,' Bronagh said, surprised.

Fatima Bazzi has got into her stride. She's dropped the angriness and moved on to show what they have been able to do with their limited resources. There is a picture of a boy sitting at a desk that is old and gouged. He's hunched over the desk – writing maybe? There's just a dark head and an arm across a sheet of paper. Look at the arm, scarred, the skin white and raised. Bronagh wonders, did she see that hand flex a little? The hand that rests on the desk. And then the child looks up into the camera and it is a slow, shy smile. He blinks, embarrassed, and then looks at the camera, the smile wider, eyes catching everyone in the room. 'Ali,' Fatima Bazzi says. Nine years old. No mother or father. Cystic fibrosis. Making excellent progress. They have high hopes for Ali.

Well, that's quite a cool trick. The animated photo. It's not super-sophisticated, but Bronagh can see the effect it has on everyone in the room. That's the kind of thing she might want to include herself. She must remember to say to Sheila about it when she gets back. Sheila used to work in IT for global securities in London but after a paradigm shift, her words, she moved back to Northern Ireland and got a job in the centre. Bronagh wonders if she had a breakdown or if a relationship went wrong. Yes, she will speak to

Sheila about this. Possibly it could be integrated at the end of the presentation. She'll maybe suggest a coffee with Sheila.

mum please strapped at pres for cash can you just send 50 quid? pleeez xxxx

Bronagh ignores Patience's flick of her eyes from Fatima to the phone and back to Fatima. She texts Donal three words: I miss you. She hadn't thought about missing him, but now that she has typed that she thinks about how lovely it would have been to have dinner with him in the restaurant last night, how they could have gone for a walk. She sees the two of them walking through Central Park, the golden glow of autumn, their breath in the air, even though it is July. She sends another message, a heart emoji. Fatima is finishing. Bronagh nods. She smiles at Patience. She goes onto the website of Fatima's organisation. It's not possible to make a one-click donation, but she'll do it later. Fifty quid. And then she sends the money to Lyness. Fifty quid. She smiles at Patience as the applause sounds for the end of Fatima's speech. Bronagh gets to her feet.

Ok, right, so there's the fucking four of us, me, Conor, Fergy, Andy J and Hoops, hold on a min, that's five, and yeah, no, Coppa was there as well, and we were walking along, must have been about half one or so, we'd been down this place, this old shop that's all boarded up but you just fucking move this panel and that's you, just shift it over, you're in, we were in there doing our stuff and next thing a rat runs across the floor big old rat and Hoops jumps up like it's going to attack him wise the fuck up Hoops for christsake it's more afraid of you but he says big rats can attack and then Andy J picks up this thing, we'd never noticed it before like a bit of pipe and says let's just kill the thing knock it to fuck but it was long gone, shot off, we need to get our act together lads hanging out with vermin in a place like this, well then get fake ID Hoops says, why don't you send off and pay for the fake ID for all of us to the guy in Croydon London, yeah let's do that, go to Thompson's, get into Thompson's sure, so we left there and were walking along we passed this guy and this girl and this other girl and they were holding hands and one was kissing the other one's neck and Hoops shouts pair of lezzers you're fucking lezzers yous love it and the girl goes that's right, we're fucking lezzers, fucking lesbians, and Hoops said glad we are agreed on that, which made us laugh, glad we are agreed on that, sounds like something an old man would say and then she shouts fucking smicks, and we just walked on because fucking smicks from a lezzer, well, know what I mean, stupid, we saw an old drunk man and he said hello gentlemen and we said shut up, shut up you old dickwad and then there was this girl who was walking along like a lone sheep with no coat or anything we surrounded her and circled her, where you going to we said, you heading to a party? you know where there's any good parties? you just on your way back from a party? from a house party? hey you! we're speaking to you! snobby bitch go fuck yourself says Andy J but I didn't think she was a snobby bitch because she went to the same school as me for fuck's sake so she was hardly a snobby bitch, I remembered her from school couple of years above me, was always sitting on the radiator outside the geography room, the geography room, fucking leave her, I said, are you ok I nearly said but I said fucking leave her because we needed to go down to Conor's house next because there was something that his cousin was going to leave off for him.

It's been slow enough even for a Saturday morning, so Boogie buys a paper and parks the car in a spot that is equidistant to three different zones, in order to max his chances of getting a job. He listens to the radio, a phone-in about new legislation relating to care homes. There's one of those places, in the city centre, that used to be a workhouse, back in time. Occasionally, not that often, he might get a job to it. When he's waiting, he can practically see the lines of pale, skeletal little kids. Never been short on imagination. Roadside memorial and he can see the crash, imagine the sudden burst of metal and light. Same thing, he can envisage all sorts of excitement for the girls, doing this and that, going here and there, but he doesn't really extend the visionary projection to himself. Just getting through the day is the basic objective. But obviously, you know, were he to watch a guy, on a massive screen, filmed carefully, some good soundtrack, buying a paper and parking the car in a spot that is equidistant from three different zones, he would find the scene of interest. What cunt doesn't realise that's how it works? Come on!

The girls will do fine. Leigh said they were better off with him than with her – never a truer word spoken. She didn't know how long it would be before she could take them back. Difficult to have them dumped on him, in that flat. Jay didn't like it, understandably. This place is too small to have two kids here, he said. Plus, Boogie, it looks weird.

Two guys in a poky gaff with wee girls. Know what I mean? Back then, Boogie had been working in a restaurant and he'd had to phone the woman and keep telling her he was sick. Plus, Misty should have been in school. He didn't know what to do about that. She asked if there was any homework she could be doing. He gave her lots of old receipts and told her to check up the addition to see that the machine had got it right. He wanted to know that he wasn't being ripped off. Misty drew on the backs of the envelopes sent to the old guy who used to live in the flat. Her drawings of houses and little people he put along the mantelpiece. But still, he wanted the kids gone. What happened to fun-time? He was only twenty.

Fair's fair, a couple of weeks, but he wasn't equipped to look after two fucking kids that really weren't his responsibility. Hard to know even where to put them. They were on the sofa for a while, covered in the duvet from his room, the one that hadn't been washed since he'd moved in. But that meant that Jay had to go to his bedroom when the kids were ready to sleep. So, he reversed that arrangement and the kids took his bed, while he slept on the two-seater. Then he lost his job. We need someone more reliable they said, and who could blame them? Round the back of that Malaysian restaurant . . . If there was one in the town he would've firebombed it. It was her decision, fucking Leigh, her decision to have the baby and the other kid was nothing to do with him. Now they were a chirping, early morning, eating, shitting reality.

Nan D brought round nappies and two sets of pyjamas.

'You should get that one toilet trained,' she said. She also said that she was done looking after kids. It wasn't her job. She'd done it, and then she'd done it again, and she wasn't going for a third time. Boogie had liked living with her, although there was the constant criticism of his mother, who had never been worthy of Nan D's son. Still photos of his dad everywhere in Nan D's house. Nan D had some idiosyncratic traditions and rules. When she boiled the potatoes, she always put the plates on top of the saucepan so that they were warm. You could smoke inside the house, even weed, but you weren't allowed to put your feet up on her sofa. You could stay out all night and she wouldn't enquire as to your whereabouts, but you had to be there for the tea at six o'clock.

'Sure thing,' he said. 'I get ya. But I don't have a fucking clue, Nan. You have got to give me a hand.'

'Have I?'

Fuck and then didn't the kids get chickenpox. He let Misty play with one of the children from a downstairs flat and she picked it up from her. She was sick all over the bed and then, when he took her to get cleaned up in the bathroom, he saw the rash. Don't be scratching them now! he said, wisdom coming from he knew not where. What was it sick kids ate? Soup? He got Nan D to bring round a couple of tins. She also came with calamine lotion, which she dabbed on Misty with cotton wool.

'Funny wee piece,' she said afterwards.

Misty was picking at the scabs, so he got toilet roll and duct tape, made DIY mitts out of them. She said that her bottom was sore. What was he meant to do? 'My bottom's the sorest of any part of me,' she said, when she woke up in the night. Jesus Christ, what was he meant to do? He couldn't look. She was starting to whimper. 'It's sore, Boogie. At the front of my bum.'

'I'll give you the cream and you can rub it on,' he said.

'But I can't, not with these things!' she said, holding up a hand wrapped in bog roll and black tape.

'I'll take that off you,' he said. 'We'll unwrap your hands, like a boxer after a fight. And you can rub on the cream. Then we can wrap you up again.'

And then the fucking baby got the spots. Jay moved out. Good luck, he said, but he did not want to live in a children's ward. All the rent was now down to Boogie. He was up all night with Geneva because the chickenpox were in her throat and she wasn't able to breathe. 'There,' he said, as he pushed damp hair off her face, 'there, bird, there you go.'

Message after message and Leigh never answered her phone. Then she got in touch one day to say that she'd been in hospital. The phone went dead after that. Nan D said that he should get legal advice because someone can't just dump kids on you like this. Had that waste of space got no relatives? Wee missy there had missed weeks of school and something needed to be done, so Nan D said that she'd accompany him to Knox Dallesandro where she'd gone a few years ago over that whole altercation with her neighbour. One of Mr Bobby Dallesandro's juniors ensured that Nan D had no case to answer.

Nan D turned up dressed for a wedding in a pale blue suit with a dainty little chain belt.

'What?' she said. 'You got to put on the right togs for these people to take you seriously.'

'More like you fancy Bobby Dallesandro.'

'Bobby's too important to be doing anything about little kids. It'll all be top crimes for Bobby.'

But still, when they got there, she was peering around, looking for him. The woman in reception watched the girls when Boogie and Nan D went in to see the solicitor, who listened to what they had to say about the situation before stating that foster care would be an option, should no one be in a position to look after the children. Social services should be contacted.

'Oh no,' Boogie said. 'I don't think I'd be putting them into care.'

'It would usually be temporary until the mother can look after them again.'

'What money does he get, if he hangs on to them?' Nan D asked.

'If he becomes their temporary guardian, you mean?' the solicitor said.

It wasn't really that difficult what he had to do. Being a parent is not something of great complexity and requiring of great skill. That's one of those bullshit things people try to tell you. The reality is that if you are able to look after, say, even a small dog, a Jack Russell, then you are able to look after a kid. You just need to get it organised: enough food, somewhere decent to sleep, somewhere warm. Try to keep them clean. But at the same time, although it's basic, that doesn't mean it is always easy. He wasn't always great. There were plenty of nights, at the beginning, when he got really wasted on his own after they'd gone to bed. And, back then, he did still hope that Leigh would feel better and would want them back. And then that became the thing he dreaded most. Luckily, all that happened was that she had them over to Scotland for a few days.

He made plenty of mistakes. He's not kidding; on that, he was parento numero uno. Take that kid's indoor play-park, when Gen was about four. It was the usual range of trippy stuff: a crazy castle, a huge piano-keyboard on the floor, nonsense noise coming from it as children jumped on and off. The three of them spent ages watching the slushie machine, the paddles churning yellow and blue ice. What colour to get? They all went for blue. Earlier on, he thought that he'd seen another kid push Gen. Inevitable, really, at a place like this. But then it happened again, on the balcony of the crazy castle, a push so hard, and with two hands, that it caused Gen to fall.

Boogie was on his feet. 'Oi, blondie!' he shouted. 'You gonna stop that?'

The girl went wide-eyed and then disappeared inside the castle.

Boogie was sipping on his blue slushie when a woman with a ponytail came over to him with her crying child.

'I'm terribly sorry,' she said, 'but as you can see my child is extremely upset. Do you happen to have some kind of problem?'

'No,' Boogie said. 'All fine. I don't have a problem.'

When her gaze remained on him, he said, 'Well alright then, I do have a problem. I do actually have a problem when your kid gives mine a massive dig in the back, but all sorted now.'

'I didn't see anything.'

'Well, she did,' Misty piped up. 'I saw it. She went like this—' and she offered a re-enactment of it. The woman looked at Misty, her tongue and teeth stained blue, her hair matted where it hadn't been brushed in days. And then she turned to Boogie.

'I would ask you not to speak to my child, or any other child, like that.'

'Fuck off,' he said.

He stared at the woman and it was a thrill to know that she was frightened. It was a delight. He took a step towards her and saw her eyes searching for someone to help her. Let her panic. He could smell her perfume. Then suddenly he stopped. 'Let's go, kids,' he said. The girls slipped on their shoes quickly and he noticed how scuffed and shabby they were, the laces grey. They were still waiting outside the playpark for the bus when the woman and her child pulled out. The little girl, no longer crying, looked at Boogie for a few seconds and then, bored, turned away.

'You need to brush your hair in the mornings, Misty,' Boogie said. 'I've told you before.'

But they have had plenty of laughs too. Like the time he did that thing out in the back yard with the Mentos and the jumbo bottle of Coke. It has to be those very specific mints. Polos or whatever and you are wasting your time. Ain't going to work. But if you use Mentos, the most insane geyser of Coke will shoot up into the air, but you got to make sure you shoot the Mentos in quick, using a funnel. The laughs of the three of them. 'Do it again!' the girls shouted. 'Do it again!' And so, he went the next day and bought more mints. And they did it again the day after that.

In the afternoon, Boogie calls home again because he'd just finished a job that was in his very own street. Gen asks him if he has had anyone funny in the car.

'Not really,' he says. 'No comedians. No wise guys. Thank god. Can do without them. Can do without big characters. Spare me from big characters. Dickheads.'

'Do you believe in the lost city of Atlantis? I just watched a video about it.'

'Don't know. Do you? What's this?' He points at a cardboard box.'

'Oh, that just arrived for Misty. She said that she was going to get a ring light. So maybe that's what it is. Not sure.'

Last year Misty did beauty at college. Sometimes she still tries to do special effects make-up. 'Look,' she said, when she came down one day with a huge bruise on her leg. 'What do you think?'

'I don't like it,' Boogie said.

'I could give you a black eye!'

'I don't want a black eye, love.'

'Boogie!' Misty shouts from the landing. 'Will you be home to give me a lift to work? I need to be down the hotel by four.'

'Sure.'

'She's such a lazy ass,' says Gen. 'She should get the bus. She should make her own way there. She should take responsibility.'

'Why don't you fill me in on this Atlantis place?' Boogie says.

Even though she moved to England many years ago when she got married, Alice Fisher and I remained firm friends. Early last year, she inherited a property, a small house off the Lisburn Road. Alice had the idea that the house could be modernised to allow for short-term lets. Alice knew someone who did this in Devon and was keen to do similar. Her brainwave was that I could be project manager, as she called it, of the renovations and take charge of the management of the property in relation to arrivals and departures. Alice would pay me, of course, and it would give me something interesting to do with my time. My time, as far as I was concerned, was already occupied quite pleasantly, but I agreed, nonetheless.

There were structural issues to do with the kitchen and upstairs there was damp. I had never overseen work of this kind before, and was pleased with how I managed. I gave Alice regular progress updates. She gave me free rein with the décor and this filled me with great excitement. I studied interiors magazines and websites for ideas. Favouring a balance of the elegant and the rustic, there was a shop in Belfast which I particularly enjoyed visiting, Campagne de Provence. I got ideas for graceful, airy spaces quite unlike the dank and rather forbidding style of Alice's late relation. Alice's two insistent points were that the interior design shouldn't be exorbitant and that it should photograph well for the booking website. I think I made a very good job of it, a very good job indeed, to such an extent that I felt, had I started earlier, I could have been a great proficient in the area of interiors.

When the house was done and prior to the arrival of any guests, I stood in the sitting room with its chandelier and rough-hewn boards, its bunches of lavender and wooden cabinets, and thought how it was such a pity that it couldn't stay in this pristine state. The main bedroom upstairs was of particular note. I had bought, at auction, antique bedlinen trimmed with French lace. On the chest of drawers there was a beautiful bowl and jug in duck egg blue. I lay on the bed myself and at a certain angle I could not see the roofs of the terrace opposite. It was timeless, classic, but not at all staid.

Of course, it couldn't stay immaculate although the first few bookings did encourage me to think that perhaps it would attract the kind of appreciative clientele who would take care of it. The first of these was a woman from Kent who was at a conference at Queen's University to do with medieval city states. She provided that rather superfluous detail when making her booking. There followed a couple who took it for a week as their base while they explored the sights of the north Antrim coast.

But then, after that, the lace got ragged. I was also responsible for cleaning the house after the guests, a dimension of my duties that had been added in a rather ad hoc fashion by Alice. I told her about the range of people who were starting to appear and she asked if there wasn't some kind of filter that could be applied on the website. But it seemed not. There were the teenage parties. Someone would rent the house as a venue for a party after a school formal or other such event. The neighbours did not appreciate this. On a couple of occasions, when I turned up in the morning, they confronted me about the noise and disruption. I said that I didn't own the house but was employed by someone who lived in England. They didn't seem terribly satisfied by that, and to be honest, neither was I, by that stage. I was tidying up one particular morning when the police appeared. They told me to cease what I was doing immediately. I pointed out the bag that I had found in the kitchen, They asked me if I had been upstairs, to the bedroom. I said no, not as yet.

They were there for a number of hours. I told Alice what I surmised about the police visit from the little that they'd said. She was anxious to know if it would mean the next booking might have to be cancelled. I said that really, I didn't know. It is always difficult to break long-held friendships. But it is also equally true that if one goes back far enough, we find we do not know the friends in question at all.

Miriam, en route to Sports JPX, walks quickly. She passes a group of women, sitting outside a bar, wearing tiaras and gauzy wings. The one getting married is the fairy with the veil. Titania looks sad. Maybe she wants a woodland vale, rather than a makeshift beer garden decorated with painted kegs. No such fandango when Miriam and Kahlil got married, just a small crowd at the City Hall, for a ceremony with all of the spirituality of a pre-flight safety talk and wasn't that a godsend? Martha stood beside her in a blue dress. Her father had wanted there to be a blessing at the Shepherd Church, the new place they'd joined. No, Miriam said. No thanks. They got married five months after she had walked up those stairs to the room above the barber's on the Donegall Road. Her parents were told of the wedding only a fortnight before. His name's Kahlil. Their mental search of bible names came back with nil result. Where's he from? Belfast. Portadown. Dublin. He came to Dublin from Egypt when he was sixteen with his brother. But he's gone back there again. Her parents were horrified at the news. 'I forbid it,' her father said, like an Old Testament patriarch. 'I'm afraid it doesn't work like that,' Miriam said. 'But maybe this is good news. His family, they're something called Coptic Christians, if that means more to you than it does to me.'

Kahlil met her parents a week before the wedding in the first-floor restaurant of a hotel. Everyone was scrupulously polite and both Kahlil and her dad wore a shirt and tie.

After, they went to Egypt for their honeymoon, where his two sisters and mother took in every inch of Kahlil's bride and were slow to be friendly. But his brother's wife made Miriam laugh with her impressions of them.

Of course there were things about Kahlil that could be ridiculous. He was always working. After the place above the barber's, it was a bigger place above a Chinese travel agent's, and then a warehouse by the docks. He moved on from supplying most of the restaurants in Belfast to restaurant properties and fit-outs. Kahlil was sentimental. He hung on to that little takeaway, Pepe's, because it was the very first place that ever had him as a supplier. He bought it when the owner retired. He went round these places, always working, even when it wasn't necessary. He should have let Pepe's go.

Plus, he could be stubborn. He never went to any of the prenatal classes for either of the boys. He thought the other men there were absolute losers. 'Are you kidding?' he said. 'Some of us have work to do! We're not all lazy ass fuckers who want to spend an hour sitting on a beanbag listening to a student nurse!' He was ridiculous too, and flashy. The next-door neighbours got a garden house built, a modest timber affair that peeked over the hedge, its fairy lights twinkling. When they came home one evening, there was, at the bottom of the garden, a giant orb, a glass and chrome sputnik. 'Get inside!' Kahlil said. 'Man, are you going to love it. Go inside! The seats are leather!' They all went into the globe, which had a circular table in its centre. They sat facing each other as though about to begin a space age séance.

'There's integrated speakers,' Kahlil said. 'Let's have some music.'

* * *

Sports JPX, not so far away now. She could call into Die Halle, if she wants. Rami's working there today. He said there's a big stock take so he'll be back late. Die Halle looks like a prison; utilitarian, brutalist. When he first got the job there, Miriam went in to see where he would be. There was a hushed reverence for these clothes that looked appropriate for mountaineering. Miriam passes the fruit and vegetable shop, Cash Converters, a rug shop. She hears a man's voice call her name, Miriam, Miriam, and at first she thinks it is one of the homeless guys who are fighting over a trolley filled with bags. She stops and looks at them, waiting for one of them to utter it again. She is shocked to see how young they are. And then her name, Miriam! Miriam! It's Jimmy. And beside him is Cyndi. They were friends of Kahlil. When their son turned eighteen, Kahlil and Miriam were invited to the party. There was an incredible four-foot-high swan carved out of ice. Cyndi is apologetic, 'We're so sorry. We are only back from Hong Kong last month.'

'Oh,' Miriam says, 'please, you were away! Of course! No apologies.'

'And you're OK?' Cyndi asks. 'The boys are OK?'

'Yes, we are all doing alright.'

'We couldn't believe it. Kahlil. Just so young,' Jimmy says, shaking his head.

'We really wish we could have been at the funeral.'

'Honestly, please don't apologise.'

'But, Miriam, what happened?' Cyndi asks. 'We heard another driver was drunk and we heard that Kahlil had a seizure and we heard—'

Jimmy puts his hand on Cyndi's arm.

'No, it's alright. He lost control of the car and hit a tree,' Miriam says.

'He was a very good friend to us, always,' Jimmy says.
'I have to go,' Miriam says.
'Our condolences.'
'Thank you. I'm sorry. It's just that I really have to go.'

When Kahlil didn't come home that night, Miriam hadn't been too concerned because he often stayed late, working. It wasn't unusual for him not to answer his phone. He liked late-night talk and a few drinks. He knew people all over the city, the kind who enjoyed telling long and winding stories, who came from all over. It wasn't unusual for Miriam to come downstairs in the morning to find him lying asleep on one of the sofas. But this time the doorbell rang at about five in the morning. He'd forgotten his keys! They had a spare set, hidden under a stone in the front garden, beneath a rose bush. Miriam had placed them there in case the boys lost theirs. Kahlil would have forgotten about that. Or maybe one of the boys had used that spare set and not replaced them. She was wearing only a nightie when the two policemen sat her down on the sofa to tell her that there had been an accident and that Kahlil had died at the scene.

No, no, no, no, no, no, no

She was taken to the police station in the days after and they gave her a bag with some of his clothes in it. A policewoman with her hair cut in a blunt bob said very solemnly, when she took Miriam into a little room and gave her a cup of coffee, that he hadn't been alone. She had a righteous look and so Miriam thought the woman meant it as a form of comfort, that Jesus always walks with you. She thought of that story, where a person sees along the beach of life their footprints and those of Jesus until there is just one set of footprints. And when they query Jesus about this, and ask where were you Lord, he replies that that was when he was carrying them.

'We don't believe in that,' Miriam said.

'He wasn't alone.'

'I said, we don't believe in that.'

'A young woman. She's in hospital.'

Jimmy and Cyndi might know about this girl. They might have heard that she was in the takeaway, Pepe's. They might assume that Kahlil was having an affair and he died, not with Miriam beside him, but his young lover. Rami and Haady were told their dad was giving a lift to someone. That's all she said at first. And later on, she said to Rami, her voice high, 'It's amazing the ridiculous things people say. Always over-dramatising. They've to make a story of everything, even someone just doing a good turn!'

'Sure,' Rami said, after a pause. 'Talkers gonna talk.'

She tries to remember, yet again, as she stares at the street preacher outside the sports shop, their loudspeaker warping their speech, what the last thing was that she said to Kahlil. Bye-bye? See you. I'll see you when I see you. She might've been absorbed in what she was doing and not even said that. She might not have raised her head. The police were very insistent. He died instantly. Could they be absolutely confident of that? There were no last words, he didn't die, you know, calling out?

Miriam could have found out, one way or another, something about this girl. But if there is even a slight chance that Kahlil might've liked her, she would prefer not to know. Better that than finding out there was something. Martha organised the funeral. She came over and took charge of everything. Miriam spent that time on Tramadol, left over from when Kahlil injured his arm. She took the tablets with red wine and the world turned glassy and slow. Martha said, Why assume the worst? He gave someone a lift. People give other people lifts all the time. You have no reason to ever doubt him. He was crazy about you. I mean, of course, Martha said, who can ever know the strange depths of others, the secret inner lives, etcetera, etcetera, etcetera, but I don't think that you should doubt Kahlil at all on this particular score. You guys were nuts about each other. It's been what I always wished for, that I would end up having something like that. It's what I've always hoped for. And then she held up her hands. Enough, she said. I'm heading to the shops because you are low on absolutely all essentials.

Miriam presents the girl to herself in various iterations: gorgeous, pouting, oozing out of booty shorts, blind, stinking of chip fat, friendly, pert, blonde, redhead, Somali, Polish, Egyptian. She imagines Kahlil and the girl on the bonnet of the car. All the different girls. She's got a single bed now, like when she was a kid. She and Martha once had beds so narrow they couldn't turn around for fear of falling out. Miriam got rid of the double. She couldn't bear to reach across and feel the cold sheet, couldn't stand the emptiness.

Sports JPX. She came here one day to get sports socks for Haady and gasped when she saw it. A mannequin that had a physique just like Kahlil. The way the fabric of the green tracksuit top stretched across the shoulders so that you could see the swell of back muscles. The slightly bandy legs and the stance, with weight on the left foot. The plastic when she touched it felt smooth and not cold. The moulded indication of a side parting, those forearms, the biceps. It was him in a green tracksuit with white and black trainers. And shorts and sweatshirt. Seven versions of Kahlil in different outfits and poses. Thank you, she said.

Misty had been to my house a few times. We'd hung out together. We knew each other. I knew she liked me. It wasn't a surprise to either of us when we had sex.

We had a teacher at school, believe it or not, done for armed robbery. Taught ICT when the other woman who wore the pink jumpers was off having a baby. Teacher was the driver. Can't remember how long he went down for but his teaching career was over, finito. People who've done that aren't allowed to teach kids. Pity, to be fair. He was OK. And certainly no worse than the woman with the pink jumpers who had the baby. Plenty of people said, me included, that if they'd known he was that kind of guy, then they would have paid more attention to him in class when he was going on about option control command shift or whatever. There was another teacher that we had called Mr Mumbles, wee man with a shit car. Don't know his real name, that was just what we called him, Mr Mumbles. There was this guy in our class called Boogie Downes and he was fucking amazing at art. Didn't really matter what it was, he could draw it. The art teacher gave us stupid ass stuff to draw, a shoe or some fucking piece of fruit in the centre of the table, and this one guy could do it so it looked 3D, like it was leaping out at you. He could just do it, no sweat. You ever been around talented people? Like I don't think I've ever been around talented people apart from Boogie Downes. Most people can't do shit. In the form room in the mornings people would ask him for pictures of their dog or a flag or somebody's face and he could just do it, just do it. We'd all crowd around and watch. And the form teacher, Mr Mumbles, would always say in his fancy voice well, let's just see what Boogie Downes Productions is producing today and he would watch too. Boogie Downes Productions. It was what Mr Mumbles always said, like it was a TV programme. Up to that point the fella was just plain Michael Downes, but then he started getting known all the time as Boogie. Ha ha to be fair, Boogie would also draw tits and people fucking but not if Mumbles was going to see it. Fast forward like, ten years, and I was actually on remand myself – do not ask! But I'll give you a clue, not armed robbery – and this older guy is playing music, what have you, and I say what's that, and he goes, that's Boogie Down Productions and I'm like, Jesus Christ almighty, there's people called that? Because obviously I'm thinking back about old Mumbles with his shit car. Mumbles was fucking having his own little private joke, weren't he? But here is the thing, the moral of this story is that you got no idea at all what people are into. No idea. Like, you could make judgements about me and I could do the same about you. And we could both be right. Or we could both be wrong. Or one right, one wrong if you want to be, you know, strict about it. If you had asked me, I would've said Mumbles would listen to orchestras and that shit. Ended up anyway that Boogie

Down Productions, I got into them. Although, times change, I got a fiancée now and she pays for the Spotify so she always gets the main say on what we play and it is usually women singing. My fiancée likes music that's fun. I do too, why not, have a laugh, but you don't need to have a laugh all of the time. Know what, I saw the man himself Boogie Downes a few years ago, pushing a buggy round Tesco with another kid in tow. Boogie! I said. Fuck's sake! Ya still doing the old – and I pretended to do a sketch in the air. But he didn't know what I was on about at all.

In the afternoon, Frankie tells Nina that she is going into Ladyhill for an hour or so. Either Elaine or Joanne will be arriving, the two sisters who are the housekeepers at the Levine house, responsible for washing, ironing, cleaning and other general duties. The arrival of the online supermarket shop is always synchronised with their presence in the house. The sisters make meals and put them in the freezer. Very occasionally, when guests sit around the huge dining table, Elaine arranges for caterers to come. She orders flowers every week and arranges them. She is a master of *ikebana*. When Barbara was there, only Joanne came, once a week. Barbara was a great cook.

Barbara was, like Neil, a villager. That's what people who are from the old part of Ladyhill call themselves. Strange term, like people wearing smocks and clogs or burning an effigy in midsummer. But the villagers here come from the Georgian terraces, and their connecting avenues, which run off the four corners of the green, rather than the newer houses clustered around the three roads that lead out of Ladyhill, or the council estate one mile outside. When Neil first mentioned Ladyhill, he said it was regarded as the most English town in Northern Ireland. English? What did that even mean? Tower blocks? The view from Jackie Boyce Residence of dirty warehouses and lockups? No, it was the village green and the architecture, the antique shops and the cricket club, the beautiful old church with its renowned stained glass. He said where he lived was five miles from Belfast. Belfast? Frankie looked it up and saw a picture of the City Hall under an apocalyptic sky.

He'd been honest with her, from somewhere adjacent to the beginning. They were in a hotel room and he said, 'I'm married, as I'm sure you probably realise.'

'Sure,' she said.

'But here's the thing, my wife isn't very well.'

She didn't reply. She was thinking about her pale blue dress and if she could wear it again that night, or if it would look dirty on the second day.

'Six months, the best prognosis. Very aggressive. We've been together a long time, you know, Frankie. Since we were at school.'

'Six months,' she said. 'Not long.'

'No. And if it's hard for me, it's even harder for the kids. For Chris and Nina.'

'That's tough,' she said.

Neil had got up and dressed at that point, embarrassed at having uttered his kids' names while in the same bed as her. But later on that night, he said, at various intervals, you understand me, you make me feel ten years younger, I just want to be happy – is that wrong? I can be myself with you, no one has made me feel so desired in such a long time. And so on.

This afternoon Frankie is going to pick up Neil's prescription. Statins. When she says to Elaine, who has just arrived, she points out that there's no need, Mrs Levine. She can pick up whatever is required this afternoon. There's no need for her to go to Cassidy's Chemists. Frankie says, no, she's going. They're always understaffed, Elaine replies. I hope you don't end up having to sit for ages, Mrs Levine. You could always ask them to deliver the prescription, you know. But Frankie says that today, she'll be going to Cassidy's, to pick it up.

She parks her car in front of the village green. So English. When they had to say bye-bye to Jackie Boyce Residence, she and Michelle got a dilapidated flat, sharing with Pili from Kisumu who was doing a post-grad course in civil engineering. We are here to make your life a total mess! Michelle said to him. They would come into his room in the middle of the night when they were back from some club, jump on his bed, wake him up. He pretended to get annoyed but he said he didn't feel homesick like he did in the place where he stayed before. He showed them a photo of his little brother in a school uniform. She and Michelle got jobs on and off in bars, restaurants, shops. Coggy sometimes slept on their couch when she'd been thrown out by her parents. I can't be bothered with Coggy, Michelle said. She's a tourist. A day-tripper. And then she goes back to Daddy and Mommy dearest. When Pili returned to Kisumu, they had to find another flat.

The French trip made it all change. Amrita had a boyfriend called Warren Jeffares and, suddenly, there was talk of them all going on holiday with him and a few friends. He'd a place in the south of France and also a beautiful, big boat. It made sense just to jack in their jobs – they were crap anyway – and fly to Nice on a budget flight. There was a car waiting for them to take them to Villefranche-sur-Mer and Amrita got annoyed because Michelle kept saying dopey stuff in French that she could remember from school. Stop being so fucking childish, Michelle! The houses were so colourful, like something a kid would draw. The bounce of light on the water was almost blinding. When they arrived at the house, there were people by the pool and Amrita went over to fling her arms around the person they supposed was Warren Jeffares. A guy in a white jacket, an actual servant, came over to them with a tray of drinks. They were strong and long, cold and delicious.

In the chemist, Frankie hands over the prescription to the young pharmacist who says that he'll have it with her as soon as possible. Frankie doesn't reply and, because there's a queue of others waiting, she takes the plastic seat at the end of a row of four. She looks at the packets and plastic tubs of the pharmacy, the notes pinned to the wall. Further along is the chemist section with the painkillers and cough medicine, the couple of units of cheap make-up. Later, there was that guy called Didier who took them shopping. Michelle got a Fendi dress but it made her sweat loads. Frankie got a swimsuit. The handles of the bags in that shop were like little pieces of twisted rope. Amrita didn't go on the shopping trip because she stayed with Warren. She thinks she's the queen bee now, Michelle said. Thinks she is better than us.

There was a boat and the tender took them out to it. On the yacht, Teo was there. When he didn't wear a white shirt, he wore a white vest. Tufts of hair grew on his shoulders. He didn't drink and he wore little slip-on shoes. The rest of him was pure bulk but his feet were dainty. Michelle loved to order around the guys who worked on the boat. Her drink was too hot, too cold, needed more ice, jeez, that's too much ice you've ruined the drink! Frankie sometimes noticed those guys looking at her, Michelle and Amrita. Those guys had contracts and a regular pay packet. Michelle and Frankie split it between them, giving Didier his hand satisfaction, as he called it. Your turn tonight, Miss Frankie

Frank Franks! I'm doing my nails. May it be quick and easy, Michelle said.

One night, Frankie couldn't sleep and she ended up standing in the doorway of space near the galley area, where the boat crew were playing cards. The one guy stopped dealing and they all stared at her. When she asked what they were playing, the dealer said why didn't she join them. She said that no, she'd just watch. But when she wasn't required to be involved with Didier, she went other nights too. By the fourth time, they were friendly. They told her that they had names for everyone on the yacht: Teo was Super Mario, Didier was SleazyD, Amrita was Pocahontas. What you call Michelle? Moany bitch, one said. What do you call me? Laura, the chef said. Because you look like a girl who used to crew on this boat by the name of Laura. What does she do now? Don't know. And someone dealt out the cards again.

In the chemist shop, a man goes past pushing a buggy. The baby drops her bottle and it rolls to land at Frankie's feet. She stares at the teat, the horizon of milk. The man picks it up, stares at her. Cocksucker, she thinks. Expects her to pick it up. He seems familiar and she wonders if she knows him from one of the schools. Got that look. There was a teacher once, the first time she had to attend one of these parents' affairs; Neil of course was away so she had to go. She put on a beautiful, tailored suit, but all the rest of the parents were there in jogging bottoms and slouchy jumpers. The teachers, and one of them might have been this guy, all said how very clever Chris was, particularly those teaching him sciences. Top ten in the year without even trying. Chris simply nodded, neither arrogant nor modest, at this statement of fact. Then they sat down in front of another woman who talked for a while about something or other before declaring that Chris had been stealing chips from the canteen. She'd a tight line of a mouth. Behind her desk was her timetable all coloured in, next to a bible verse and a picture of a sunset. She said that Chris had stolen chips quite a few times now and quite frankly the canteen staff were fed up with it.

'Chris doesn't need to steal chips,' Frankie said.

'He doesn't need to steal them, I think that is quite obvious to us all, but that is what he has been doing.'

'Chris,' Frankie said, turning to him, 'have you been stealing chips from the canteen?'

'No,' said Chris, staring at the teacher.

'That's it then,' Frankie said, smoothing her fine wool pencil skirt as she got up.

Schools. Colleges. Frankie thought she'd escaped all of that for herself. And yet, when she and Michelle returned from that trip to France, Frankie had actually wondered if she should return to education of some type.

'What?' Michelle had said. 'You? Why? Are you fucking kidding?'

'Might be a good idea. To do something. Make something of myself. Max my assets.'

'What? Babes, you are making something of yourself. You've come back with loads of designer gear from a crazy long trip to Villefranche Frenche Fruncherama, a party extravaganza.'

'Yeah, where a woman was nearly murdered.'

'It wasn't that bad, Frankie. Don't be daft.'

It had happened during the final week of their stay, when everyone was hanging out at the house. There were two new girls there, petite, dramatic, from Slovenia. They talked to each other in their own language, giggling little chats which involved whispering in each other's ears, looking around, laughing and then smiling demurely. One of them had a scar at her throat. Tracheotomy, Michelle said. Seen it before. There were other people who came to party at the villa, a man from the town who owned a string of restaurants and a couple of businesspeople that Didier knew. And other girls. The mood drifted and bent, depending on the configuration of people who were there. One night, Frankie sat up with the Slovenian girl with the scar. The other one wasn't well. She had been sick since the day before. On her own, she was fine. Michelle was in bed. There were big, guttering candles and lights in the trees. From somewhere, there was distant bass. They were drinking wine. There was the noise of the crickets. And then suddenly the Slovenian girl started singing and it filled the night, and although Frankie didn't know the language she knew it was a sad song, and maybe also about love. The girl didn't look at her but Frankie watched her, as she sang, and she looked so young.

The next day there was a group of them, lazy at lunchtime, sitting in the sun outside. Frankie was in the pool. Teo had been in an agitated mood the past day or so, always on the phone, always shouting in some language. He had argued with one of the friends of the guy who owned the restaurant. He had held up his hands, OK! he had said, OK! and then he had left. The Slovenian girl, the one who had been sick, came out and she said something to Teo, who was now sitting under the vines. Whatever it was, he didn't like it and told her to come back. She didn't, she continued walking, and then he got up and caught her by the arm. She said something else and then he hit her, with the back of his hand, so that she was knocked off her feet and landed hard on the path. He lifted her by the hair and punched her in the face. Everyone watched this spectacle. It was over quickly. Teo rubbed his fist and went back inside. The girl lay there and it was Warren and Amrita who took her, immobile, to her room.

The pharmacist calls Levine but Frankie doesn't move from her seat. She's watching one of the people who have come to the special hatch just a little further down from the pharmacy counter. The chief pharmacist speaks to the woman and she is given a liquid to drink. Frankie knows that gauntness. She watches her take the methadone. Frankie feels a momentary softness, it hovers there, as she sees the flutter of the woman's hands as she puts down the cup, her mother in a mauve smudge of a memory, putting on a skirt, zipping it at the side, her hand reaching out to touch Frankie's hair. Levine? the man calls again, and she is up to get the statins. She gives him a brief nod and puts them in her bag.

And so, yeah, after France, Frankie investigated courses in ICT and marketing. She even thought, briefly, about university access. But then the job turned up, working for Skyline, on private charters, flying out of Farnborough. She did that for a couple of years. The passengers were nearly always preoccupied men. The pilots seemed to talk a lot about their kids' school fees. And that was where she met Neil. She thought at first he was Scottish but he said no, Northern Ireland. It was strange that for such a wealthy guy, he was so amazed by her. When he eventually asked her to marry him and to come and live in Ladyhill, she wasn't sure. She looked around her room, thought of that sofa with its slash sealed with duct tape, taking turns with the microwave and how much longer it might be before anyone else came along. And so they got married, with Michelle as a witness. Coggy sent flowers from New York, where she was now studying sculpture.

When Frankie gets back to the Levine house, everything is pristine and orderly. The food has been put away in the cupboards. Elaine has left instructions for the chicken that is in the fridge and due to be roasted. The fruit bowls are now a riot of shape and colour. Frankie looks at the three-foot-high flower arrangement in the hall. She asks Chris if he wants to go for a run with her later on, but he says no. He's leaving soon because he's working tonight. Maybe he'll go on somewhere afterwards, he's not sure. Chris's weekly allowance is triple what he earns in the hotel. The job has more of a social dimension. Nina says that she could come. No, Frankie says, you couldn't keep up.

I worked for many years when I was younger in a café, situated in a picturesque village outside of Belfast. It was olde worlde, from the wooden beams across the ceiling to the Bakewell tart we used to serve. We had our regulars, whom we would greet by name, even at times bringing out a bowl of water for their dogs. Sometimes there were others, possible trysts in an out of the way spot, holding hands beneath the tables, or men with younger, well, lads, I would say, at times. Uncles and nephews maybe. Fathers and sons. There was a time one of the lads started to cry. The older man looked round, embarrassed and impatient. Perhaps the young lad had suffered a bereavement. Or possibly he had broken up with a girlfriend. It was only later that I found out, when I came across it in a newspaper, that a favoured location for Special Branch handlers to meet their low-level informants was, in fact, our café.

I did it after Chris, except I couldn't do it. So, I just pretended. I just pretended I was doing it. I don't know what happened. I wouldn't want to hurt anyone. But then that bottle was in my hand.
  I don't know what I was thinking of.

In the hotel there's loads of different outfits, from the chefs in their whites, to the reception staff in those black suits with gold buttons. Upstairs, there's a small bar and restaurant that's only open a couple of nights a week. It's for the top people. It's called Erito. The chef is Japanese. He gets ingredients flown in specially. Misty has tasted a spoonful of a pudding from Erito. It was being photographed for a magazine and ended up being left in reception. They all had a scoop of it. It tasted nice, like a milky Haribo. The staff in that restaurant have to wear shirts with little cufflinks. Fucking pain, Tom, who works there, says. He uses instead those little pieces of green string with plastic on each end. They're used to join pieces of paper. Same difference, he says. The shirts are made out of mauve silk, the same material as the dresses that the girls wear. Most of the people who work there are German. They're in Belfast on placements from somewhere they study hospitality management.

In the bar and restaurant where Misty works, it's way more relaxed. The guy in charge, when they were recruiting people to work in the hotel, said about this particular part of it, that there should be a buzzy, clubby, speakeasy feel. Do you know what I mean? the man asked Misty, in front of everyone. She had looked round at the polished metal and dark wood and the old advertisements in frames and the green and gold lights. It was nothing like a club! What was he on about? But she said, yes, I get ya. The man had been impressed by another girl called Harlow in a white crop top. Harlow's described as a hostess which means she greets people when they arrive and shows them to a table. She doesn't need to touch any dirty dishes. One night, Misty was watching some old film with Boogie and there was a scene in a place that she realised was what the restaurant was trying to be like. 'That place has a buzzy, clubby, speakeasy feel,' she said.

'That's because it *is* a fucking speakeasy, you dummy!' Boogie replied. 'Your man there has been running it and now these others are muscling in. He's gonna get shot before too long.' Boogie has never been to the hotel but he says he knows what it's like, having dropped plenty of people off there. He doesn't need to go in.

Misty moves between the bar and the downstairs restaurant, just going where she is required. Although she's not meant to be a kitchen porter, she will also load the dishes, if that's what's needed. She can make coffees. She did the morning's training and got a certificate emailed to her. Her own outfit is an apron, a blue and white striped shirt and a pair of baggy black trousers. When the place first opened, everyone's trousers had braces, but to be fair they only looked good on a handful of people. If you had big boobs, then it was hard to know where to place them because if you put the braces over them, the elastic of the braces formed a triangle of air between the boob, the braces clip and the shirt. It was the kind of thing that you would have been asked to calculate the area of in maths. And if people put the braces at either side of their boobs, then it made them look even more enormous! So the braces went. That's just the way. Things evolve in terms of outfits.

Misty sees that the pinstripe shirt is squashed at the bottom of her bed, between the mattress and the frame.

Shit, and there's something on the collar. That's a pain. She goes to the bathroom and rubs at the spot with Gen's toothbrush. Is it ink? How could she have got ink on the collar? There, with a bit of scrubbing using the handwash, it is pretty much gone. She puts Gen's toothbrush back in the glass. Misty bends over and sprays the dry shampoo lavishly. A nice feeling always, an icy blast. It must be what food feels like when it's being frozen. She rubs in the dry shampoo at her roots and then brushes it out. Misty ties her hair up on the top of her head, twists her ponytail around, sticks a few clips in it and then washes her face with a wet wipe. They always say that you shouldn't use them, that they just move the dirt around on your face and, worse than that, right now in Belfast, in the sewers, there are massive fatbergs, created by fat dripping down the drains from all the fast-food places and then getting mixed with wet wipes. The fatbergs look like dirty snow.

She gets the big palette and does her eyes first, with the rose gold and pink. She does a little commentary as she uses first the fluffy brush to get the main colour down and then works on the crease with a smaller, angled one. As you can see, she says, I'm using brush 6A. Her eyelashes, well, she always gets Russians. She doesn't go to a salon. She gets them done by a girl who works from her own house. She lies on her sofa while the woman glues on the lashes, her kid padding about and watching cartoons on the TV. But she always has the radio on as well, people talking about sport. Are you into sport? she asked her. She said no, but her guy listened to it. Well, he is never there but still the sports chat booms out in the woman's house. Misty peers at her eyes. She should really have gone back for maintenance because most of the lashes have fallen off apart from a clump in the middle of her left eye. Oh well, no one will really notice, especially if she does her eyeliner thicker on the right to achieve some balance. She puts on her foundation, just to even out my skin tone, she says brightly in this commentary voice that sounds a little like Lynchie. And to add a lit-from-within glow! She always feels a bit sad when she thinks of that because *lit from within* is basically a person feeling happy about something in their life and there really isn't a way that putting on shade 20NC nude honey that's going to make you look as though you are full of joy in terms of what is happening in your life. Clue is in the description: lit from *within*. But yeah, I am applying this for freshness and lit-from-within glow! She presses the brush one final time on each cheek and then she cleans her teeth. She lines her lips just beyond her lip line but just in the middle because it gives the best illusion of volume. Would she say no to fillers, if someone walked in right now with a fully loaded needle. Nope! Are you kidding? That stain really hasn't gone away at all. It is mysteriously revealing itself again, on her collar, just slightly fainter than before.

'Misty!' Boogie shouts. 'You ready to go?'

'Nearly! Has anybody seen my jacket? Gen, have you seen my denim jacket? Geneva!'

Oh, never worry I'll just wear this one, she mutters to herself. She pulls where it is hanging over the banister, a cropped, fake leather jacket, its belt dangling from one loophole.

'Coming now!'

Boogie's car is always so clean. He takes it every week to that old bit of waste ground, with the patchwork tarmac, that's occupied by the Albanians. They're only young, the ones who do the work. They dress up just to clean cars. They dress up as though they are in a music video. One time she went with Boogie and they sat on the wall while the guys, and one girl, did the work. It was actually embarrassing, sitting there, while they did that. One of them in a yellow tracksuit and big puffy Jordans smiled over to her. He smiled so sweetly. But she looked away. She didn't want to go out with a guy who worked at a car wash.

'Oh, come on, love,' Boogie says, when someone doesn't edge out to make a left turn. 'We gonna be here all day.'

'Sexist.'

'Aw shush you.'

'Sexist.'

'I'm not sexist in the slightest. This is all about empirical evidence.' And he tapped the steering wheel to emphasise the point. This phrase has been used a lot in the house since Gen had introduced it, after a history teacher had said that this was what they should be presenting in their answers. I have empirical evidence that you did not flush the toilet. I have empirical evidence that you did not do the washing up.

'Yeah,' says Boogie. 'I'm basing my comment on empirical fucking evidence because I spend a lot of time on the roads, believe it or not, and what I have empirically observed, on many occasions, is that, empirically, women can't drive for shit.'

When the person makes the turn, it's an old man.

'Your empiricalness has let you down,' says Misty.

Boogie parks around the corner from the hotel because it allows him to swing back out of the town more easily without having to negotiate the one-way system.

'OK,' he says, as he reaches over to give her a quick kiss. 'I don't know what I'm doing tonight but give me a shout if you need a lift home, sure.'

I want to tell you about something I have never told anyone. This is the first time that I have ever tried to articulate what happened, and I don't know if it is even a sensible idea to do so, because for a very long time I have coped, I have managed, by starting each day with a to-do list that has maybe thirty or forty items on it and working through this in order until they are all ticked off. If thoughts re-surface, I look at my list and what I still need to accomplish. By the end of the day, I am formulating the list for tomorrow. So, I don't know what the good is in explaining what happened, really, when I have never told a soul. When I was sixteen, I had a baby. Obviously that was a long time ago. Fifty years, in fact. It was never an option for me to keep the baby and so for the last few months of my pregnancy I was sent across to Scotland, to a farm outside Girvan, to stay with a couple that people in my church knew. They were very kind people, very kind, and I look back on that time, when I stayed with them, as the best of my life. I would help her with sewing and mending things, and in the evening we all watched the television in a little room and ate toast. It had always been made clear to me that I wouldn't be able to keep the baby and so what happened was that, after he was born, he was taken to be adopted by a 'good' family, although I didn't know who they were. I returned home and life resumed. I was always quick with numbers and so I got a job in the accounts office of a big company. Eventually I got married to Ian, who has been a great husband to me. I told him about the baby boy, when I knew that we were getting serious. He said that he was sorry and that a similar thing had happened to Irene, his favourite relation, his great-auntie. But then, what happened was, when the boy was in his early thirties, he got in touch with me, out of the blue. He was living in Ayr. He wanted to meet. I asked Ian if he thought it was a good idea and he said he did. And so, I went. I flew to Prestwick. We met in a café. He's called William now. I always imagined him as Jack. He was nervous and talked too much. I felt such a wave of tenderness for him. He said that he had not had a happy childhood, that the people had children of their own who they constantly favoured. He had moved out when he was sixteen and had ended up living in a hostel at one point. I felt responsible. I said I was sorry. I put my hand on his. He said that he went to the gym every day, but he looked thin to me. After we had had a cup of tea in the café, he asked me if I would like to go back to his flat and I said yes. It was very tidy, a bedsit really, a tea towel hanging over the oven handle. There was a poster of New York on the wall, and a picture of an angel. We talked for a while more. I mainly listened. At one point he told me something funny, a little story, and at that point I gave him a little hug. We were sitting on his sofa. And he kept hugging me. I'm sorry, I said, but I didn't have any choice. And then I felt his hand on my breast. His fingers were gripping me quite hard. But for some reason I thought that it was part of the joke, that he was playing, like the way you might tickle someone hard. And so, I hugged him again and said, it was so good to see him but what happened then was that he swept me backwards and I hit my head on the wooden arm of the sofa and after that, well, he, I don't know how to say it, he took advantage of me. He called me names while it was happening which I do not want to repeat. And still I thought that there had been some kind of misunderstanding, that it wasn't happening. He got up afterwards and got a drink of water in the kitchen. The tap was rushing as I fixed my clothes. I didn't speak. I couldn't speak. And then, as I got up to go out of the door, it happened all over again. I have never told anyone about this. I said to Ian that it had gone well and that William was a nice young man but he had his own life to lead. The names he called me. He hated me. I have never in all my life heard of someone do that to their mother.

There was absolutely nothing to give me, or us, any indication that it wasn't what everyone wanted. Seriously. I'm more the kind of guy sitting on a sofa, eating a pizza and watching a box set with his girlfriend. I'd never really experienced anything like that before?!?!

There was an article in a men's magazine, between adverts for isotonic drinks and expensive aftershave. It was about the writer's experience of being with women who, although not 'tens', were brilliant in bed. Indeed, the writer suggested an actual causality between these two aspects of the women concerned. I came across the magazine in the waiting area at my physio's. She's called Ellen Hoogstra. Just off the ring road.

Frankie leaves a voice message for Neil in San Francisco. Hi, babes, get back to me, she says. It's urgent. I do mean urgent. It's about Chris. Speak to you as soon as.

Michelle says that Frankie's accent has changed. The last time Frankie saw her was when she went to visit her in Mallorca, at the wellness centre. She said how the fuck do you move to Ireland and end up speaking like you are off *Downton Abbey*? And I don't mean the maids. I mean Lady Mary. That's what she called Frankie for the rest of the trip, Lady Mary. Frankie was there out of season, but there were still a few stragglers, stringy women in their fifties, going down to the beach for a swim, having reiki healing or massage. Frankie laughed when Michelle listed off all that she could do. 'Shuddup, I got certificates,' Michelle said. 'Dance workshop, wait till you see it, you'll be moving about like you did when we was teenagers. That's cos I am keeping it real. Not like you, Lady Mary.'

'Keeping it real with all of this bullshit,' Frankie said, laughing.

'You and me both then, Lady Mary. Hadn't heard from you in so long thought you'd forgotten about me.'

Within five minutes Neil is ringing her for a video call. His disappointment that she is wearing a t-shirt is obvious. He sometimes likes to touch himself when they do these calls, although it is always out of shot and neither acknowledge it, beyond her doing some industrial grade arching of her back while wearing something gauzy.

'What's up? Looking good, Frankie. What's wrong with Chris?'

'Chris has just been arrested. The police have just left. They've taken him to the station. They went up to his room and searched it.'

'You are kidding. *Chris?* They've arrested Chris?'

He asks if it's about drugs and she says that no, it's sexual assault. He repeats the words, incredulous. She has got to be kidding! He asks Frankie if she contacted Loretta immediately. Well yeah, of course. Loretta is employed by Neil as an administrator. Loretta could run the Northern Ireland office standing on her head, he always says. She's a sixty-five-year-old genius who, when not working for Neil, spends her time doing jigsaws. Loretta said she would get legal representation sorted without delay. 'Leave it with me, Mrs Levine,' she said, as though she'd been asked to sort out coffee and biscuits. Neil says that he will phone Loretta right now. 'What does sexual assault even mean these days? he asks Frankie. 'Brushing someone's arm as you walk past them?'

This situation, Frankie reckons, will be sorted out quickly by Loretta and the lawyers. Chris isn't going to have sexually assaulted someone. The idea of it is stupid. And anyway, being arrested isn't such a big deal as all that. She and Michelle had it happen to them a few times, like when some girl accused them of stealing her bag in a club. They'd looked inside it and Michelle had taken the bottle of perfume, but they hadn't taken the bag and whatever else was in it. They were kept in a cell and then let go. It's not the worst thing that can happen. Frankie doesn't like the way she appeared on the screen during that call. Her lips have lost a little of their volume since the last time she got them done. It isn't that she has them pumped up in an obvious way because the place she goes to is excellent. It's not some hairdresser with a syringe – it's a guy whose main job is as a reconstructive surgeon. That might be something to do in the next few days; they can always sort appointments for her. She is tracing a finger over her lips as Nina comes in. She puts her arms up and does a little pirouette in the middle of the room.

'What do you think of these leggings on me?' she asks.
'Nice.'
Nina lowers her arms. 'Nice nice, or just nice?'
'Nice.'
'Could you take a photograph from the back so I can see what they look like?'
'Sure. There,' Frankie says, handing Nina the phone.
Nina scrutinises it. 'I like to see myself from different angles. And this is one that is not very nice.'
'Leggings are leggings.'
'I'm scared about what's happened to Chris.'
'I've just spoken to your dad. He'll get it sorted out.'
'I'm going to wash my hair,' she says. 'Maybe later we could do something?'
Jackie Boyce Residence, the clothes on the floor, those bottles of perfume, lying on Michelle's bed while she leans out the window to have a smoke, laughing as they crept back in the early hours of the morning. Frankie slept in the same bed as Michelle in Mallorca. She said she was going to book a hotel but she didn't. She could have slept in one of the guest rooms at the wellness centre but she didn't. Michelle's room had only a tiny window, high up, on the opposite side to the door. 'Fucking Lady Mary, you were hogging those covers all night!' Michelle said.

'I don't know, Nina,' says Frankie. 'We'll see.'

I was extremely happy with the service McCullough's Funerals offered. They were dignified, sensitive, and there was careful attention to detail. For us it was the most extraordinary, surreal thing – death. For them it's their daily business, yet the way they treated us was never perfunctory. It was so full of care.

Mrs McCullough and the young girl were excellent. The cuff of Charlie's suit had got turned up a little, just the edge, when he was lying there. The young girl fixed it, straightened the sleeve, gave him a little tap on the hand, as if saying, there, there you go.

Charlie was always immaculate.

Lloyd Ferguson had a Catalan girlfriend once, although doesn't that seem a misnomer? From the beginning it was clear she was an autonomous individual who had no intention of becoming something – a girlfriend – that sounded as retro as a mop-top beat group. He met her when he was studying in London. Nothing seemed trivial with her. Her parents were both Marxists and her grandfather had been executed by Franco. She was a disciple of Herbert Marcuse, dedicated to pleasure and revolutionary change. He loved to watch her eat. She was always talking so everything would end up being used to stress her point. A slice of toast would be pointed at him as she expounded on some theory. Her skin looked jaundiced in the winter. She left him, of course, as he knew was always going to be the case, and it meant he did badly in his exams. He became a cop. His mother was ill and that meant that he would move back home, with the choice of the civil service, the fire brigade, the prison service or the police. He passed the medical for the last three. The police interview was the first one he had, he was offered a job and then that was that. When he told the Catalan woman, who had moved back to Barcelona, she sent him a postcard with a photo of a mountain on it. On the back was a drawing of a sad face. He still has it on his fridge. Periodically, he turns it around the other way; sometimes the face, sometimes the mountain.

It's five o'clock. He and Colin Shaw have dealt with a minor road traffic incident and have arrested a young man on suspicion of involvement in a sexual assault that occurred the day before. They have also dealt with a burglary. Not much in the house seemed worth stealing, but still a door had been jemmied open. What did they think we had? the woman kept saying. The young guy they arrested lived up a dirt track but the house was like an upmarket medical centre. The woman wasn't very helpful. She stared at him and then at Colin. He could see her nipples through her t-shirt, even though his eyes didn't move from hers. Some young girl, round one, had sex with three guys; round two, had second thoughts. One guy, one girl, that's old-fashioned nowadays, played out. Three Little Lord Fauntleroys. And then one of them was that lanky guy in the black sweatshirt who lived in a medical centre.

'Your woman in the t-shirt,' Colin says. 'Funny how a sour old attitude can make someone less attractive.'

'Funny how a sour old attitude can sometimes make someone more attractive. It's called sultry.'

'That's dark hair. Sultry is a chick with dark hair.'

'No. It's attitude,' says Lloyd.

When we went to that hotel there was no one that I fancied who worked there, people had said the guys were hot but they were NOT, not hot at all. There's this bar in the town where I once saw this wee guy, middle of winter, just wearing a black t-shirt and black jeans, with a toothbrush in his back pocket, and wow he was a total dreamboat. But in that place it was all older guys at the bar, with suit jackets on and those wee slippety slippety shoes. The ones that work there, our waiter thought he was just the coolest. His name badge said Chris. What's that short for, Marie said, Christos? Christian? Christianopolis? He just blinked really slow, like, shut up, you dick. He was no fun. He was too skinny. I like guys more pumped than that. I like guys who, before they go out on a Saturday night go to the gym in their good clothes, just to get a bit of a pump on. There, in their good going-out clothes and their aftershave. But not ones wearing those wee slippety slippety shoes.

The banner hangs in the kitchen, Happy Birthday. A square tray of brownies has a single candle. There is a pizza menu on the table. 'Well,' says Miriam's mother, when she comes into the room, 'isn't it good that I brought some things with me?'

'She baked the wheaten bread this morning,' her father says.

'And I made the stew yesterday.'

'Well, thank you,' Miriam says. 'Maybe we can have it tomorrow. I've got pizzas ordered. I don't know if stew and wheaten are really birthday fare.'

'And pizzas are?'

'More than stew. Can I get you a drink?'

'Just tea for us, dear. Just tea for us.'

When she makes them tea, Miriam puts together a drink for herself.

'Do you have any sweetener for your dad?'

'No, I've got sugar.'

'I'm not meant to take sugar,' he says.

'Well, I've got no sweeteners. Why don't you buy one of those little boxes – Sweetex or whatever – and take it with you when you go out for a cup of tea?' Miriam asks.

'We don't go to cafés much,' her mother says.

'But you're out now,' Miriam says.

'We brought bread. And we brought stew. And we brought presents. We just didn't think we also needed to bring sweeteners.'

'Where's the birthday boy?' her dad asks.
'Upstairs, still in bed.'
'Ah,' he says, smiling. 'Teenage boy.'
This from a man who never lay in bed in his life beyond half past seven. But with age and failing health has come softening, indulgence. The Abrahamic patriarch has become cuddly. He dotes on his grandsons. Miriam shouts for Haady to come downstairs immediately.

'I was hearing,' her dad says, 'that you lost the birthday cake. How does someone go about losing a birthday cake?'

'Rami made brownies,' Miriam says, pointing at the square tin.

'How does somebody lose a birthday cake?'

'Same way anyone loses anything. By leaving it somewhere.'

'Good that Rami was able to come to the rescue.'

When Haady comes down the stairs, his grandfather is eager to show the presents they have brought. One is a boxing game: a red ball, attached to a string, attached to a headband. The object is to punch the ball repeatedly, before it inevitably swings in an unreachable direction. Haady puts on the headband, tries, manages five touches.

The other present is a kite. He takes it outside, the bobbing ball still dangling from his head.

If only Miriam could leave them to the kite, the brownies and the headband and sit with her phone and its photos of Kahlil, happy, sad, taken unawares, smiling, what did I maybe say to make you laugh that time, and there's five videos, she has no idea why, all identical, of him sitting, adding something on a calculator, and he looks to the side, out of the window, then goes back to totalling up. What's he thinking?

'Shall I heat up the stew?' her mother says. 'I mean, I do quite agree with you, Miriam, it isn't the usual type of party food, but it's just one of Haady's favourites.'

'Sure – stew and pizzas.'

'Oh, look there's Rami!' her mother exclaims.

'Granny.' Rami hugs her. Their hair is cropped short as each other's.

She has read that in Belfast during the conflict there were séances because so many were taken unexpectedly, leaving behind unanswered questions and husbands, wives, children who didn't get to hear or say a last I love you. Who couldn't understand why they wanted an ectoplasmic gush of revelation or reassurance? All bullshit of course, but a dark table in a house, a woman in a mantilla, Miriam would go there, if she knew of such a place.

She has tried the glass. She took one from the cupboard, polished the table, laid out pieces of paper with letters, called on Kahlil to spell out whatever he needed to say. But the glass remained immobile. She stared at it hard, willing it to move, but no. The glass didn't move but seemed to speak primly, confident in its own good sense. Don't be so ridiculous, it said. Expecting me to move like some cheap trick. He loved you. Or did he, entirely? Contact the girl and see! Later she gave Haady a drink of lemonade in that glass. See, she was saying. You are so lacking in any significance that I use you for the kids' drinks, bitch.

They eat the birthday tea, Miriam's dad expressing amazement that pizzas are delivered by bike. They have generous squares of the chocolate brownie and sing happy birthday. When the others all go out to try to get the kite flying, Miriam and her mother do the dishes.

'Well, that was nice,' her mother says.

'Sure.'

'How do you think your dad is looking? Frail?'

'Not really. Just the same as usual.'

'It takes such a lot out of him. Those long sessions in the hospital.'

'Can't he watch a film during the dialysis? On a laptop?'

'He never grumbles or complains.'

'He looks fine. No frailer than someone else his age. And still in the land of the living.'

'Don't know if it's the day for a kite.'

'Let's just see.'

'Can you remember that man at Kahlil's funeral? The one who had come from Cookstown? Do you know who I mean? Well, he was on the television the other day talking about the difficulty of importing meats. I recognised him as soon as I saw him.'

Miriam lifts a white bowl and slowly wipes around its edge. 'Don't remember him,' she says. 'There were so many people.'

'When I say meats, I mean salamis and that kind of thing. We never really eat that sort of food. Miriam, this little wooden chopping board that was in the basin here. You shouldn't submerge it in water. You'll ruin it. You should just give it a wipe.'

Miriam puts the white bowl in the cupboard.

'So, you don't think he's looking frailer?' her mother asks.

'No, I don't. What about you? Is it you who's feeling frail?'

'No, not at all.'

'Message received loud and clear about the chopping board,' Miriam says.

'It's just because it's wood.'

'Sure thing.'

Her mother puts another plate on the draining board. And suddenly the kite is in the air, Haady holding the strings. It dives to the right, rips through air, its tail looping then ribboning straight. Its smiley face looks down benevolently.

'There's someone at the door,' her mother says.

'I didn't hear anyone.'

'Well, I'm almost certain I heard someone. Yes, there it is again! There's somebody at the door.'

Two members of the police stand in the same spot as the ones who arrived to tell her about Kahlil. Have they come to tell her again? Is this a repeat? They're positioned exactly as they were before. The older one speaks. He says he is Detective Sergeant Lloyd Ferguson and he asks for confirmation that Rami Abdel Salam lives here. DC Ferguson names the man beside him as Detective Constable Colin Shaw.

'Yes,' she says. 'He's my son.'

In the kitchen, the officers see the cake on the table, the candle that has been discarded at the side of the serving plate. They take in the banner, the pizza boxes, the round, surprised eyes of the older lady who is wearing yellow rubber gloves and who has turned from looking out of the window at an elderly man and two kids.

Haady, in the garden, stares at the two policemen who are standing at the patio doors. Slowly, the others follow his gaze. But the kite is tenacious. The smiley face grins as it fights to remain in the sky.

'Oh look, the police!' Miriam's father says. 'You boys run on in and I'll be there presently when I've reined this thing in.'

Haady looks on in amazement as the cop asks Rami his name and date of birth and then tells him that he is being arrested on suspicion of sexual assault. Miriam's father comes in holding the kite just as the other policeman says that they need to take Rami's phone and the clothes he was wearing the night before. There will also be a search of his room. Other officers are arriving to do this.

'My stuff's in the dryer,' Rami says quietly.

'You've already washed it?' DC Ferguson asks.

'Is that so unusual,' Miriam's mother says, 'that someone should wash their clothes they've worn the day before? Surely not.'

'It's necessary for you to hand over your phone,' DC Ferguson says, as he looks from the granny to the suspected assailant.

Rami's phone is in his bedroom and when he comes down from fetching it, he wears the coat that Kahlil got him for his birthday. A ridiculous price, but Kahlil had said it was worth it. An investment! Lifetime warranty with Canada Goose. It's a warm day, even if it was breezy enough to fly a kite. But there he is, leaving, in the padded coat that Kahlil got him. They all stand at the door, watching Rami get into the back of the police car.

'Man, what a fourteenth birthday,' Haady says. 'The feds took away my brother! The feds took away my brother on my fourteenth birthday. What we going to do, Mum? Somebody's framed Rami! It's obvious!'

'Let's pray to the Lord,' says Miriam's father.

Normally McNeil lets me get on with things in the way I know how. He's been doing what he does for over thirty years, so there's no need for him to turn up on site. He lives in hotels most of the time and he'll be sitting playing online poker somewhere in his underpants. Sometimes, if gallery people or journalists contact him with questions, he answers with one word, Dorothee. My name.

They're all labelled. They all have a co-ordinate. The pieces. So, when people say they are moved by the work, that it's something about polyphony or it embodies the ideas of some philosopher, I'll just see E47, E88, F12 and P110 adjacent, sixty degrees. It's a job.

There's something, I guess, that's very true and I once heard a cop say it in a film. If you're a prostitute and you start coming with the customers, that's when you know it's time to quit. I'm like that. The day I go into a gallery and any of this stuff moves me, is the day I throw in the towel, the day I phone McNeil and say, buddy, you are on your own.

I don't come from a fine art background. I worked at a speedway track and I met a girl who got a summer job there. She was a photographer and then, through her, I worked with KUNK collective and then that led me to McNeil.

On that trip, I flew in from New York. When we went to Dublin and Belfast the woman who represents McNeil in London was there. She tried to call the shots. Back off, lady, we've been doing this for years. It was something to do with Wintering 02, something to do with the light, and how she felt it 'had lost a dimension of its power' in the Belfast set-up. I was also pissed because I was splitting up with Mary. We had had these arguments for six months straight that left me exhausted. I thought I had something wrong with me, like cancer, because I felt so bad all of the time, but it was actually just the fights with her. I thought that we could get back to being how we once were, but then the wheels were off again. She wanted to take Sandy, and I loved that dog, but I ended up saying you have him, because I couldn't face another fight. So he stayed with Mary. I was crazy about Mary at the beginning. I drove one time, back in the beginning, for eight hours solid, just so as I could be with her for an hour and a half. But when the call came through in that hotel in Belfast, and it was Mary to say that she was gone, all of her stuff was gone, well, I could not have felt better. I felt like I had just sipped cold water from a crystal glass. And then when I went downstairs there was a message left for me to say that the gallery woman was heading back to London in unforeseen circumstances. I went to the hotel restaurant and sat waiting for a long time to be served, but I was buzzed. I didn't care.

I watched a girl spill ice all over the floor. She was in the restaurant and she was carrying it through to the bar. I thought, wow, didn't it look pretty fucking magnificent as it tipped out of the bucket. You wanna scoop it up, I asked her, or should we let it all melt? Better scoop it up, she said. I helped her do that, then asked her to get me a drink. When she brought it, I gave her a tip. You sure? she said. Oh yeah, I'm sure. Good times.

After the Kids' Breakfast, certain people were invited back to Mary Donovan-Leitner's apartment. Bronagh travelled with Jill and Duff Krauss, who asked lots of engaged questions and talked about their holiday home in west Cork. The Donovan-Leitner place, small stained-glass panes in its bay windows, has an austere Irish country house elegance. Easy to imagine that in the kitchen someone is churning butter, occasionally tucking behind their ear a stray lock that has escaped from their cap. Strange to exit this apartment into the honey and beige stone of the lobby, the noise of traffic outside. There should be fields.

Hair and teeth the same pearl, Mary wears black clothes with pin tucks in unusual places, like textile origami. She's constantly engaging with life's issues. When someone talked about their beloved dog getting old, its final appointment at the vet's imminent, Mary Donovan-Leitner turned the conversation to some poet woman's response to Abu Ghraib. Bronagh really wanted to hear more about the dog. A couple of people, sitting in that austere and beautiful room, asked a little about Finn Anderson. They had enjoyed that aspect of Bronagh's presentation, and really, didn't she think he was one of the finest young actors around at present? Mary Donovan-Leitner started talking about Peter O'Toole, some story involving him in Wicklow, that moved into a consideration of the Irish War of Independence. A very fine actor, a woman in a brown jacket said. Peter O'Toole? Or Finn Anderson? But Bronagh was thinking of Johnny, bleeding out alone in a dirty room, as she looked at the linen. What must he have been thinking, when it was ending? He never had that buried contempt. There was often that, with the kids, in that they despised you for being necessary to them. At his funeral, his mother posed for photos with Finn. She was wearing a check miniskirt. Bronagh came home from the funeral to find that Lyness hadn't gone to school. He was lying in bed smoking weed. Chill, he said when she told him to get up, open the window and have a shower. Don't tell me to chill, she said, I've just been to the funeral of a young man. Then maybe, Mama, you should, you know, have a smoke, he said.

'And a very versatile young actor,' the woman in brown said. 'We saw him in that excellent movie about the family who lived in the village.' She turned to the others who were sitting there. 'Did anyone see it?' Leslie Leitner came in to say that tea was served, with a little butlerish bow – comic irony from the multi-millionaire. He looked like he could model for one of those catalogues of expensive knitwear, old, tanned and lean in board shorts and a cashmere jumper. Over the food, someone mentioned how they had found Patience Johnson highly informative. Others nodded in agreement. 'Where was she from again?' someone asked. 'Liberia,' Bronagh said. 'Patience Johnson is from Liberia.' Patience and Fatima Bazzi had ended up going off for drinks together, along with a couple of Lebanese women. 'Liberia,' said Mary Donovan-Leitner, 'such a complex situation.' But she didn't elaborate further. The food had been very disappointing, Bronagh had to say: cold chicken and an under-seasoned set of salads. There was also a soup with barley floating in it. But the drink earlier had been served in beautiful glasses. There was an inch and a half of crystal at the base of Bronagh's tumbler and the cocktail was crisp. It wasn't self-aggrandising to think that as a result of her trip, lives might be changed to some degree. She had told them as much, during her speech. It had worked well; the Andersons, the two brothers on two paths narrative. Just generally, she had blamed no one, made nothing sound too hopeless or complicated. And it worked.

Bronagh had flown business class on one occasion and it was blissful. She could recall every detail of it, from the grey slouch socks she was given, to the film that she watched – an immersive historical queer drama – to the yellow and black striated sky she could see when she woke up from a gorgeous sleep, as a result of the complimentary roll-on bottle of lavender oil. But here she is, moving her bag so that a young man can sit down beside her. When the plane takes off, they both get their work out. She can see that he is looking at some kind of technical material and she monitors whether or not he glances at what she is working on, but he doesn't even incline his head slightly in her direction. She's considering documentation in relation to the purchase of a piece of waste ground near the centre. As usual with these things, there are difficulties, namely people declaring that this scrubland is tantamount to some kind of bird sanctuary. She wonders momentarily if she should book a break for her, Donal and Lyness at the end of August. Donal could surely spare a couple of days. She likes the idea of preparing a simple but delicious meal, then carrying it out to somewhere sunlit. Opera is playing. She is looking at a picture of one of these supposed birds that have this graffitied waste ground as a habitat when the woman in front moves her seat back. Well, of course you are entitled to move your seat but why not turn your head a little, just to herald that you are going to do it. No need to speak but there should be slight acknowledgement of the person behind, surely? She'll text Finn Anderson later on and let him know how much it mattered, his association with the centre. Patience and Fatima probably spent the rest of the day together, telling funny stories, shrieking with laughter in some bar.

When they bring the drinks, Bronagh takes a mini bottle of white wine, the young man beside her a glass of water. He puts away his complicated reading material and takes out a magazine which is about music, it would seem, but is also complicated. There's dense text and small pictures of guys with keyboards. In putting her own work into her bag, Bronagh succeeds in knocking, fairly gently, the head of the woman in front. She takes a few sips of the wine and says to the young man, 'Nice to get a drink, isn't it?'

He holds up his bottle of water.

'I'm being a bit more rock and roll,' she says.

He doesn't reply.

She nods in the direction of his magazine, even though it is patently from the more intellectual end of the spectrum.

'Believe it or not,' she says, 'that's what I used to be involved in.'

'What is?' he says.

'Rock and roll,' she replies. And takes another sip of wine.

'Right, I see,' he eventually says.

'Yes, but really, I don't know if that's what the band I managed would have considered themselves to be. They might have said they were actually anti-rock and roll. They were influenced by some philosopher but I can't recall his name. I've moved on to other realms anyway.'

No answer.

'Are you a musician?' she asks.

'No. I'm doing post-doctoral research.'

'In what?'

'Synthetic chemistry.'

'Sounds hard!' Bronagh says. 'Synthetic chemistry. Wow. I'm involved in children's services,' she says.

When he asks what that entails, she tells him. And then, there seems to be so much to tell this young man, in an unburdening which includes how she had once lied about having an affair with a man she didn't like, while sipping a drink she didn't like, a brandy sour. The young man says nothing. 'I've never fitted in!' Bronagh suddenly says.

A little later in the journey, the young man, who tells her his name is Patrick, says that he's been staying with a friend outside the city. It's only recently that he has been feeling well again. For the previous year, he has been ill, in and out of hospital. Cancer.

'Oh no,' Bronagh says. 'Oh Patrick!'

'Testicular cancer.'

Bronagh looks at his crotch and then out of the window.

But all seems well now and he's just had two good weeks of rest. He's looking forward to going back to work.

As Bronagh makes the drive from Dublin airport to Belfast, she resolves not to tell Donal about how she had this conversation with a stranger. It would seem tawdry in the recounting. She turns in to Sprucefield retail park to buy some presents for the boys. The selection of whiskies isn't wonderful, but she finds a twenty-year-old malt that she knows Donal will find acceptable enough and in another store she buys Lyness new headphones. He's lost his, again.

When Bronagh eventually turns off the ring road, she notices that they've refilled the hole that had been dug in the week prior to her departure. Something wrong with the pipe system and so everyone had got used to seeing clusters of guys in hi-vis, looking perplexed. But now, there's only a flutter of red and white tape from a lamppost as a reminder that they were ever there. She turns into the long, tree-lined road that connects two of the arterial routes running out of the city, waving at Hilary Doyle, who is just coming back from a run, her cheeks blotchy. It's not too late for them to get a takeaway tonight, if Donal hasn't already eaten. She likes that Thai place but Donal thinks they use too much chilli. Nonsense, she says. The problem is that they don't use enough! Their hedge needs cutting, she thinks, as she turns off the engine. There's a police car parked on the other side of the road.

I don't know about the Rami guy, but in terms of the others I've nothing positive to report. I knew them from Prep, where I was as a kid. I'd met them another few times since, over the years. They'd turned into just the kind of unimaginative, complacent non-entities that I would have expected. Isn't Line-up's mother some kind of social justice crusader? That's funny. I saw the girl and she didn't fit in with all the others at all. She was wearing some kind of work attire, but really, it wouldn't have mattered how she was dressed. But yeah, I've tried to avoid people like Line-up and Chris. So, it is not that there is any love lost. And I did feel a pang of something for that girl because she was trying to fit in and overcompensating in a way. I have not told you about my arm. I got sepsis as a two-year-old, nearly died, came back from the brink, but they had to take away my arm. It's not such a big deal. But here is what it has done. In every situation I look around and see the person who is not like the others. The thing is that sometimes they see me and they know what I am thinking and they feel aggrieved because they want to say, I'm not like you with your sad little face and your one arm. Don't think we are alike at all, buster. I watched her drinking very ostentatiously, being overly animated. And I knew. And I don't like Line-up and Chris. But, that said, what I do have to state are my views on the whole idea of consent. Most of the time, people do not want to be where they are. They would rather be somewhere else. Most of the time people are doing things that, in an ideal world, they would rather not do. Most of the time the views that people express are different to the ones that they actually truly hold. We say that we are fine when we are not. They shouldn't have presumed anything about what it was they were doing. But no one should presume anything at any point about anybody.

I can see why someone would look at a pair of Yeezys for a four-year-old kid, a few hundred pounds for what, a couple of months of wear, and think that it's madness. I get it. But at the same time, I've always made sure that my own kids have been dressed in proper gear. Branded sportswear. Everything has got a logo. More than that, I take great care that the clothes are kept good. It's because it was never that way for me, when I was younger. It was never that way for me.

Gen had studied a poem in school about how you shouldn't fear traditionally creepy things such as haunted houses, hidden assassins or being alone at midnight, the witching hour. What you *should* be wary of is the power of your own mind because that is where the true horror lies. That night, Gen was feeling that the poem got it wrong because traditional creepy was terrifying. Boogie had called earlier to say that he'd unexpectedly given a lift home to a very old friend of his that he hadn't seen in a long time. He was going to finish driving for the night and have a few drinks with him. This guy didn't live far away so he'd walk home before too long and then pick the car up in the morning. Would she be alright until Misty got back? Misty probably wouldn't be late. 'Sure,' Gen said. She told him to have a good time. But it got to after midnight and no one was back.

A creak on the stairs. That wardrobe door! It seemed to move. The eyes on her posters followed her as she went to turn on another light. No response from Boogie. She texted Misty, rang her, left a message on her voicemail. Come on, hurry up! A guy high on crystal meth could chance upon the house and rape and strangle her. Maybe there was a satanic presence here. This place could've been an ancient burial ground. A woman might have strangled her five kids here. Right! Get out of bed! She'd put on bright and bouncy music and she'd make pancakes.

No one would be killed by a devil or psycho while melting a bit of butter or pouring batter into a pan. Or maybe – involved in doing something innocent and straightforward – that'd be exactly when a person would be killed. Girl in a frilly apron, pickaxe through her head, still holding the whisk.

But she got up and went downstairs. It didn't seem so bad. When you thought about it, a whole other world was up and about right now: DJs, clubbers, women breastfeeding babies, security guards, the police, doctors, nurses. And right now, she was part of the night crew! Gen had a bowl of cereal, not enough milk for pancakes now, and watched a programme about child stars, where are they now, followed by a film where a woman's husband was having an affair. Cool to be part of the night crew really. Once you got used to it, the dark was actually so peaceful.

At about two in the morning, the doorbell rang. Gen, unsure whether she should answer it, crept into the hall to see if she could sense who it was. When it rang again – and again – she shouted who is it and heard Misty's voice.

When she opened the door, Misty went straight upstairs.

'Where were you? I've been ringing and ringing! Oi! Why don't you answer your fucking phone? Oh well, be like that. Be self-centred.'

Gen felt sorry for the woman in the film when it finally dawned on her that the husband hadn't been any of the places he said he was, although, to be honest she had been extremely gullible because many of his explanations were daft. She yawned. He wasn't even that nice looking. She switched off the TV and went upstairs.

Misty was in her bra and pants, running a bath.

'I need to go to the toilet,' Gen said.

'Well, I'm in here. Can you not see?'

'I can. But I want to go to the toilet. And then you can get into the bath. What happened to your feet? Jeez!'

'What?'

'They're terrible! Look at your feet! They're bleeding.'

'I walked home.'

'Where from? America?'

'Hurry up and go to the toilet and let me have a bath.'

Gen went down to the kitchen, to what they call the 'medical cupboard', with its crusty old bottles of Calpol, half packets of Rennies and various vitamin supplements, bought over the years. There was a roll of crepe bandage. Gen took the few blister pads left over from when she did that sponsored walk for teen suicide awareness and put them outside the bathroom for Misty. It was nice now, getting into bed. The pictures on the wall, before she switched the light out, were their usual friendly selves. All just in your head. She pulled her duvet round her. All just in your head and the poem was right.

But she couldn't get to sleep. As she lay there, she heard Misty go into her bedroom again, and then there was the burr of a man's voice. On the Bennyz. Wouldn't you know – talking to sleazes. Gen banged on the wall, and before long they stopped. But Misty was still fussing about, going into the bathroom again, switching the light on and off in the hall, going into her room, tramping up and down the stairs. 'Shut up!' Gen shouted. 'Go to bed!' And then the light went on once more. 'Right,' Gen said as she threw off the duvet. 'That is it.'

Misty was sitting at the top of the stairs.

'Will you stop dicking around and go to bed please?'

'There was no hot water. Only cold. I couldn't even have a shower.'

'Oh yeah there's something up with it. I forgot, Dad's going to look at it. He was meant to be back ages ago. Did he message you?'

'I don't have my phone.'

'Why where is it?'

'In my bag back at that house.'

'Why's your bag in a house?'

Misty was twisting her ponytail.

'Why's your bag and your phone in a house?'

'Just is.'

'Sounds a bit weird.'

'Shut up, Geneva.'

'Shut up yourself.'

Misty was twisting her ponytail.

'Stop doing that,' Gen said. 'I mean it, stop. It's not nice, the way you're doing that. Put your hand down! What's wrong with you? You're getting on like a nut. Put your hand down.'

'Just leave me alone.'

'Not until you stop acting like a nut.'

'I had a bad time tonight,' Misty said.

'What you mean?'

'A bad time.'

Gen looked at the little box of plasters still sitting outside the bathroom door.

'I thought we were friends. I thought they were friends of mine.'

It had been a nice place, with ornaments and lace and stuff, like an old person's house. There was a tree outside. At the very end of it, when there was only Line-up left, she got patted on the head. She got patted on the head the way you would pat a dog. A wee dopey dog in the park. That's what Line-up did. And so, what she said to him was, do you know what I could do? Do you? I could go to the police.

Because you're not allowed to do that to people. She could tell the police what happened, what they did to her. He said that he didn't think so, shaking his head, laughing as he said it. And then he patted her on the head again, like this. Misty patted the top of Gen's head, ruffled her hair, like she was a good-natured little mutt.

'Then go to the police!'

'That's what Mike said.'

'Who's Mike? Was he at the party?'

'No, Wyoming.'

'Where's that?'

'The middle of America. He's a Bennyz guy.'

'You told a Bennyz guy about this? You already been sharing this on Bennyz?'

'No, I didn't share it, Geneva. I told Mike.'

'I don't know if it's the best idea. To put it out there on Bennyz.'

'Are you not listening to me? I didn't put it out there. I told Mike!'

Misty should go to the police. Gen had her birthday money, if Misty needed her to pay for the taxi. And she would go with her because police stations weren't over-eighteen. But just in case, she would do her eyes that way, with the smoky palette, to look older. She could wear Misty's black dress. But shouldn't they wait until Boogie got back? Misty said no. They should just go. Mike was right. Gen was right. She was going to do exactly what Line-up thought she wouldn't.

'I should bring my clothes. I should put them in a bag. Could you find me a bag, Gen?'

The taxi sat eight people. It was more like a van, the way the door slid open and the two girls sat tiny in the back.

'You're travelling in style tonight,' the driver said. They didn't reply. 'You're travelling in style tonight,' he repeated.

'Yeah, to a police station,' Gen replied.

Misty had an initial interview. Then she and Gen waited for a while. After that, they were taken, by two women, to another place, a little like a hospital except there were soft seats. Gen sat on one of them while Misty was taken down a corridor for more questions. There was no music. Maybe it would help if there was music – something low and gentle, clarinets or glockenspiels – for all of the people who'd got assaulted to listen to. But there was just the sound of the electric light above her. Misty reappeared briefly then had to go to another room.

This place was no way as interesting as the hospital that Gen used to love visiting when she had those pains in her legs. It was great, brilliant, when the appointment card fell through the letterbox because that meant another trip through that big revolving door, where the people were outside in their pyjamas for a smoke, where that doctor tipped her head to one side when she wrote down what you said. It was a disappointment when, after four or five visits, they concluded that there wasn't anything really wrong as such. The pains would go away, they said, of their own accord.

Gen stretched her legs out straight, pulled the fabric of her dress tight against them. There. No pain. In the taxi, Misty had said the names of the three guys: Chris, Rami and then Line-up. But they didn't all do the same thing. She didn't say too much more.

The loudest shout in the world had the same decibels as a pneumatic drill or a jet engine. She'd read that. Gen tried to think when she'd ever heard Misty yell. Maybe that time when she burned her arm on the metal rack in the oven. For months, she had a purple line on her arm, fading to a pink line. But Misty didn't seem to have made too much sound at all during the, you know, assault. Gen had seen a penis in real life. An old alco was lying in the centre of the town with it hanging out. He was comatose! A woman went over and put a canvas tote bag on top of it, hiding it from the world. But Gen had seen. Like something you could have as your key ring. She has a stuffed sheep. But when she thought of these guys, their dicks were throbbing and purple, outsize. They were slavering like French bulldogs. Suddenly there was a message on her phone from Emma from school, inviting Gen to go to La Glace today. They've got loads of new ice-cream flavours. And then after, they could all go to watch the boys practising nets? Gen knew the walk from La Glace to the cricket ground, imagined their lazy, lolloping steps as they passed the houses where big front lawns are being mown. No, she replied. I can't sorreee xxxx

How long was it now? Did Misty realise going to the police would be such a complicated thing? Gen had thought it would be a bit like telling on someone in school. She remembered Mr Winstanley nodding slowly when she told him, in that room that had all the old medicine balls and the old textbooks, about Emmet Kane's bruises on his ribs. Gen saw them when he hung upside down on the climbing frame. Touts out. Snitches get stitches. But she let them know and it only took a little chat with Mr Winstanley. Emmet moved to another school the next year.

Her phone rang and she thought it would be Emma but it was Boogie, who had just seen all the messages. He was in the car, heading home from his friend's house. A few drinks and so on, he'd fallen asleep there. The battery was dead on his phone when he woke up. When he asked if everything was alright she said that no it wasn't, but not to worry. Conversations she'd had with Boogie: arrangements about being picked up, Atlantis, homework, why they lived in their house and not somewhere else, existence of God, why he needs to buy her a new hole punch, what she wants for Christmas, what is better KFC or Burger King, Dominos or Apache, Subway or Yardbird, who's a bitch, which teacher is good.

'Dad,' she said, 'we'll be home before too long.'

The way in which I view our home – I mean, the flat we share – has definitely changed, since I started the new job. Probation services aren't anything I don't know about. I've worked in that field for a couple of years. But this new job, the people, it all just seems more fucked up. During the day I find myself dreaming of taking my key out of my pocket, turning it in the lock, then closing the door behind me. I love to get home. Quite often I have an hour or so before Suzy gets back. We've got one side of the living room done with wallpaper, William Morris. It's got blue and green foliage, birds, strawberries, strange big budding flowers, but it's very orderly, very symmetrical, even though there's lots of curling leaves and entanglement. And that's what I appreciate. I sit and look at it, the patterns. Because it's chaos out there.

Boogie had woken up on a sofa, with a fleecy blanket over him. Above was a lampshade decorated with a Tokyo street scene at night, which he recognised as being from Ikea. They had it at home, before he redecorated. Boogie, he heard a voice say, would you like a cup of tea?

He realised where he was. Jay's house. That was Jessica. He must have fallen asleep here.

'Sure,' he said, sitting up quickly. 'Thanks very much, Jessica. Shit I'm sorry. Looks like I can't handle a late night anymore.' He started to fold the blanket very precisely, first once and then twice.

'You two were still chatting away when I went to bed. When I came down for a drink of water yous were both asleep, but I managed to get Jay upstairs. Eventually! You want something to eat?'

She put two slices in the toaster, but he said that a cup of tea was all he wanted.

'I'm sure not used to it these days, can't lie.'

'Not used to what?'

'Staying up drinking. Having a smoke.'

'I normally go to bed at nine. I usually work early shifts but today I'm on a later one.'

'Doing what?'

'Psychiatric nursing.'

'Must be full on that.'

'You take milk?'

'Yeah, a bit of milk.'

The edge of a tattoo on her back was visible when she reached down to the bottom shelf of the fridge.

'What's your eighteen-year-old do with herself? I can't remember if you said last night.'

He told her how Misty had done a couple of courses at the Met. Beauty and make-up. But she wasn't too sure what she wanted to do, although she worked a few days a week in a hotel in the town. Gen, he said, was only young, still at school. He asked her how long she and Jay had been together.

'Three years,' she said. She handed him the tea. 'So, it's just you and the girls?'

She looked like she went to the gym.

'That's the score.'

'Well, that's nice.'

'Yeah. It is.'

'That's good. Cos I never knew my dad at all. Cleared off when I was about two and that was it. I've thought about trying to contact him, get in touch but then I just think, why bother.'

'You never know with these things,' Boogie said. 'Could work out well. Could work out bad.'

'That's it.'

'You wouldn't happen to have a phone charger that I could borrow, would you?'

'iPhone?'

'Yeah.'

She passed him a charger that was sitting beside the cooker. It had a pink mark on it.

'Jay was always nicking my charger, saying it was his. So, I had to put that nail varnish on it to show it was mine.'

'Did Jay tell you about the time we took the kids to the zoo?'

'Yeah he did,' she said. 'He made it sound like the most surreal thing, the most bizarre day of his life.'

'Yeah, well it was. Although everything's surreal,' Boogie added, 'when you really look at it. I mean' – and he nods at the draining board – 'the way that wineglass is upside down and next to half a tomato. Plates all at an angle. Weird. Everything's surreal if you really look. Just generally. I don't mean art.'

'I always think that when I look in the bin,' she said. 'All of the different stuff there.'

'This is not a pipe.'

'What way do you mean?'

'This is not a pipe,' he said, taking a sip of his tea. 'This guy, we did it in school, he painted a picture of a pipe and wrote under it, this is not a pipe. Surrealist. Because it's not a pipe, it's just a bit of paper.'

'When I was in school we got this new teacher, Miss Barrett, who was kind of posh. And when everyone was talking she said, Pipe down! Pipe down, please! And one of the fellas said, Miss Barrett wants the pipe passed down to her! Lads, pass the pipe down to Miss Barrett cos she wants a toke. And then after that every day somebody drew a big cannabis leaf on her whiteboard.'

'Pipe down!' said Boogie, laughing. 'Ol Miss Barrett liked the ganja.'

Boogie surveyed the kitchen, the plants on the windowsill, the photos on the wall. 'It's a nice place you got here.'

'You think? Dunno,' she said. 'Always imagined I'd live somewhere else.'

'Like where?'

'London maybe. But a bit of London that's like here. I would still do the same job. Like, I imagine me doing the same job, and living in the same kind of place, except I would get the tube to work rather than the bus. Like, I can actually imagine myself sitting on the tube.'

'That doesn't show a whole lot of imagination, Jessica.'

'No? What would you like that's different from what you have or haven't got at present?'

'Don't know. Nothing really.'

'Well then.'

She tucked her legs up underneath her on the seat and took a bite of toast. 'Jay won't be up for ages,' she said.

'I'm going to need to go,' Boogie said, getting up from the sofa. Now his phone was charged, he'd seen the missed messages from Gen.

'Right now? Is all OK?'

'I need to go. Thanks again to you and Jay.'

'Is something wrong?'

'I need to go.'

Jessica watched him as he went down the driveway on his phone, as he opened the door of the car, as he drove off.

Yes, but what is it that's happened, exactly? Where are they right this minute? Why can't she speak properly? Gen's voice is a whisper, says it was guys at a party. What do you mean guys? What guys? Ones from Ladyhill.

'It was guys at a party,' Gen says again, but she doesn't want to speak too loud because the place is quiet. She doesn't want to be broadcasting what happened. 'They were meant to be Misty's mates,' she says. 'But we did the right thing coming to the police, do you think, Dad, because one of the guys you know that, well, assaulted her, he said oh you won't ever go to the police, so you won't. We just were like, let's go, and maybe we should have waited for you but we didn't.' She tells him to hold on because there is a woman that needs to speak to her and then Boogie hears

Gen ask if she can put her on to her dad. The woman calls him Mr Downes. They would like to interview Geneva as the first respondent. But that won't happen for another hour. She gives him the name of the station and the address, although he already knows it. Yes. Sexual assault. Her voice is calm.

Boogie hardly knows where he's driving to, but he finds himself swerving into the car park of the big supermarket, through an archway of promotional yellow and orange balloons. When he gets out of the car, a woman on a mobility scooter with a dog shouts over. 'Have you got a badge? That's a disability spot.'

'I don't give two hoots,' Boogie says. 'Mind your own business.'

'But it is my business. Because I could report you if you don't have a badge. You are meant to leave those spots for people who need them.'

'Well, what I need is for people like you to mind their own fucking business.'

He starts to walk towards the shop. 'People like you are a disgrace,' she shouts. 'A disgrace to humanity.'

He turns back and comes close to her. She looks up, pale eyes blinking, from the mobility scooter.

'Let me tell you something, love. I just heard something. I just heard my kid has been sexually assaulted. And I'm going into this fucking shop so that when she comes back to the house after being at the police station, things are nice. That is where I'm going to. I don't give a fuck right now about the disabled spot.'

'Cut off his balls!' the woman says. 'Cut off his dick!'

Boogie walks off in the direction of the trolleys.

'Cut off his dick!' she shouts across the car park, shaking her arm in the air. 'And ram it down his throat!'

He fills the trolley with cleaning products: carpet shampoo, bleach, bathroom spray, kitchen spray. He wants anything that smells sharp, of lemon or lime. Ladyhill, that place where they tried to open a KFC near that pisspoor square of grass in the middle and that pathetic crowd got up a petition to stop it happening. Yeah, he knew Ladyhill with its flower baskets and fake voices. At the other end of the trolley, he piles eggs and bacon and soda bread and potato bread and sausages. He buys orange juice. And then he puts in the trolley the cereals the girls liked when they were younger, the ones in all of the little boxes. As he walks to the till, he goes through the shambolic, cluttered clothing section, but what he pulls into the trolley is a dressing gown, peach velour with a sleepy-looking hedgehog appliqued on it. He looks for another one, but there isn't a smaller size so he lifts another, made in the same soft fabric, but a deep pink and with ears attached to the hood. He's had feral guys in the taxi, turned up the radio so he can't hear what they're saying, the talk of fucking, sneering, boasting, any sound to cover them, dance, hymns, those radio plays, doesn't matter. Cut off their balls. Cut off their dicks. Stick their dicks in their mouths. You are right, love. 'Boogie!' somebody says, when he is putting his stuff into the bag. Ladyhill, though. Ladyhill money, Ladyhill lawyers. 'Boogie!' It's Andy Mahood, a taxi driver, in his seventies, and he's saying, 'Boogie, how are you doing, good to see you!'

'Hiya, Andy,' he says. 'How's it going with you?'

'All good, all good. You are never going to believe who I gave a lift to the other day.'

'I don't know, Andy.' People are still gentle with Andy because he lost his son years ago, battered to death outside a bar. 'Some footballer?'

'The guy who knocked over the wall outside the off-licence.'

Everyone in the area had marvelled at the miraculous occurrence of some driver managing to leave the road and mount the pavement at the angle that would allow him to knock over the wall outside the off-licence.

'He brought it up,' Andy says. 'Celebrity status.'

'Andy, I got to go,' Boogie answers. 'Sorry I can't talk longer.'

'Are you ever down at the Willowholme Bar?' he asks. 'That's my new local.'

'Andy, I got to go.'

We have all of our old school magazines here. We're only a junior school, I know, but I still think this forms an important archive. On the cover here we have Jacob Hetherington. He was a very talented young boy, you know, one of those children who can turn their hand to anything: sport, music, study. There was some issue, I think I can remember, to do with his father's business, so they upped sticks and went to England. Here's Lyness Farrell and Christopher Levine helping to plant a rose bush in memory of our beloved Mrs Agnes Taggart who worked here for nearly fifty years. It's still there. One cold winter we feared for its health, but it is still there.

In terms of questioning, what I'm doing initially is working out who was where, who came in, who went out, the basic chronologies. A friend said it was like somebody blocking a play. I don't know about that. I'm not into drama, or theatricals generally. When I'm talking, my tone is probably more one of curious interest, rather than, 'We got you bang to rights, you cunt.' And so, with these interviews, what I established was that X was on the bed with A, involved in sexual activity. Then B entered the room but before he could leave, A asked him to stay and he took a position beside the bed. B began activity with X and sometime during this, C entered and, after B, began activity with X. A, who had been standing by the bed resumed activity with X, followed by B, briefly. A then left the room. B then left the room. C then had activity with X. Do I think this, durationally, was entirely non-consensual? No. Do I think this, durationally, was entirely consensual? No.

Miriam is in the car park opposite the police station. She sees the drugs deals, the crawling cars, lowering their windows when the hooded teenage boys come over. It must be prearranged, what it is that they have ordered, the boys running to a black car to pick up the packets. They've no fear, that crowd, doing it so close to the station. One of the boys notices her watching him and she looks away quickly. Maybe the police actually know. Or maybe they don't care. She gazes up at the top floors of the station and wonders which room Rami might be in. Is it really so very unlikely to think he has been blamed for something he didn't do? The thing is, he's not quick or hard or unflappable. They could get him to say the wrong thing. Rami Abdel Salam. They'll make all sorts of assumptions. What a birthday party. Her parents took Haady home with them, along with the kite and the boxing game.

Before they left, she'd called the office of Scott McCloy, who had been in her class at university. His place, like all the others, had a twenty-four-hour helpline. She found it hard to speak on the phone, her breathing quick and shuddering. Haady was texting his friends to tell them what had happened and she snapped, 'Stop that! Have you any idea how stupid what you are doing is?' Her dad put his hand on Haady's arm. 'Well, it is,' she said. 'It's ridiculous.'

'The feds framed my brother.'

'Oh, grow up and stop that silly, silly talk!'

That sent him walking out of the room.

'Don't look at me like that!' Miriam said to her dad.

She'd got a message from someone at Scott McCloy's to say that they thought Rami would be free to go at some time around nine, although they couldn't be sure. Miriam has been sitting here for some time. At the right-hand corner of the windscreen, where it meets the plastic, there is a triangular aperture that allows a glimpse of the entrance of the police station. Could she possibly have missed him, watching those teenage boys running to and from the black car? It seems unlikely. Maybe she should get out. Opposite the building, there's a huge billboard, its paper torn and hanging. Half a giant smile is sheared away to reveal an advert for what, a fast-food restaurant? Miriam stands back to let a crowd of girls walk past. She hears their Liverpool accents.

Rami comes out of the station and she watches as he stands there, dazed. Although she wants to shout to him, she finds she can't. He has his arms folded and he's looking at the ground. And then she waves. He doesn't see her. She waves again. Two passing guys with rucksacks look from her over to Rami. 'Oi!' one of them shouts. 'Oi, she's waving. She's waving at you!'

When he gets in, she can smell that he's been sick. She's always been like that with the boys, she could always tell when they were sickening for something, long before they felt it themselves. It was the lightest flush on their faces and a milky smell. When they vomited, Miriam could discern the bitterness, on their clothes, on their skin, hours after. Before she even asks him what's happening, he shakes his head. No. No. He retreats into the carapace of the Canada Goose coat. 'Rami, sweetheart,' she says. He shakes his head again, bent over now so his head is on his knees. 'Rami, sweetheart.'

'Just drive away, Mum,' he whispers. 'I want to go home.'

She takes a circuitous route that heads in the direction of the Donegall Road. Miriam says that she loves him, everyone does, and no matter what it is, there is a way through it. Everything she says feels like a new slide on a PowerPoint entitled 'When Someone Is Going through Difficult Times'. They pass Kahlil's old place, but the barber's below it is long gone. Now there is a tanning and nail place where a huge decal of a woman looks orgasmically at coffin-shaped acrylics. An upstairs window is cracked, weeds sprouting from broken brick.

'Alright,' Miriam says, 'nearly home.'

At the kitchen table, where he always did his homework, even though he had a desk in his room, he tells her that this is nothing that he ever imagined he would have been involved in and that he doesn't know how to explain it, that it is not the kind of thing that he ever thought he would have to speak to his mum about, that he is ashamed and it isn't who he is as a person.

'OK,' Miriam says. 'Keep going.'

He had stayed because they were doing a stock take. And for the stock take, for some reason, the guy had paid them cash in hand and so they thought they would go to a bar for a couple of drinks but the one they went to was closing early for a private function and then he bumped into a couple of guys he knew from when he used to work in the restaurant in the hotel. They said that they were heading to a party on the Lisburn Road, somebody had a house for the night, an Airbnb, but they said not a full-on party, it would be quite chilled. And so, he went there, they all got a taxi after they had got a carryout from a place that Chris knew. At the party, after a while, he ended up in a bedroom upstairs with Chris and this girl. Yeah he knew her from before although they had never really spoken. She was just one of those people always hanging around. Always hanging around. They were upstairs and Chris started kissing the girl. It was obvious that she fancied Chris, everyone knew that. And then he was kissing her too. That had happened before one time. It was just kind of messing about really, stupid, because he didn't even fancy her. And then Chris was kissing her and things went from there. He thought he should leave when they started, you know, Chris and her, but then Chris gave him a look that it was alright for him to be there too and then when Chris had finished, he went over and the girl didn't say no. The girl, she's called Misty, she didn't say no. She definitely didn't say no.

He breaks off here and says, 'No, Mum, I can't be telling you this kind of stuff. I don't want to say any more.'

'Yes you can.'

'I don't want to. I don't want to say any more.'

'Doesn't really matter whether you do or don't want to say any more because we will be going tomorrow to the offices of Scott McCloy and I will hear all of the details then. For a start, have you been charged?'

He says that he hasn't. He is on bail but not charged. He has to give his passport in to the police. They have his phone. He can't make contact with, he doesn't want to say her name, Misty; he can't make contact with the girl.

So they might still charge him. 'They might still charge you,' she says. 'What happened next?'

He said that he couldn't really, you know, do it, he wasn't able to, do it, so he just kind of pretended to, and that anyway, Line-up by this stage was beside him and then next thing it was Line-up.

'And the girl, she didn't say anything, didn't say stop?'

He shakes his head.

'Then it went back to Chris again,' he says. 'And I still couldn't do it, so I was holding a bottle and I used, I used it once or twice but she made a noise like it was sore so I stopped and then Line-up started and that's when I left and then Chris left.'

'You should have left, Rami, before it began. I mean, Jesus Christ.'

'I know,' he says.

'The bottle,' Miriam says.

'Mum, no. I've told you enough. I've said enough. Please don't keep on.'

'Don't keep on? Are you for real? I want to know why somebody that I have never in my entire life witnessed doing anything wilfully cruel stuck a bottle in some kid.'

'It was only a couple of inches. It was only a bit. She didn't say no. And I stopped when it seemed sore.'

'Why reach for that bottle? Why do that? She didn't say no but she didn't ask you to do that.'

'Because it was something that was, hard.'

Miriam stares at him.

'I swear, Mum, I have never felt so ashamed.'

'The solicitor, from McCloy's, did you tell him everything exactly the way you've told me?'

'No.'

'Good,' she says.

It is not your job in life to be tender and trusting. It hasn't been your job to be tender and trusting since, oh I don't know, the 1960s. Or before that. You need to get up, get your make-up on, get out the door, earn your own money. I pull up my own metal shutter in the morning and I close down my own metal shutter in the evening. That's not a metaphor or anything like that. I've got my own business. A funeral business.

When I was a kid, I got on a bus and there were girls, singing this over and over again: Life is just a piss in the air! Life is just a piss in the air! They were punk rockers. I suppose they were trying to be shocking. But I've always remembered what they sang. Life is just a piss in the air. We're not here for long. But, you know what, that arc is golden.

But what I listen to is country and western. Both types of music. Old joke!

Merhaba kardesim we said when that boy Rami first came to get his hair cut because we thought he was Turkish, but he wasn't. We put his photo on our Instagram a few times. He has good hair. Skinfade.

Last night Lyness returned from the station with Donal's old friend Barney, who said that it had done no harm him turning up, rather than one of the more junior members of his law firm. He explained everything to do with the bail conditions. Barney told Donal that no, he didn't want to come in because it was already late and he needed to be up early in the morning to take his wife and Ellie to the airport. Ellie was auditioning for a dance company. 'I've two left feet,' he said. 'Don't know where she gets it from!'

Bronagh was sitting in the kitchen when Lyness came in.

'I'm starving,' he said. 'I've had nothing to eat for hours! Like I was actually locked up in a legit cell! I mean, what the heck! How was New York, Mum?' he asked, putting on an approximation of a New York accent.

'I'm waiting for an explanation. I arrive back to see my son disappearing into a police car.'

'Yes,' Donal said. 'Your mother just sat there watching it as if it was a TV programme. Why in the name of God didn't you get out of the car?'

'Well, I am sure Barney has filled you in on all the details. They were just asking about what happened at this really quite pathetic party. I could tell the cops were thinking, what is this all about, guys? They were just, what do you say, going through the motions. Somebody accuses you, they have to arrest you. Do you know who else they were questioning? Chris Levine. I mean, are you for real? Chris

Levine. Half the girls in Belfast want to get off with Chris Levine. Is it too late to order a takeaway?'

'It's not a normal occurrence, Lyness,' Donal said. 'Yet you are very casual about it. Being questioned by the police. Being arrested.'

'Well, Dad, as Barney says, they have to investigate these things, whether they want to or not. And as a result, people like me and Chris Levine have to answer questions, whether we want to or not. Why not just order pizza?'

On Monday morning Bronagh makes a phone call to a chief superintendent she has encountered through her work at the centre. They always have to be very careful about how they position themselves in relation to the police because it could have a negative impact on attendance or create issues of trust, if they're seen to be too closely aligned. Yet Bronagh knows whom to call for some information, when necessary.

She joins Donal on the sofa, folds her hands in her lap.

'Well?' he eventually says.

'Well. That was very interesting.'

'What was very interesting, Bronagh?'

'There were three boys. And this girl, to some degree or another, she'd been physical with two of the boys before. Chris Levine. And she didn't ever say no.'

'Three,' says Donal. 'That seems excessive, doesn't it?'

'Another thing. There were drugs in her bag. And according to some person, she had supplied drugs to the boys on previous occasions. And god knows who else. I mean,' she continues, 'by no means am I saying this girl is a piece of work or anything like that, and, as you know I have experience of dealing with all sorts of different kids, but, well, I think it is important for us to know that not long after she got home from the party where she was apparently assaulted, she went on Benefactors.'

'What?'

'She has a Benefactors account.'

'What's that?'

'Oh, for Christ's sake, Donal. It's not appealing, you know, that whole who is this beat combo they call the Beatles kind of shtick. Benefactors.'

'I simply don't know what you are talking about, Bronagh.'

'Benefactors. You sign up and you take pornographic or semi pornographic pictures of yourself and make pornographic films of yourself for perverts to access on a global scale.'

'There's pornographic film studios in Belfast?'

'You do it from your own house obviously. Your bedroom. And here's another couple of things. This girl doesn't live with her parents. She lives with some guy who used to be her mother's partner. I mean, not even a stepdad. And guess what, Donal. When they examined her, she had bruises that she'd drawn on herself.'

'Well,' Donal says. 'She certainly sounds a bit of a loony tune. How did Lyness even end up coming into contact with somebody like that? But did she have actual injuries?'

'Oh, I don't know,' Bronagh says. 'Probably not. But as you say, obviously a very troubled person. Trust Lyness to get himself involved! I'm not surprised that Barney doesn't think it's too significant.'

'No,' says Donal.

'He did give you that impression, didn't he?' Bronagh asks.

'I don't think he seemed too worried.'

You might look at me now, behind my desk at the travel agent's, and you might think I'm unfit and you would be right, but it wasn't always that way. Not at all. I was actually a pretty good footballer back in the day. I was on a team that won the under-17s schools cup. That's a big deal, pal. And we weren't one of those schools, your St Columb's or your Ashfield Boys, who everyone half expected to win each year. We weren't a team like that at all. We nearly went out in the quarters, but a guy called David McKay scored two late goals to pull us through. He went on to have trials for Aston Villa and Sunderland, although I don't think anything ever happened for him. We got through the semi easily and then the final, I was so nervous I was puking all morning. When we won, it was the best moment of my life. To win something like that, with a load of fellas who are your friends, most of whom you've known since you were kids, well you can't put a price on that. It was sheer euphoria. It was pure. It was obviously quite a few years ago now, over fifteen. Nothing that has happened since has surpassed that time, if I am being honest. I feel lucky to have experienced it.

As he slept on the flight back from San Francisco, Neil Levine dreamed of fucking Frankie. He imagined her, not in a hotel room, but in the actual first-class cabin, sitting astride his seat. That was where, after all, he had first encountered her, on a plane. That uniform. He had asked her to wear it quite a few times when they first got together. The little hat looked like something a girl guide would wear. When Neil opened his eyes an air steward *was* standing there, a young man, asking him, sir, if there was anything else that he needed? Neil looked at the tracker and saw that they were somewhere over Utah. The air steward, looking at Neil's crotch and seeing he had a hard-on, didn't give so much as a smirk. Well, so what anyway? Neil thought it was very romantic, wholesome even, that thinking about his own wife in the sky would cause such an effect.

When the plane neared Heathrow, he started to think about what he was returning to. There were meetings this week involving some quite major projects that hadn't gone according to prediction. There was nothing to concern him in terms of any significant repercussions, but it would involve a complex enough interplay between his lawyers and a few key participants. And then there was this thing involving Chris. The way it was presented at first, he thought that it was laddish high spirits of the kind that were demonstrated at virtually every teenage party. But then, when Neil has spoken to him on the phone, Chris seems, well, he can tell that beneath the composure he's slightly concerned. About what? Something that boiled down to 'being there'? What was that about? We are now complicit in everything that our friends do? But these things grow legs. He's seen it before. When the misinformation settles, it hardly matters in the end what happened originally. Loretta has kept him informed about what's been happening. Chris has the best lawyers in town. It was funny though. He detected from Loretta a discernible degree of disapproval towards the whole goings-on, something that had never manifested itself when she was party to any of his more unorthodox business practices in the past. But yes, people could be odd.

He thinks again about the teenage party, how actually, in reality, this was something that he never went to. They were happening of course. He could remember how, at his school, there were the guys and girls, free and easy, who talked on Monday mornings about what had happened, who had got off with whom. He could remember that girl, a sprinter, who everyone was crazy about. She went on to be a Miss Northern Ireland contestant. There was always the anticipation among the lads about who might be lucky enough to get off with her. There were those discos, too, in local hotels but they weren't in his orbit. There was a maths teacher they had, Mr Nolan, a visionary really, who converted the tiny store off his room into a computer suite. A few BBC computers. Sinclair Spectrums. Only three of them were really interested, a girl called Linda Hull, Desmond McQuitty and him. Twenty-four-carat nerds. Neil's parents were old-timers, retired when he was in his last year of primary school. When Nolan told them that their son would benefit from having his own computer at home, they duly bought him one. It was regarded in the house like the ark of the covenant.

Can you remember your first blow job? Yeah? How long did it take the guy to come? The first time somebody told him that joke, Neil could have said, about two minutes. And then, after that, Desmond gave me one, and I lasted not much more. Him and Desmond McQuitty, one time, at his house, programming all night, his parents in bed. It was one of those things, needs must, like finding a temporary fix for a software issue. Neither of them had any guilt about it or questioned their sexuality. It was just a pragmatic action. Of course, they would both rather have had some kind of activity with Linda Hull, but she was in some kind of intense correspondence with a guy from Imperial College whom she met on the Larne–Stranraer ferry.

He speaks to Frankie from the lounge where he waits for his connecting flight to Belfast. 'Back soon, babes,' he says. 'Yes, not too tired, looking forward to seeing you. Nothing further with Chris?' he asks.

'Nothing further.'

There is only a very outside chance, an absolute outside chance, that this whole thing could go further, to trial even, and Chris's role seems so peripheral, so marginal anyway, But you shouldn't bet against the black swan. 'No,' he says. 'You never want to bet against the black swan.'

'Sure,' says Frankie. 'What's the black swan?'

'Bad things can still happen,' he says. 'I suppose that's what it means. But I'll be home soon.'

My son was killed, three months short of his eighteenth birthday, by a sniper, Belfast, 1970. The British Army returned his possessions to me, with no note, in a large brown envelope that had ripped along one side.

Misty takes off that dressing gown that Boogie bought her and puts out the light so the room's cave-like. Very sore when she gets into the water but it eases off when she has been there for a minute or two. This morning, she went to the unit for some tests. They'll let her know the results in a bit. It wasn't the same woman as before, the one who called her pet, and had an assistant. Even though she hasn't put it in the bath, she can smell Gen's cookies and cream foam bath. Misty plunges under the water, shakes her head. Boogie got the thermostat working this morning when she was out. That rushing sound in her head, like someone scribbling on a pad with a biro. She comes up once more and exhales. The police said that she couldn't have her phone back. The boys, they told her, had been arrested. She'd imagined Line-up's face, when he was arrested. He must have been so shocked. Maybe he remembered what he'd said. The police gave her back her bag.

    She looks at the dressing gown lying on the bathroom floor, its dopey hedgehog. Bit of a random purchase from Boogie. They won't investigate it too much further is what she reckons. That was the vibe from the other woman, although she didn't say anything in particular. It was just the way she was writing things down. Misty sees the four crescents on the side of her arm, made by four nails. The doctor woman had looked at the bruise on her shoulder and Misty had said, oh no, don't worry about that one, it's just me messing around. I did beauty and special effects last year. I mess around still! When the other one asked questions, it was like back in school when you thought you understood photosynthesis or the Plantation of Ulster and then they would ask a question and you'd realise that you actually didn't really get it. You just knew a small piece of it or maybe you didn't understand it at all. How did you know it was a bottle? Were you on your back or was that after he turned you around? Who do you remember being in the room at this point? Line-up couldn't just pat her on the head. Chris did nothing to help. It happened so quick but it lasted for ever, isn't there a word for that? Chris at the beginning, OK, and then Rami, well OK, she supposes, OK, but what did Rami even do, and then Line-up, it happened so quickly, she didn't say no. But no, not Line-up. And then it all started again. So, did you consent the first time? Did you consent the second time? The cops will think she's a scuzz, and everybody else too when they hear about it, so she should have just left it. Rami is not a bad guy. Chris is not a bad guy. Was Chris frightened when he was arrested? Chris was only a kid when he lost his mum. Everybody will know, from the party. So, know what, who gives a fuck if everyone knows? Because otherwise it's Misty Johnston, who we can treat any way we want because we can. Things got a little crazy! they might say. Just partying hard. Hey, come on, nobody was out to be mean and shit just happens and everyone gets carried away and Misty, you're the Bennyz one, aren't you?

After her bath, she goes to her room and tips the contents of her bag on the floor. There's a packet of sweets, a leftover croissant squashed into a napkin, a hairbrush, a can of body spray, a notebook with a cat on the front of it, one sock, her phone charger. The bag sits looking miserable, slumped to the side. At one corner the plastic frame pokes though the artificial pebbled leather. What must her face have looked like, surprised, tired, frightened, wincing? They didn't look at her face. Nobody looked in her eyes. Line-up's hair was stuck to his forehead. Line-up's face was screwed up before he turned her round. The ring light in the corner of the bedroom looks like a shocked mouth. Misty takes off the hedgehog dressing gown and hangs it over the circle, before putting on her clothes.

When she goes downstairs, Boogie and Geneva are sitting in the kitchen.

'Was the water hot enough?' Boogie asks.

'Yeah. Nice and warm.'

'Good. Did they say if you need to go back again for more interviews?'

'No,' Misty replies, as she gets herself a glass of water. 'They didn't mention that, but I've got a special woman who is the one who is always going to be in touch. Naomi McCrory.'

'Well,' says Boogie. 'That seems sensible, doesn't it?'

'Why's it sensible?'

'Rather than having a load of random people. To have one point of contact.'

'Suppose so. Have we any bread?'

'There's a fresh loaf bought today. But at the same time, you are still going to have to talk to a lot of people about what happened, over the next while. Lawyers, police, all of that. There'll be more interviews. That's just par for the course.'

'Par for the course? What you on about?'

'Just the way it is. With these sorts of things. They'll be building up a case.'

'I didn't know you were an expert on all of this,' she says, tightening the belt of her dressing gown.

'Well, as you know, I'm not, Misty.'

'Then how do you know what's going to happen?'

'Alright, doesn't matter,' he says. 'I was just saying. I'll shut up.'

'Well, I don't want to talk about any of it.'

'Fair enough,' he says. 'Do you want me to make you something to eat?'

'No.'

'No need to get on like that,' Gen says. 'He was just asking you some basic questions about it all. And stating the obvious.'

'Who asked you to get involved?' Misty says.

'Get involved? What do you mean? I'm sitting in my own kitchen in my own house, so I think I can join in any conversation I want and I can, as you call it, get involved whenever I want. Yeah?'

'I don't know why you two are being so mean when I just came back from having to speak to the police about what happened.'

'Nobody,' Boogie says, 'is being mean. Nobody is being mean at all.'

'Yeah you are.'

'No, we're not,' Gen insists.

'Yeah you are and don't think I don't know why.'

'Why then?' Gen says. 'Why don't you tell me?'

'Because you don't believe me. You don't think I should have gone to the police.'

'But I went with you!'

'I mean you,' she says to Boogie. 'You don't think I should've gone because you think what happened, I brought it on myself.'

'That's total rubbish,' he says. 'Total and utter fucking rubbish.'

'Why you picking on him?' says Geneva.

'I sat in that interview where Gen told what happened when you came home and what you told her and I have never felt more sad in my life,' says Boogie. 'And that's the truth.'

'You'd be more upset if something like this happened to Geneva.'

'That's just not true,' says Boogie, getting up from his chair. 'Let's not talk about this anymore.'

'Good idea,' says Misty. 'Good fucking idea. Gen, can I borrow your phone? I need to send a message to the hotel that I'm not going to be in today or tomorrow.'

'You can borrow mine,' Boogie says.

'I asked Geneva.'

Gen passes over her phone slowly, without speaking.

'Thanks,' Misty says. 'I'll be down in a minute.'

Upstairs, she phones the hotel and gets put through to one of the managers in the restaurant, the new woman who doesn't know everyone's names yet. 'Yeah, Wednesday or Thursday will probably be fine,' Misty says. 'I've got the cold. Well, it's more like a flu.'

When the call has ended, she looks at Gen's contacts. Her mum's phone number is there; the last message sent to her was over a year ago. Mum, she types. And then deletes it. And then retypes, a sentence explaining what has happened to her. She signs it Mistyx. Her mum phones back almost immediately. Oh my god! Her voice is high-pitched. I can't believe this! My baby girl! Misty suddenly doesn't know what to say. Why did she do that? This is Geneva's phone, she says. I'll ring you back in a bit when I get my phone back. No worries. All is fine.

As she is deleting the call and the message, there is a knock at her door.

'Just checking you're alright,' Boogie says. 'Sorry about that.'

'I'm sorry too,' she says.

They give each other a sad high-five.

I had someone else with me yesterday, a trainee, and so I first had to ask permission for that. It meant that, more than usual, I had to provide a commentary on what I was doing. The trainee kept saying, OK, each time I said something. It was a little irritating, so I was glad when she stopped doing that and moved to a more discreet nod of the head. I began by trying to elicit specific details about the types of injuries sustained. Mouth? Breasts? Vagina? Vulva? Rectum? And to ask if there was any bleeding or abrasions. I asked too, according to the usual protocols, about which orifices were penetrated and how, and, if known, whether ejaculation occurred and whether, if known, a condom was used. And then I ask about the assailant's, or assailants', use of aggression and weapons or objects. At this juncture I can also ask for a description of the assailants.

I've done this for a long time. It's not useful to anyone for me to be emotional. But sometimes I'll use the word, pet. I fill in the information on the forms. In this case I had to make a note about the use of a vodka bottle. The patient was not sure if she was talking about two or three people. After that, we proceeded to the actual examination itself. Each step needs to be explained and of course the patient can refuse any part of the examination. If the patient permits it, then I can take photos of possible injuries. I examine the mouth, breasts, vagina, vulva and rectum. I say the word thank you, to acknowledge that this is something that they are permitting me to do. Obviously I have seen many injuries over the time I have been working. I have seen a perineum ripped three inches. I have seen intestines protruding from an anus like a red cauliflower. This time there were injuries, lacerations, caused by the bottle, in my opinion. There are the samples to be collected: smears of the buccal, vaginal and rectal mucosa, samples of scalp and pubic hair, blood and saliva samples. If available, semen. Everything, as I showed the trainee, is labelled, dated, sealed. There are tests to be done at a later date: a pregnancy test, serologic tests for syphilis, hepatitis B and HIV.

A perfume that Bronagh uses sometimes is Fracas by Robert Piguet. She was introduced to it by an actress she met at a dinner once at a London gallery to celebrate some Irish painter or other. Bronagh just had to say, what is your perfume, since it was so comfortable and elegant, just like the woman herself. When she said it was Fracas by Robert Piguet, Bronagh resolved to buy it the very next day. When she investigated online, it said it was a fragrance of refined simplicity, enjoyed by women such as Madonna, Kim Basinger, Stella Tennant and Courtney Love. By this stage, a year and a half later, Bronagh now has the Silkening Body Wash and the Silkening Body Lotion. Just as much as the scent, she likes the name, Fracas, which is a fight. But the word makes it seem kind of chic, a little pushing and gesticulating in a piazza, on a sunny early evening. Someone at the centre, headbutting a fifteen-year-old, the bubbling blood running down the wall: that wasn't a fracas. Contretemps. Good too. It made a disagreement charmingly trivial and ridiculous. The word that she had come up with to describe what Lyness had ended up getting involved in was not fracas. No, it was a hoo-ha or even better a hullabaloo. She doubted whether anyone at the centre would have heard about what had happened, but she knows that the word she will use is hullabaloo. She thinks, too, that it would be a good idea to get in touch with the mothers of the other boys who have been arrested, if she can. She eventually manages to get

Chris's mother's number through someone who has the same cleaners and Bronagh sends her a message to see if she would like to meet. She wasn't able to get in contact with the other boy's mother. Bronagh has thought carefully about where the venue should be. Going for a drink seems frivolous. They need space. She decides on the café of the Ulster Museum because it is large and not particularly indulgent in its sensibility. OK, when? came the response to Bronagh's text, some hours later. Wednesday at eleven, she replied.

Kids from a scout troop are jumping on and off the steps, a few of them climbing up the abstract metal sculpture at the entrance. Frankie parks her car on a terraced street nearby. Two guys removing a window turn to look at her in the middle of their precarious operation. She hasn't been to this place before. When the woman contacted her, Frankie wondered if it was a good idea or not. She thought about it and decided yes. She goes to the counter and buys a can of diet Coke. She doesn't know what the woman looks like. There's one sitting in a multicoloured tasselled cardigan. Another is reading a book. And then there's the one with a yellow folder on the table. Frankie sits down, pulls the ring of the Coke. Let whoever it is come over to her. Her mouth is tender, as it always is, after the Restylane. They apply numbing cream, but it never works totally. Everyone knows that's how it is with lips. Don't get them done if you're going to be a pussy about it. She takes a sip of Coke and presses the cool can to her mouth. She watches as one of the scouts loses his footing on the sculpture and slips. He gets up, laughing and rubbing his leg.

'Hi!'

It's the woman with the yellow folder. She sits down opposite Frankie.

'I'm Bronagh and I am presuming that you're—'

'Yeah,' Frankie says.

'Well, here we are. Thanks for coming.'

'No problem.'

'I thought it might be useful.'

'Could be.'

Bronagh says, 'I really like your dress. It's so well-fitted. I'd love to wear something like that but I've developed a fairly unerring sense of what suits me and what doesn't.'

She laughs and Frankie doesn't reply.

'Anyway, I think I'll grab another coffee here, before we start to have a chat. Can I get you something? Would you like a coffee or something to eat?'

'No thanks.' Frankie holds up her can of Coke.

A woman struggles with a buggy and two children, making their way along the path towards the gates of the park. Frankie can't hear, but it looks like the woman is shouting at the bigger child and he is walking along now with his head bowed. A girl in bare legs and a plastic mac sits on one of the park benches by herself.

When Bronagh returns with her coffee she puts, in the middle of the table, a slice of cake and two forks. She looks around the café. 'It's really very nice here,' she says. 'It's airy, isn't it? I'm rarely over on this side of town because I work on the opposite side of the city. But I must say, I do very much like it here. What do you do, Frankie?'

'In relation to what?'

'In relation to work.'

'I don't.'

'Oh,' says Bronagh, taking a small piece of cake. 'I see. Well, it's not compulsory, is it? And I'm sure you're extremely busy just with life in general. I work in young people's services. Integrated support services. I'm CEO of the 411.'

'Right,' says Frankie.

'The reason I mention it is that I am pretty aware of youth behaviours, of all types.'

Frankie puts down her Coke.

'You said young people's services. So you work with kids in care?'

'Well, not exclusively,' begins Bronagh, 'but certainly we do act as a service provider for many young people in the care system. Although we would prefer the term looked-after.'

'Girls or boys?'

'Both.'

'OK,' says Frankie.

Bronagh smiles.

'So, you know kids, girls, who live in residences?'

'Well, yes, I do. But the thing here is that our approach is innovative and it has proved to be pretty transformational for a lot of our kids. I've got a terrific team. We're multi-disciplinary. I mean, of course not everyone is aware of our work, but we do have an international reputation.'

'Right,' says Frankie.

'Yes. For example, I just came back from New York the other day. I was there as a guest, as part of a fundraising initiative. But what do I return to? I'm getting out of the car and what do I see but my son getting bundled into a police car! I'm just off the plane from New York! I mean, can you imagine?'

'Not really. But,' she adds, 'if it happened, it happened.'

'That's really where we are now, Frankie, isn't it? This hullaballoo and the boys. No criticism of the police. Everything has to go through due process.'

'The kids you work with, that are in care. Are they over sixteen, yeah? Are they still in school? Do they have jobs?'

'It depends. I mean, obviously there's a range of settings and situations. So obviously, due process is absolutely crucial but at the same time it's good if we are there to support the boys in any way that we can. Because it really isn't pleasant, is it? Even a brush with this kind of thing isn't good at all for them. I'm not saying that teenagers can't behave very badly, of course they can, and I'm not saying that on this occasion they behaved like monks, but this situation! From what I understand from Lyness, it's an absolute misunderstanding.'

'Sure,' Frankie says.

'Chris is wanting to do medicine?'

'That's his plan.'

'Lyness couldn't really choose. He went in the end for business. It'll be all change for them in September!'

Frankie presses her lips together again. She puts her finger to the place, on her top lip, that feels tender.

Bronagh lowers her voice. 'I've actually found out a little about this young woman. I don't want to go into all the details, but she has a Benefactors account, she was covered in fake bruises, she deals drugs, she doesn't live with her parents and' – she remembers a detail she forgot to tell Donal – 'she turned up with this little child who was wearing an evening dress and who was all done up. Now that is someone who needs help really more than anything else, don't you think so? She just needs help.'

'Who was the kid in the evening dress?'

'Oh, I don't know, some relation I presume. Not sure. But anyway, I am so pleased we met. And that we are on the same page, so to speak.'

'Sure,' says Frankie. She says sure again a few times, as she listens to Bronagh talk. When they get up to leave, only Bronagh has touched the cake.

My granny was in the final of the Miss Lovely Legs back in the day. Like this was pure back in the day, the 1970s, I think. She had to wear denim booty shorts – they all did. Although she calls them hot pants. The contestants were allowed to wear their own shoes and my granny says that hers were gold and strappy with stiletto heels. All the judges were men who owned businesses in the local area. Nowadays she wears these slippers with pom-poms.

I saw a girl being sick at the end of my driveway. She bent over to vomit, straightened up, then lowered her head again. She looked young. There's a streetlight positioned beside the gatepost, so the scene was well illuminated. I hoped that it would rain in the night, a consistent dark and heavy downpour, so that by the morning the sick would be sluiced away.

'Would you mind wiping the condiments?' the supervisor says when Misty returns on Thursday. Boogie had wondered why she was going back so soon. Maybe she shouldn't go back at all. But she likes the hotel. Is she meant to stay in the house for ever? 'I don't like to be asking,' the supervisor says, 'but before the condiments could you sort out that disabled toilet cos the floor is soaking wet – hold on, get yourself sorted, and I will get you some rubber gloves.'

'Sure,' Misty replies, 'no problem.' She's happy to take orders from this supervisor who is always strictly business.

When Misty goes to the staff area, Harlow's there. Harlow watches her take off her coat, fold it up, put it along with her bag in the square storage space.

'Are you alright?' Harlow eventually says.

'Yeah.'

'I'm actually surprised to see you, if I'm being honest.' Harlow plays with her necklace, running it along her white bottom teeth.

'Well, I'm fine. I'm alright. Just getting back to work.'

'You certainly look fine.'

Misty stares at the new rota pinned to the wall.

'So yes,' says Harlow. 'I didn't think you'd be back here.'

Misty fixes the collar of her work top. 'Why did you not think I'd be back here?'

Harlow gives a little tinkling laugh.

'Why did you not think I'd be back here?' Misty asks.

'Well,' Harlow says. 'I thought you might have been traumatised or something. Know what I mean? Is that not how people usually are? Obviously you know that Chris won't be here because part of his bail conditions is that he has no contact with you. Hence he is not on the rota. Chris Levine on bail for sexual assault. I mean, what the actual fuck? And Lyness Farrell. And the other one too. Three guys.'

'If you'll excuse me, I just want to go out there and get on with what I've been told to do.'

'Chris is a good friend of mine,' Harlow says. 'I've known him for years.'

Harlow's standing in front of the door.

'Do you mind? I need to get out.'

'Have a nice day,' Harlow says. She gives that fluting laugh again.

Wiping the condiments involves getting all the salts, peppers and sugars. After you've filled, or replenished them, as one of the managers calls it, you then use diluted D10 on a cloth to get them clean. There's that music playing. She's heard it before but she doesn't know who it is.

When Misty goes to the kitchen to get the bag of peppercorns and salt crystals and the funnel that she needs to use to put them into each of the pots, she asks Krzysztof, the kitchen porter, if he knows what it is.

'No. Sounds like it is from a long, long time ago.'

'I like it. The woman's voice.'

He agrees that she makes a good sound. Krzysztof says that he's going back to Poznań at the end of the month because his mother isn't well. Once before, he showed Misty a photo of her on his phone. She was out in a garden with two children, Krzysztof and his sister when they were little. His sister worked somewhere, he told her, with politicians because she had studied hard at school and knew many languages. Whereas he, he had not studied hard at school. 'You've still got time to do courses,' Misty said. 'If you want to. What would you study?' He had thought for a minute before answering.

'Maybe staring out to sea,' he said, finally. 'I am joking. Electrical engineering maybe.'

'Jeez,' Misty said. 'Electrical engineering. Think I'd get electrocuted on day one!'

But he still has another few weeks here before he heads to Poznań. It's unlikely, he says, that he will return to Belfast. 'But, Misty, you need the fucking salt and pepper. And the fucking funnel!'

'Yeah, give me the fucking funnel,' she says.

He gives her arm a little punch. 'Stay strong.'

They make different sounds, the peppercorns, the sugar and the salt. Even with the music playing, she can hear the smooth slide of the sugar, the rattle of the peppercorns. She wipes each salt cellar in the same way, three times around the middle, then she runs the cloth over the top and bottom. After five bottles, she re-sprays the D10.

Later, the manager directs her to helping with the drinks orders for the early lunchtime customers. There's a couple with their two kids, who are both holding cuddly toys from that place where you get to build the bear yourself. You choose a heart to put inside the bear. Boogie took Geneva and her, when they were younger. The woman has a white wine and the guy a beer. The children get strawberry milkshakes. Neither the children nor the adults say anything when the drinks are put down. She goes over next to a much larger table where a group are wanting various permutations of vodka, gin, slimline and non-slimline tonics. They keep changing their minds about the kind of gin. Misty laughs and is patient while a man goes on about how he once met the guy who owns Lenaghmore House gin. He also owns a racehorse, he says, and guess what, didn't he once win a grand with a bet on it? Lenaghmore House gin, it's all I ever drink, he says.

When Misty brings over the drinks, one of the women at the table says, 'No, love, I'm slimline!'

'I'm sorry.'

'And I'm not the vodka. I'm the gin. Is this definitely the Lenaghmore House?' the guy asks.

'Yeah it is, I made sure—'

But then Misty sends a bottle of non-slimline tonic cascading over the lap of a woman in a sequinned skirt.

'Jesus fuck I'm soaking. You just knocked that whole bottle right over me!'

'Aw shoosh, you'll dry off,' another man says.

'It's fucking sequins, you dick, they don't dry off!'

'What are sequins made of? Plastic, so if they are plastic then just wipe them.'

The woman says to Misty again, 'I'm soaking. I want another drink and I'm not paying for it. In fact, I don't want to pay for my meal when I'm sitting here soaking.'

'I'm sorry. I'll get the manager.'

Wee bitch liked being fucked in a Rangers top, dirty wee slut wanted everything she got. Did she have big funbags?

Wee bitch liked being fucked in an O'Neill's top, dirty wee slut wanted everything she got. Did she have big funbags?

Nan D's flat, along the Shore Road, feels like a psychedelic padded cell to Boogie. Take a spongy step across the deep pile carpet to a sofa that feels like red velour quicksand. Even the walls, with their heavy embossed patterns, are soft. There's photos of his dad on the mantelpiece. Easy enough when she lost her husband, she says, but devastation when it was her son. She hates talk of Boogie's mother.

'Still injecting steroids into each other's asses?' Nan D said, when Boogie came back at Easter from the visit to his mother in England. She and her partner had both become bodybuilders, senior division. 'Don't be mean,' he said, 'they actually eat a lot of very healthy food. Their freezer is chocka with those bags of frozen fruit.'

'She was a useless mother to you,' Nan D said. 'But fair's fair, many others are useless too. Leigh, for example.'

Nan answers the door with her hair wrapped up in a towel turban. 'Michael,' she says, 'you're early. I've not even got my face on yet.'

He sits downstairs watching a detective programme while she blow-dries her hair. The TV colour is turned up to full saturation. He looks for her remote to adjust the balance, finds it under a plush cushion. He turns it to black and white and then moves it back again to where Nan D had it. Up to her, really. But the detective's hand is the colour of brick.

When she comes down, she makes him a coffee in her usual way, boiling the milk in a saucepan and then splashing it over the instant granules.

'There's nothing except for those fondant fancies,' she says. 'And you don't like them.'

'No probs.' He takes a sip of coffee. 'What's new?'

'Nothing to report, Michael. Nothing special. Well, I tell a fucking lie, something quite incredible did happen and it happened last night. At the church there was a man speaking in tongues.'

'Was there indeed.'

'Aye there was. A sight to behold.'

'Well, you know what I'm going to say. You know I'm going to say what a load of old bollocks.'

'You can say what you want but I know what I saw and I know what I heard. The Holy Spirit.'

'Great, the Holy Spirit is calling in on the Shore Road.'

'The fella who was speaking in tongues, it was the one, believe it or not, who used to run the newsagent's near the football ground. Can you remember it? It was about the last place in the city where there was a top shelf, know what I mean, the last place where there were all those magazines and not in plastic or with stickers covering the women up. You'd see the kids go in for an ice lolly and then their eyes would be out on stalks with all of that tits and ass. Well, he's a different proposition now and he is speaking in tongues.'

'Funny person for the Holy Spirit to choose.'

'Everyone's sinned. It was incredible. The way he was making these sounds.'

'Very good, but a change of topic,' Boogie says. 'I've something I need to tell you.' And he sits back on the red velvet to begin.

※ ※ ※

The clock on the little table, with the big golden spheres rotating one way and then the other. The detective walking to his car. She doesn't speak. Boogie talks quietly, deliberately, as the golden spheres continue their course. 'So that,' Boogie concludes, 'is what I know.'

'So, what kind of cunts are they?'

'As I said, well-off ones.'

The clock, round and round. The detective, meeting up with the ex-wife he is still in love with. His brick hands long to touch her.

'I tried to change the colour balance on your TV,' Boogie says. 'But I just put it back again to where you had it. The colour balance.'

Nan D reaches into her bag to get a compact foundation. Looking in its mirror, she applies the make-up briskly. 'Big Geordie and the other ones who used to drink in the Aleppo. You remember that bar? Time was you would have walked in the Aleppo and you would have supplied old Geordie with all the details and then all would have been taken care of.' Now she takes out a lipstick, 'All would have been taken care of. The Aleppo was dark but it was clean.'

'All would have been taken care of, except if one of Geordie's compadres was involved. In that case, I don't think too much would have happened.'

Nan D ignores this.

'So, what's next then?' Do you want a drink? A whiskey?'

She goes for the bottle of Powers and two cut-glass tumblers.

'I'm getting the vibe,' Boogie says, 'that she wishes she'd never gone to the peelers.'

'Michael. Here's what I'm thinking. Just you sit and listen while I talk this through.'

'Off you go.'

'In any situation you got to, like, look at the odds. And the odds are fucking stacked against our poor soul here with these Bennyz goings-on and the three of them and what have you. I mean, did you know about this Bennyz thing?'

'Not until she told me the other night.'

'Alright. They're who they are and she's who she is, and we've got all the rest of it, so the odds are against her. And the odds anyway are against folk speaking up about this kind of thing.

'Sure.'

'And these guys, these excuses for fellas, from their big houses, they can be pretty sure that no matter what they done, they can just cruise on. What age you say they are?'

'Same as her, from what I hear.'

'Probably going to university. They probably already got the sweatshirt. They probably already got their name down to take part in that boat race.'

'Probably.'

'But here's the thing, Michael, there is just a wee outside chance that they could be charged. That it could go to court, and not only that, but there's a chance that Misty could end up with one of those lawyers like off the films, a young underdog, nice long hair like your woman, can't remember her name. She's been in loads of things. From the wrong side of the tracks, underdog, but sees something in Misty that reminds her of herself, you know what I mean? And works night and day. In libraries at midnight and grafting grafting grafting. And she turns a whole jury around, our girl. And those guys are going down and their lives are just grubbied up for all time.' She takes a drink of her whiskey. 'They got to know that that's a possibility. Like a really slim one. But still a possibility.'

'Alright,' Boogie says.
'So. Exodus.'
'What you mean?'
'Exodus, you never heard about it?'
'Course I have. Movement of the people. Everybody knows Exodus.'

'In Exodus, the Israelites were liberated from their bondage under the Pharaoh. There was a man talking about it the other week, so there was. And when they were liberated they got gold and silver from them as reparations. The Egyptians forked out.'

'Your train of thought, I am right in thinking, your train of thought is that in order to avert potential risk, they should be given the chance to pay some money?'

'You got it. You are fancying it up there, Boogie, the way you are saying it. But yes.'

'Why would Misty not take the chance on going to court along with your grafter woman with the nice long hair?'

'Because she doesn't exist.'

'Does she not? How do you know?'

'She doesn't exist but Exodus does. It's called reparations. It's about paying up.'

I was downstairs, sitting on the couch with a couple of people I know, and this girl Ellen says, hey did you know that Line-up is, you know, upstairs? With that skanky wee weed dealer? So what? I said, with a shrug. That's what I did actually say. I'm not retrofitting it now. You know how people do that? Well, I just turned right round to her and I said this, this, this and this. And in actual fact they just sneaked away, sad and resentful and said nothing. But no, I actually did say, So what? I'd gone out with Line-up for four months earlier in the year. He wasn't a bad boyfriend, as boyfriends go. There were things about him that I really appreciated, such as his generosity. If he was eating a sandwich, like a Subway, he would offer to give you half of it. I wouldn't take it, but it was nice that he would make that gesture. And in his car, in the glove compartment, well, I don't know, I always think guys are going to have something unpleasant in there, not necessarily a gun, but an object like that. He had a paper bag full of sweets, those old-fashioned sweets that you can only really buy in a few places, like cola bottles and wafer planets. He reminded me of someone you would get in one of those funny movies where a bunch of guys get into crazy situations together.

Those were the things on the plus side. But then, what I would have to say is that I didn't find Line-up that physically attractive. I remember the first time that I saw him, standing at the end of my bed. I couldn't think what it was he was reminding me of, and then it dawned on me. It was a picture book from when I was really little that had Goldilocks and the Three Bears in it. He was the same shape as Daddy Bear. It's probably the main reason why we split up. Call me shallow if you want! But that's why I wasn't bothered at all by this apparent revelation about the skanky wee weed dealer doing whatever upstairs with Line-up.

Miriam wants the boys to go into town with her on Sunday afternoon. She says it's non-negotiable, but Rami immediately says no and that she can't just pretend everything is continuing as normal. He's lost weight. His face is sallow. He's always scratching at the eczema that has appeared on his neck and at his hairline.

'You can't hide yourself away in the house all of the time,' she says.

But it seems that is exactly what he can do, as he slowly goes up the stairs once more, to his bedroom.

'We can go shopping,' Miriam says to Haady, when they get out at the multi-storey car park. 'I can buy you something.'

'I got my birthday money,' he says. 'I don't need you to get me anything.'

'We can go to Sports JPX. Let's look there.'

'Skip that place. You joking?'

'Why?'

'It's a smick shop. It's a total DLA shop.'

'What's that?'

'Disability Living Allowance. AKA, shit.'

'No, it's not,' she says. 'I didn't realise you were such a snob, Haady. And the thing is, anyway, Adidas is Adidas and Nike is Nike.'

'It's actually not. There's DLA Nike and then there's Nike. Jeez, everyone knows that.'

But they are walking in the direction of the shop, anyway.
'What you think is going to happen to Rami, Mum?'
'Nothing.'
'You don't know that though, do you?'
'Absolutely nothing is going to happen to him. I won't let it.'
'Mum, you say that, but what you gonna do? Take everyone out with your Beretta?'
'We are going to make sure that everything turns out alright. Oh look, Sports JPX!'
'Mum, honestly,' Haady says, 'I'm just not into these brands anymore. What about going to Rami's place and using his staff discount?'
'Football boots. They're functional. They're necessary. They aren't something you want to spend your birthday money on. Let's get football boots. I don't know but I just like this place. Maybe it's the colours. Or maybe it's the way they display the trainers in those white frames. It's futuristic. Space age leisure.'
'It doesn't look any different to any other sports shop,' he says. 'It's like JD.'
'Even the music in this place, I love it. It's uplifting. It's positive. They've got it just right.'
'It's like everywhere else. Calm down, for god's sake.'
When the assistant comes over, Miriam says that they are looking for football boots. He directs them to the back of the shop.
'What do you have in mind?' he asks. 'Firm ground? Soft ground? Astroturf?'
'Well now, that's a good question,' Miriam says. 'Haady, what is it you are looking for?'
'Whatever. It doesn't matter. Soft ground.'
And the assistant points to the selection.

'I like those ones,' Miriam says. 'Don't they look good? Kind of sculpted.'

They take a seat on two green cubes when the assistant goes off to get them in a size nine. 'Mum,' Haady says, 'can you imagine it if Rami went to jail? Like, he would be one of the last people in the world who would be able to cope with that. He's not tough. Well at least he wouldn't get called a ballroot because scuzzbag whatsername was over sixteen.'

'Rami is going nowhere. Why keep bringing it up, Haady? Stop going on about it. We're getting football boots.'

'I'm not going on about it. I'm just saying.'

'Well don't.'

'Tell you something,' he says, 'I'm only ever going to go with girls who have high morals and respect for themselves.'

'What century is this?'

'There's certain kinds of girls that you just want to stay away from. Trust me, Mum, every guy knows that. Stay away from them if you know what's good for you.'

'That's simply nonsense. You might as well say that there's certain kinds of guys that you just want to stay away from. Every girl knows that. Stay away from them if you know what's good for you.'

'My total point, Mum! Let all the freaky headcases go with the freaky headcases and leave everybody else to get on with it.'

The assistant comes back and says that they don't have those particular boots in a nine, but they do have them in a ten. And with thick football socks, a ten might be better anyway.

'Alright, sure, we'll take those,' she says. 'And what about socks then? Maybe you actually need socks? Why don't we go upstairs? There's a better selection of clothes up there.'

'We don't need any more stuff, Mum. Why don't we get out of here and go for a burger?' But she is already on the escalator.

They have changed the clothes since the last time she was here. The one that she liked before in the white polo top is now in a more autumnal brown tracksuit with a bag over his shoulder. He looks as if he is on his way to college rather than the park. But that leg, the way the weight is placed on it. You can't see the back muscles as distinctly through the heavier zip-up top.

'I wish your dad was here,' Miriam says.

'Dad would not be cool with all of this. He would be mad.'

'What do you think of that?' she says, pointing in the direction of the brown tracksuit and the moulded face, the broad shoulders.

'I think that that is the most DLA outfit in the whole shop. Can we just buy the socks and leave?'

My earliest memory of feeling dubious about the bible, and by extension, religion, was when at Sunday School we were told the Parable of the Talents from the gospel of Matthew. For those unaware of this tale, a master, going off on a journey, gives one of his servants five talents and another two. A third servant receives one. The servants who received five and two talents trade and turn a profit, whereas the servant who got the one talent buried it for safe keeping. The master, when he returns, is both pleased and angered. 'Who can explain why?' the Sunday School superintendent asked. I raised my hand, sure of the answer. He was pleased with the man who had kept the money safe and angered by those who had gambled it. The Sunday School superintendent said that was the wrong answer. The servant who had not made a profit was cast out into the outer darkness where there was weeping and gnashing of teeth.

I still recall the burning embarrassment of having, in front of a crowd of other boys, got an answer so definitively wrong and then the creeping feeling that my parents, with their earnest prudence, their extolling of the virtues of saving, would too have been castigated by the master.

Of course, the Parable of the Talents is sometimes interpreted as the allocation of 'personal abilities' to be made the most of, rather than wealth, or 'gifts from God' to be appreciated and used. I find neither suggestion terribly persuasive. Neither addresses the fact that everything was rigged from the beginning: those with more could afford to gamble. The one talent, one shot servant could not. And so, the rich get richer and the poor get poorer.

So, religion's obsolescence, its ideological malleability, its illogicality, its downright cruelty, I'm not going to disagree with you on any of these things, but I do still enjoy visiting churches.

When Misty gets home from work on Monday, Nan D is there.

'I got talking,' Misty tells her, 'at the bus stop, with some ones I used to go to school with. Like Natalie. She's back from a holiday. The swimming pool in the hotel had a glass floor and below that was a garden bar.'

'Great opportunity,' Nan D says, 'for all the scrotes of the day to cop an eyeful.'

'It didn't sound that kind of place.'

'Everywhere is that kind of place.'

'Well, she's back from there.'

'How was work?'

'It wasn't that good,' she says. 'I made mistakes again today. That's just been happening.'

'Your dad told me.'

'Nan D,' Misty says, 'I don't want to talk about it.'

'I get it.'

'I'm going to give up the hotel.'

Nan D brings two mugs and a plate of biscuits on the tray with hot air balloons.

'That's Gen's tray,' Misty says.

'Listen, people with their own fucking personal trays, I'm not paying any attention to whatever nonsense you have in this house. Do you know,' Nan D says, 'that people in other countries think it's weird that we have different flavours of crisps? That, say, a mum could be eating smoky bacon, a da having cheese and onion and then three kids all having different flavours. For these people in other countries, it's all about the one big bag. They think everyone should all be sharing the same big bag. Like the way you would a cake or something.'

'Funny,' Misty says.

'I'd rather have separate bags rather than everybody's dirty sweaty paws sticking into the same one.'

'Know what you mean.'

'Yeah. The people are from Italy, who think that. Or Spain.'

'Are they?'

'I know you don't want to talk about it,' Nan D begins, 'but—'

'Yeah, I don't.'

'I know, but there's something I want to explain. Just listen, Misty. Let me tell you. You know those old black and white photos of kids in the back streets, some wee girl wrapping a tea towel round a brick to pretend it's a baby doll? Well, that was me, kind of. But there was something that we always thought and that was that no matter how much of a shithole we lived in, it was better than the people in the west? Like, they were the lowest of the low. You know a pin-up, like a sailor's tattoo of a woman?'

'Yeah, loads of people got them these days.'

'Jacqueline Stewart, a girl I used to know, she looked like that, but the only problem was her teeth because she'd taken some medicine that made them this colour. Like porridge. But she was beautiful if she didn't smile. What a rocket. First person I really heard say fuck. I don't mean fuck this, fuck that. I mean fuck, for having sex. She was about fourteen years of age and she said, I had a great night the other night. What happened? I fucked a fella.'

'OK,' Misty says. 'Keep going about Jacqueline Stewart.'

'Well, Jackie was going with somebody from away out of our area and she said to me, I dare you to come up with me and see him or are you too feared? I said fuck away off I'm not feared, I'll go wherever I like! And so I went up with her and the house was more or less the same as ours. Fella was out somewhere anyway, but his ma took us in and gave us both hot chocolates, Cadbury's.'

'That was nice.'

'Don't really like hot chocolate. First sip is alright then it feels like it's sticking to your teeth.'

'Don't mind it.'

'Even used to think,' Nan D says, 'that there was another city centre up there. One for them. But we all go to the same one, everybody goes to the same shops, goes through the same pile of jumpers to get the right size. Buys the same towels. Know what I mean?'

'Sure,' Misty says, taking another biscuit.

'There's people with things in common. Like, let me explain it another way, hold on, let me put it this way. There was this fella I knew, best of laughs, and then he got all serious. He got into all the up-the-workers theories. You know what I'm on about?'

'No.'

'What you have in this country is Man United supporters fighting Man United supporters, is what he said.'

'Like, hooligans?'

'No, you're not getting it. This is it. You've some guy eighteen years of age, IRA, supports Man United, and you've some wee guy over from Bolton. British army, eighteen years of age, supports Man United.'

'OK.'

'So, this fella I know, on the side of the workers, Che Guevara, told that story and one of our crowd said, Just let them kill each other, they both support Man United, so who gives a fuck.'

'He didn't get the point,' Misty says.

'Yeah, but do you get the point? Anyway,' Nan D says, 'anyway. Here it is from the other way round. When I was a kid—'

'OK, no more. I get the point. Everybody is just the same. We're all just human.'

'That is actually the fucking opposite of what I'm saying, love. The polar opposite is the point I'm making. Listen to this. So, when I was a kid there was actually a mission to our part of the city. You know the way you might think of these missionaries heading to Timbuktu, mud huts, getting boiled in a pot, well, the ones who couldn't hack that came along to us.'

'Yeah?'

'Yeah. And we went along to their hall in the evenings because it was warm and a place to go. I've always been neat with my hands. And I liked to help them cut things out, you know, pictures of Jesus and all of that, bible tracts. And there was one of them, about sixteen, seventeen, she would talk to me sometimes, ask me what I'd been up to. Nice voice. I sometimes used to read things out trying to do her voice.'

'Wish I'd a nice voice,' Misty says.

'For a long time, I never told her anything. But then I started to tell her this and that. And one time,' Nan D says, 'one time, I told her something and she put her hand on my arm and said, oh. I looked at her hand and she took it away again. She always had her hair clipped over to the side. Like she had no style. Granny mush. Anyway, one time I was coming out of the mission, it was over for the night, and I heard one of the others, an older woman, say to her that we were a bunch of kids of low intellect. And my one she didn't reply. She didn't say, no they're not, or some of them are alright, or anything like that. She said nothing. So, the next time, I didn't go to the mission but I waited till she was leaving and I hid behind a wall. And then I threw a stone at her and it hit her on the side of the head.'

'That was a bit much! Just because she didn't reply when the other woman said that?'

'She should have said something. Stood up for us.'

'But,' Misty says, 'she wouldn't have known anyway it was you who threw the stone. And even if she knew it was you threw the stone, she wouldn't have known *why* you were doing it.'

Nan D pauses and then continues. 'You were with the wrong crowd. They weren't your type of people.'

'They were friends of mine.'

'They weren't your type of people.'

'I said right from the beginning I didn't want to talk about this.'

'Me and your daddy were saying they should pay for what they done.'

Misty shakes her head and says that she just wants to forget about it and that she can't be bothered trying to make people pay. Reporting them will have given them a fright but she doesn't want to do more. She tried to phone to say she wants to drop it, if that's alright with them, but couldn't get through to the right person. She'll ring again tomorrow.

'No,' says Nan D. 'No. Keep them on eggs. You can do that. Leave it for a bit. Keep them on eggs, Misty, for a bit yet. I think that's only right.'

* * *

And so, when she goes back again to the police for a further interview, she tells them again what happened, and it is starting, in the retelling, to have more substance, like she's sitting in the multiplex darkness, and in the unspooling, once more, she's becoming calmer, watching it, one hand slowly reaching into the cardboard of the popcorn. It's a cinema with red velvet seats, and her face when she is watching it is serene, almost curious. Another handful of popcorn, a swig of Coke. Rami's face on the screen is embarrassed. Rami with a bottle. The noise that Line-up makes. She still has to close her eyes. Two policemen give her a lift home in an ordinary car. They've music playing and the one who isn't driving sings along. The driver asks the other cop what he is doing that evening and he says that he is heading to the gym because he hasn't managed to go in a week. 'Why, what are you doing, Lloyd?' he asks.

'I,' he says, 'am going home to read my book and have a beer. That's what I'm doing.'

'What's your book about?' Misty asks.

'Crime. Bit low rent. Bit trash. But that's what I like.'

'Well, know what,' Misty says, 'if I'm reading a book I need to find a person to be in it, like I want to be one of them, and if there is nobody that I feel is me, then I can't get into it.'

'That'd be easy with your book,' the other cop says to Lloyd. 'You're the detective.'

When they stop at the garage to get some coffee the other cop asks Misty if she wants anything.

'Maybe a bag of Starbursts or something,' she says.

When the other cop has disappeared between the buckets of flowers and the revolving sign saying firelogs milk firelogs milk firelogs milk, the one called Lloyd says that he isn't the detective. He is Philomena Hannon who works in the bar where the suspected killer used to drink and who doesn't really know what she is doing. 'She has red hair,' he says. 'The writer always says that she has red hair. I am Philomena Hannon.'

The other cop grins when he comes back with the coffees and a giant packet of Starbursts.

'Here we go!' he says.

I'm interested in the problematics inherent in technology, imaging and the body. I started off doing installation work, mainly with video and text, but these days I've been going back to painting, on large canvases. There's such freedom to that. I've become more intuitive in what I do, for sure. I've just done a series on girlhood and aperture. There's an arrogance to all art, isn't there, in the sense that you are saying, this is my particular take on the world, and please spend some of your time paying attention to it? I mean, there's that thing, what is art but a corner of reality seen through a temperament? But even the simple act of speaking is asking someone else to pay attention to you and what you are. I started off studying PPE. I did a year of that. But all of the time I was yearning to create. No, it's not the same, arranging something in a bowl, integrating creative choices into the quotidian. I wanted to be an artist. That's what I am. I applied only to the UK's top, most competitive art schools.

There was no way that they were meeting in Bronagh's house, the place where Lyness had blown out the candles of his birthday cakes, blasted out a few bungled notes on the French horn, sat wrapped in a blanket watching a favourite cartoon. They were not going to have that kind of a discussion there. Bronagh had decided on Belfast Castle. She now had Miriam Abdel Salam's number via the solicitors, Scott McCloy. When Bronagh texted to suggest they should meet at Belfast Castle, the Abdel Salam woman responded back with, where? In the Dungeon Tea Room? Bronagh didn't reply with no, it's *actually* the Vault Restaurant. Instead, she just added that if the weather was nice then they could sit outside in the grounds. Donal said that he didn't know what she was trying to achieve and that he didn't think Barney would necessarily recommend it. Did he prohibit it? Bronagh asked. No? Well then. It's been two weeks since all of this happened. It will be good to talk.

Bronagh arrives early and takes a spot beside one of the huge splashy flowerbeds to the front of this baronial castle, high on the Cave Hill and looking over Belfast Lough. She sends a text to the others to let them know of her precise location and orders a coffee. A bus tour has just arrived, old people, in little clusters, making their way slowly down the path, two being pushed in wheelchairs. She thinks about Patrick from the plane as she watches a cruise ship slowly make its way towards the port. The unexpected significances of travel. When she had looked at the music magazine website, there wasn't a single person she had ever heard of. A woman sits down beside her. 'Miriam,' the woman says. In some vague way, Bronagh had imagined her to have a sallow face, peaky even, looking out from under a headscarf. That's not her.

'Mrs Farrell!' says the girl who brings the coffee. 'Oh my god, Mrs Farrell, do you remember me from the centre?'

'Of course I do,' says Bronagh, getting to her feet and giving the girl a hug. 'What are you up to now?'

She says she has a little boy, two and a half, and that she's working part-time at the castle.

'Can I get you something?' the girl asks Miriam.

'Black coffee.'

'And what about Finn Anderson!' the girl says. 'Isn't it incredible? I can't believe that I used to know a real-life megastar. I mean, wow!'

Bronagh smiles and nods.

'These coffees are on me!' the girl says. 'Seriously! I'll comp the coffees.'

Bronagh smiles beatifically. 'Brilliant.'

As the girl goes off, she turns to wave at Bronagh midway in her journey to the kitchen.

'I can't go anywhere!' Bronagh says.

'Why's that?'

'Well, I'm CEO of 411. That's the Anderson connection. Finn Anderson used to go there. And I just see the kids wherever I go.'

'He's a good actor, but I didn't enjoy the last film at all. So manipulative in its sentimentality.'

'Really? The critics seemed to think it was very good. I'm actually just back from New York,' Bronagh says. 'He was everywhere there. I was over raising funds. I met some great women from Liberia and Lebanon.'

Miriam laughs. 'Did you only meet people from countries beginning with L? Maybe you encountered someone from Lesotho?'

'Abdel Salam,' Bronagh says. 'That's an interesting name.'

'Is it?' asks Miriam. 'Why's that?'

The girl brings over the coffees and shortbread. The shortbread is comped too, she tells them.

'You're too kind!' exclaims Bronagh. 'Too kind.'

They both take a sip of their coffee and look around the grounds of the castle.

'Yes, you have a very interesting surname,' Bronagh says. 'Oh look, there's Frankie! Frankie! Over here! I know Frankie already. We've already met.'

She gets up to wave at Frankie, who is approaching in slouchy fringed boots and an outsize pullover over a soft leather dress. She already has a takeaway cup. Bronagh rises to her feet, ready for an embrace, but Frankie sits down.

'I'm Miriam.'

'Right,' says Frankie. 'I'm Frankie Levine.'

'What a lovely bag,' Bronagh says, nodding in the direction of Frankie's pebbled tote.

Frankie moves it further under the table.

'Remember when bags were a thing?' Miriam says.

'How could bags ever not be a thing?' smiles Bronagh. 'We're always going to need bags to carry our stuff.'

'I mean when people were encouraged to think an overspend on a bag in the shape of a horse's saddle was some kind of declaration of their essential self.'

Frankie looks like she is going to laugh and then lifts her cup.

'Well, people can spend their money how they like,' says Bronagh.

The three women look at two bridesmaids who have come out onto the lawn for a photo, their heads weighted down by flower crowns.

'Have you been on holiday anywhere over the summer?' Bronagh asks.

'No,' says Frankie. 'We'll go in September.'

'We haven't been anywhere,' Miriam says.

Bronagh says that they haven't been anywhere either. She's travelled, but it has been for work. 'Sounds like we are all due a holiday!' she says. 'You know,' she continues, 'Lyness has never been in trouble with the police. And I'm sure the same holds true for your boys.'

'Yes,' they both say.

Bronagh suddenly recalls the time when Lyness was involved in that car crash, but really that was something else entirely. 'So, that's what we are dealing with,' she says. 'Boys unused to being in this kind of situation.'

'For sure,' Miriam says.

'Someone from my particular professional background,' Bronagh declares, 'is always going to be concerned about matters of consent and agency.'

'Well, I think anyone,' Miriam says, 'regardless of their particular professional background, should be concerned about matters of consent and agency. Right, Frankie?'

'Yeah. I suppose so.'

'And the thing is,' continues Bronagh, 'no one should apply a bourgeois morality to a young woman, or anyone really, who chooses to have sex with multiple partners.' She has found this term, bourgeois morality, retrieved from conversations with Steven during her management days, useful over the years.

'Given the situation, I don't think anyone here is best positioned to apply bourgeois morality,' says Miriam.

'Well, regardless, it's a situation that has got out of hand.'

'Guys and their dicks,' Frankie says.

The other two look at her, startled.

'I know it's not been terribly long,' Bronagh continues, 'but at the same time, it's over two weeks. I would've thought that everything might've been dropped by now, that they would've made their enquiries and realised there wasn't a case to answer.'

'Yes,' Miriam says. 'Difficult to think of this continuing for weeks, months. I can hardly envisage that.'

Frankie stares at the fourth seat at the table, the one where no one sits. It is moulded black plastic, a hardy chair out in all weathers on the side of the Cave Hill. She looks at where an old, discarded serviette is trapped under one leg.

'Chris had sex with her first,' Frankie says.

'And then Rami, although Rami actually didn't,' says Miriam.

'And then when it happened again, it was Chris who was first,' says Frankie.

'And at the very end, Lyness,' Miriam says. 'At the end each time, Lyness.'

'Yeah,' Frankie says.

'All of the boys are implicated,' Bronagh says.

'Are they?' Frankie asks.

Miriam, taking a sip of her coffee, agrees yes, but it seems that they behaved differently.

The bridesmaids have been joined by one of the groomsmen who is lighting a cigarette, cupping his hands around the flame.

'The girl,' Frankie says, 'she's been in our house. Hanging around with Chris.'

'Have a look at this,' Bronagh says. 'It's from that site where you put up photos and videos of yourself in return for money. It's quite ridiculous, but she calls herself Elizabeth Barrett Browning. That's just her profile picture. In some of the other photos she is wearing less than that blouse with its little bow. Elizabeth Barrett Browning. Obviously trying to make herself sound like some Knightsbridge-dwelling It Girl.'

'She was a nineteenth-century poet,' Miriam says. 'Married to Robert Browning.'

'Oh. Well, you learn something new every day.'

'Can I see what she looks like?' Frankie says. 'I mean, in the pictures.'

Frankie swipes through the few that Bronagh has captured. Sitting on the edge of the bed, her legs skinny. She looks like she could leap off and start playing a skipping game. What is it she has on her windowsill?

'Well, what I would like to say here,' Miriam says, 'is that I would appreciate candour. Let's have that. There has been quite probably some really horrible behaviour.'

'She's got freckles,' Frankie says. 'She's young.'

'They're all young. Her and the boys. They're all young,' Miriam says.

Frankie lifts her bag and puts it in her lap.

'You know that she sold them drugs?' Bronagh says to Miriam.

Miriam is watching the arrival of another two bridesmaids. One, the freshest faced and most curvaceous, the youngest, has a different dress to the others although made with the same fabric.

'And,' Bronagh says, 'she had those fake bruises. Bruises that she had drawn on herself. In addition to this whole Bennyz thing and the drugs and so on. I mean, what can we say?'

'Well anyway,' says Miriam, 'are we all in agreement that we hope the boys have learned a serious lesson from this and that, if at all possible, we want everyone to move on without further repercussions?'

'Yeah,' says Frankie. 'Definitely.'

'That's what I've been saying,' replies Bronagh.

'Let's hope we don't have to be in touch again,' says Miriam. 'But we all have each other's details if we do.'

The mother of the bride and the bride's father are on the lawn now. She walks with a stick and has a calliper on one leg. Her husband guides her tenderly, carefully.

'Lyness was premature, you know,' Bronagh says. 'They didn't know if he would pull through. They thought he might not. He was so tiny.'

The forest has always been there for me, as it were, has always been a part of my life, right from when I used to be taken for walks in it as a child, as a baby, in a pushchair, along the tarmacked paths that cut through the darkness, the denseness of the pines. And then later, when we used to go there at the weekends, we'd drink, smoke, later on take acid up there, our music, no matter how big and full and bass-y it was, made fragile by the forest. And then of course when I got married and had the kids, well by that time they had built a playpark by the entrance, a place then where I pushed swings forwards, forwards, forwards, the pink carousel around and around. I have a mind, when the time comes, to die in the forest, like others before me, to lie down on the soft floor of pine needles and to crawl into the trees, into the darkness until I am made immobile by the branches and the black.

'Shut the fuck up!' one of them says. 'Shoosh, I mean it, shut the fuck up!'

But it's delivered in a way guaranteed to encourage the person to do the opposite.

'I said, what a fucking nonce! What a ballroot!' Laughter. More laughter. 'Rent a ballroot, dial his number!' Bronagh is walking down the corridor of the centre when she hears all of this. She goes out to her car to fetch a folder that she left on the back seat.

Later she hears similar words. There is a guest speaker who has come on Wednesday night to talk to a group of kids about finding your own voice and anger control. They sit on beanbags to listen to him. She enters near the end to say a few words of thanks and she thinks that the girls, over in the far right-hand corner, are looking at her. With what? Curiosity? It's surely not pity? Why? What's up with them? The guest speaker says how impressed he has been with the centre and all of the kids he has encountered. These guys are the future, he says, and the future is looking good with these guys. Yeeeohhh! a few shout. Bronagh smiles graciously. 'So many people say that,' she replies. 'I really love working with these young people.' And she smiles again.

There is one girl who has started going to the centre who always wears her school uniform. That's unusual. All of the others want to remove it as soon as they can. But she keeps it on, possibly because she has no other clothes. She is whispering to her friend, loudly, 'Did you hear what she said, she said that she loves working with kids and innit so funny because her son loves abusing them!' Her friend makes an amused face. 'Did you hear what I said, I said that she says she loves working with little kids whereas her son loves abusing them!'

Bronagh wants to go over to her and say, I heard what you said and that is an utter lie. She could grab that girl by her school tie and push her up against the wall and say, you have no idea how dangerous and unfair what you are saying actually is. But she knows to ignore it and focus instead on a door that is not opening properly when pushed. She moves it backwards and forwards, observing the mechanism where it meets the frame. Mick McConnell appears.

'That still up to its tricks?' he asks.

'Yes,' she says. 'Are you happy to close up tonight?'

'Sure, of course,' he says. 'The new guy's staying late and he'll give me a hand.'

'There's a few things due to arrive tomorrow,' she says. 'All the new furniture for the study zone. I think it should look really nice. It's actually the same furniture that some big design agency in London has. It'll be very smart. I've seen the photos.'

'Cool.'

'Plus, I have got these academic publishers to give us lots of free licences for study guides and workbooks on pretty much every subject known to man. They'll be able to access a total wealth of material.'

'That's great,' he says. 'I really think a lot of those lads, you know the whole Nicky Higgins crowd, they're getting the idea of the importance of qualifications.'

'Good,' she says. 'Mick, I don't know if you were in the group with the guest speaker tonight, if you popped your head in, but there seemed to be quite an unsettled mood.'

'Well,' he replies, 'would you not say that that particular crowd are the living embodiment of unsettled mood?'

'For sure. But that's not quite what I meant.'

'What did you mean?'

'Oh nothing.'

'No, go on, say. What did you mean?'

'Just that, I thought, well, I don't really know.'

'You thought the kids seemed preoccupied or something?'

'Yeah, I suppose so.'

Mick takes a seat on one of the squashy orange sofas in the atrium area. 'This may not be at all what you are alluding to, so forgive me if this is way off beam, but I have heard a few of the kids talking. And this is totally something and nothing because you and I absolutely know the way that kids talk.'

'Talk about what, Mick?'

'Well.' He gives a sigh. 'Well, talk about your son. It's pretty unbelievable what they are saying, but the word among our troops is that he's been done for sexually abusing a little kid.'

'That's not true at all. I can assure you that that is just not true at all.'

'This is none of my business, of course,' Mick says. 'I'm not into tittle tattle and people whispering. I wouldn't have said a thing to you if you hadn't asked about the kids.'

'Yes I know.'

Bronagh runs her hand down the orange fabric.

'There was an incident,' she eventually says, 'involving several people, all over eighteen, at a teenage party a few weeks ago. One of those parties that gets a little out of hand.'

'Sure. Happens a lot.'

When he looks at her, she realises that he does so with no malice. She wonders how there has ever been animosity between her and this person, looking at her now with green eyes that, yes, are frank and, yes, kind even. When she looks down she notices that on the orange sofa those hands of his have their nails bitten to the quick.

'Just teenagers at a teenage party. The police ended up speaking to a few people. That's all.' She smiles sadly.

'Sure thing,' he says.

'There's always going to be talk,' Donal says, when Bronagh gets home and tells him what the 411 kids are saying. He continues to watch the TV.

'But it's absolutely crucial that I have the trust of the kids who go to the centre!'

'I spoke today to Barney,' Donal replies, as he changes from a news programme to a film. 'And he has spoken to all the other legal eagles. And all of them feel that there is a very slim chance indeed of this making the threshold for evidence for Public Prosecutions. Extremely slim. The chances of them being charged are next to zero. And the lassie is so compromised really by her own behaviour and so on.'

'Well, that's good to know. But it's still there, you know what I mean, Donal? It's hovering.'

'I think tonight I'll have a Laphroaig.'

Bronagh makes herself a cup of tea. The kettle fails to click itself off the boil and she only realises she has been staring at it, oblivious to its fandango of steam and bubbling when Donal comes through and switches it off. They sit beside each other on the sofa, and Donal drinks his whiskey from a heavy glass.

'I can't say I'm not very disappointed in Lyness,' Donal begins. 'I mean, that's just a fact. I don't know what they're thinking of nowadays,' he continues. 'Young people. They've lost the run of themselves.'

'What do you mean?'

'Life's got too complicated. They can't keep it straightforward.'

'That's the world for you. Not young people.'

'Well, Bronagh, let me put it this way. When I was Lyness's age I had a girlfriend, who I know I have mentioned to you before, Mary O'Leary.'

'Yes, I've heard all about her.'

'Well, me and Mary used to meet every Friday and Saturday evening, if we could, at eight o'clock. She was from a big family who'd moved up the hill and she spent a lot of her time looking after the young ones, so it wasn't always that she could manage to get out.'

'Yes I know. You've told me.'

'We could've gone to one of the bars in the town but instead we met down by the river and when I think back you know' – the hand holding the whiskey tumbler is suspended in mid-air – 'when I think back it's a haze of summer, the water moving slowly, glassy, like it had a skin. The odd whip and cast of a late-night fly fisher.'

'What is this, Donal? Water moving slowly, glassy. Are you thinking of entering a short story writing competition?'

'Mary was quite serious. You know how some people are: you get to know them and they have this hidden sense of humour, well, Mary remained quite serious. Quite often we just sat and talked. She was interested in politics, whereas I wasn't. Never was and never will be.'

'They sound wonderful evenings indeed. Talking about politics.'

'Well, obviously there was more to it than that, you know? But there was always total respect. Total and absolute respect.'

Bronagh lifts the camomile tea bag out of the cup and throws it a couple of feet across the room into the bin.

'I've always half expected her to appear on the TV on one of those current affairs programmes or on an election poster on a lamppost. But I've never heard tell of her. The family upped and moved away.'

'You could have walked past her many times in the street.'

'I doubt it. I think I might have remembered.'

'Then you have a better memory than mine if you can remember people you hung out with thirty-odd years ago.'

'I think I could, Bronagh.'

'Where's Lyness?' she asks.

'Oh, out with friends somewhere,' he says, finishing his Laphroaig. 'I'm just going to have another. And maybe another one after that.'

There had been a heap of problems with the machines that NutCo had rented and the site manager was going crazy on the phone. They were working over the weekend. I needed to send the mechanics out to have a look but I couldn't do that until the next day and so the site manager went apeshit. There was no way we could send out replacements because they weren't available, and even if they were, by the time they would get transported to the NutCo site, the mechanics would have arrived. I went for a beer after work with Dwayne Longenhammer who had also had a bad day. He had been courting a deal with a big outfit up in the north of the state but it had fallen through. Dwayne has been a salesman with us for ten, fifteen years. He lives with his wife in a house that he built himself. He lights up, when he talks about that house. We were joined for a while by Wendine, who runs the bar. Things were slow and she had time to chat. She was feeling down too, because a lot of her customers have started going to the new place just across the road. The beer wasn't any cheaper but they had these big screens and two sisters who wore cut-off jeans. They'll come back, Dwayne said. They'll grow tired of the screens and the shorts. Wendine said she wasn't so sure. Well, Dwayne had to go, so I had another drink and talked to Wendine a little more and then I headed home. I ate a pizza. I drank another beer. There was a game I wanted to watch, but it wasn't being shown till later. I went on my computer to see if Elizabeth or CallieXT were around. Elizabeth Barrett Browning. She's only eighteen. I don't look at eighteen-year-old girls when I see them in the street any more than I look at anyone else. If I was given the choice, if I could have my pick, I would go for a woman in her late twenties, maybe Latina, with a great ass. But I've ended up talking to this kid in the North of Ireland, where they had the war. I've never moved off the basic Bennyz level with Elizabeth. I'd thought, one time, that I would, that I'd ask her to take some of those old librarian clothes off, but all of the talk, as it went on, made me not want to do that. The more there was talk, the more it moved from the point where I would say that. Whereas with CallieXT, she would shake about and bend over for the camera. There is no, how was your day? with CallieXT. CallieXT is always drinking a can of Dr Pepper or eating a pretzel. But it was Elizabeth who came on that evening and she looked like she was in a bad way. She said that she had been out. Well, that's good, I said. No, it's not, she replied. She was wearing something, like a robe, something pink, not her usual things. And I said, so why is that bad? And she said that something had happened, people had been bad, and I said that it was good then that she was home and back in her bedroom. I saw that CallieXT was available and so I said, well, I hope you can get some rest now, Elizabeth, and she said, well, Mike, and I could see her face was puffy, she said, well, Mike, I was sexually assaulted. I've just walked back all the way, and I was sexually assaulted. She said that it was three guys. Three guys when you were walking back? No, in the house, she said. My friends. The three guys are my friends. Well, I think you will find, I said, that these guys are not your friends if they did that to you. They didn't, all three, they didn't all do— You need to tell somebody, I said. You should tell your mom. She didn't say anything to that. You should go to the police, I said. You should go to the police, for sure. They shouldn't get away with something like that. She said that she had to go and I said that I sure was sorry that that had happened to her. CallieXT had gone by then, or was involved with another guy, so I went and got another beer.

In the Shepherd Church they have been looking at joy, pure and unadulterated, captivating and thrilling. They've been visited by a man with wild eyes who's been going on about Thomas Traherne, somebody from the past, big into happiness. The man, to Nan D, seemed as if he was on drugs. He kept saying the word ecstatic.

Nan D does not reckon that joy has played a massive role in her life. Well yes, there's been temporary satisfactions and some great payback times when people got their comeuppance, but she struggles to think of any joy in the way this man talked about it. For sure, she remembers her son, him being born, their closeness, her letting him win at cards, them peeling potatoes, but then it curdles into anger at his loss. If they continue talking about fucking joy for too many weeks she might have to consider a different church that aligns more with her own views where God is a lake of fire or an enormous white bird with tearing claws.

After the session they move to the café. Don't take the sausage rolls, someone says to the Traherne expert. They've been there since last week. He laughs and takes a cherry scone. Some of the others around the table talk about how inspirational they found the session and how joy can be found in the minutiae of life. The man asks them if they know a poem by Stevie Smith about 'The Airy Christ', which for him presents the idea of lightness and yes, joy, in God. Nobody knows it and so he starts to recite it, emphasising the word 'airy' each time it appears. Others tap along pleasantly on the table as he becomes more rhythmic in his delivery. This is he we had not thought of, this is he the airy Christ. Nan D stares at his cherry scone. Looks like pure stodge.

When he finishes his recitation, they sit in silence, until a woman in a patterned jumper pipes up that she is going to have to get the bus home. The people who normally give her a lift haven't come today. In fact, they hadn't been about the entire week.

'Some problem with his dialysis,' a person offers. 'Doesn't he always look so yellow?'

'It's nothing to do with dialysis,' the woman in the patterned jumper answers. 'Although he does always look yellow.'

'Is it her? Maybe she's the one who isn't well?'

The woman reaches forward to put a spoonful of sugar in her tea and she stirs it very slowly. 'It's not that. It's their grandson. Their daughter's boy. He's been involved in some funny business.'

She puts down her spoon. 'Sexual,' she mouths.

'What?'

'Sexual,' says the Traherne expert.

'It happened at some party or another. Three of them, believe it or not. Three of them.'

Nan D looks at the appliquéd wall decoration of a bible verse, its gold and silver threads.

'Rami? He was always such a lovely boy when they used to bring him here,' someone says. 'It must be a mix-up.'

'Must be a mix-up indeed,' Nan D says. But she knows that her God is the right one, and He is illuminating the path. They can forget about their tripping joy, these airy Christs floating around like white balloons because her deity has got an enormous black ledger book and steel-toed boots, twitching muscles.

She goes, afterwards, to Boogie's house. He is cleaning the oven with a chemical that makes her catch her breath when she comes into the kitchen. 'It is so fucking caustic,' he says, 'but can you see the way it has cleaned everything?' He holds up a plastic bag that contains the wire racks floating in rusty water. 'Mental.'

'Wait till you hear this. You thought that speaking in tongues was just a lot of bullshit.'

'Didn't think it, knew it.'

'Do you know who has a granny at the Shepherd Church? One of the three boys. Route to reparations becoming manifest.'

The doorbell rings.

'That's those people again,' Boogie says. 'Trying to sting me for a direct debit to stop dogs being put down. I mean, like, good cause and all that but that's the third time they've been round. They need to be told. Give me a minute here and then we can have a chat about this.'

He puts the plastic bag in the sink.

When all of them are gathered around the kitchen table, Misty says it feels weird to think about asking for money. Did it kind of make her a prostitute?

'No,' Boogie replies. 'It's not the same.'

'Is it any different to Bennyz?' Gen says.

'Who asked you?' Misty snaps. 'Nobody.'

'Sorry!'

'Today I applied for two new jobs,' Misty says. 'Working in a funeral parlour and working in marketing. I just want to get on with things.'

'Misty,' Nan D says. 'Think about it. If you fall down a pothole in the street, and the council are liable, you get a payout. That's how it is. You get money. No one is saying that the money makes it alright that there are potholes. No one is saying that the money makes it acceptable that people fall down potholes. But the money makes the people who have fallen down the potholes feel that bit better.'

'So, out of interest,' Boogie says, 'how much does somebody get if they have fallen down a pothole. Let me have a look here on my phone. Alright, potholes don't feature here to do with people. They are related to cars here. No, we're looking at tripping on pavements. Same kind of idea sure. So according to this, moderate knee injury is £14,840 to £26,190.'

'That's a lot,' says Misty.

'You would need medical evidence, empirical evidence,' Gen states.

'If that's the minimum then definitely no less than fifteen thousand quid in this case,' says Nan D.

Busy service always at the weekend and I am always on my best behaviour: yes ma'am, no ma'am, yes sir, I smile, I smile, and I see the women blushing sometimes, occasionally there is one that is not convinced by me, and then I cool a little, collect the menus quickly, pour the wine precisely, but I respect them because they know that it is all an act and that I think as little of them as they do of me. I was a very good chess player when I was fifteen. These people, they do not impress me, flabby with their money. What's up, my man? I say to the well-to-do boy, but in my own town I would not deign to acknowledge him. I like Martine though. She is a good woman. She reminds me of my grandmother.

Finished reading that detective book today and the ending, well, it all turned out as I thought it would, which you could say is reassuring. It certainly wasn't unwelcome even if it was unrealistic. I got realism daily, realism galore, thank you very much.

In the hospital café, two nurses booking a holiday keep attempting to get a better price by changing the dates, passing the phone to each other. At another table there's a couple in their mid-thirties, their faces a similar shade of ashen. They don't speak as they sip from paper cups. A man sits by himself, doing a Sudoku in a newspaper. He sees Miriam looking over at him and averts his eyes back to his configuration of squares and numbers. Miriam checks her phone. She sees the message from her mother; there's been some problem with the dialysis this morning but she'll be down in a few minutes. Miriam looks to see if there is a response from Rami to the message she sent. Not as yet. And she reads again the email from work, asking her if she feels that she is ready to return. Its tone is bright, hopeful.

Rami, the other day, asked Miriam to withdraw his university application. 'Don't be silly,' she said. 'You are being daft.' But there's little chance of him being able to go, if he continues staying in his room. She brings him up his food on a tray. I want to take you to the doctor, she said, sitting on the edge of his bed. No, Mum, he replied. I don't want to go to a doctor. She said for him not to worry. He smiled and shook his head. Miriam can't imagine going back to work. She'll have to contact them. She looks at the three pretty girls sharing a plate of chips, their exposed skin. One of them has a hearing aid. They can't be any older than

Haady. She imagines him and the girl with the hearing aid out on a date, them watching a film, with giant drinks, them holding hands. Surely everything isn't always going to be complicated. Is it? Is it?

'Hello!' her mother says. 'Sorry to have kept you waiting!'
She produces a packet of biscuits.
'I always bring these,' she says. 'You want one? No?'
'What happened?'
'Oh, some issue with the fistula,' she says. 'But they got it sorted.'
'Good.'
'I've left him reading a book.'
'Good.'
'But he normally dozes off after a while.'
'I'll wait around and see him when he finishes.'
'Well, that would be nice,' her mother says. 'He'd appreciate that.'
She says that she wants to tell Miriam about something very untoward that happened yesterday at the church. It's better to talk about it here than in the house.
'Why?' Miriam asks.
'Oh, just in case anyone hears.'
She had been doing her shift in the day crèche, where parents could drop children in for a couple of hours. Her mother says she's usually paired with an ex-nurse called Sherilyn. Sherilyn is retired now and if she isn't at the church she's hill-walking. 'She makes me feel very inactive,' her mother says. But yesterday, Sherilyn wasn't there and in her place was a woman who, yes, she'd seen at church many times but who'd never been involved in anything to do with the children before. And little wonder! You should have heard the way that she barked at them. Oh, give over, you

wee scrote, was what she said when one little boy was annoyed that another child had taken the felt tip he'd been using. It happened again when two of the kids were arguing over a game. She simply packed it up, put it in its box and told the kids to shut up. Usually, she and Sherilyn had a cup of tea and a chat, when the children were having their orange juice and toast, but this woman sat on the opposite side of the room, watching her. 'I tried to ignore her,' her mother says, 'but every time I looked over, there she was, staring. So eventually I said, I'm terribly sorry but I've realised that I don't even know your name. And I introduced myself to her, because I suppose it was odd that I hadn't at the beginning. But she leaned towards me and said that she was Misty Johnston's great-grandmother. And then she called Rami a word I won't repeat. Well, I just didn't know what to say, Miriam.'

She looks around the hospital café and further lowers her voice.

'One of the children at this point knocked over an entire jug of orange juice. It was pouring off the table onto the floor, but I just stood there talking to this woman. She said that she wanted to get a message to the parents of these young men, letting them know that if at this stage they were willing to offer some kind of recompense, some kind of reparations, then the family would give it due consideration and would be prepared to act accordingly. And then, Misty Johnston's great-grandmother said that I'd better go and mop that up. The orange juice.'

My mother was widowed at thirty. She had three young sons and an alcoholic father to look after. Granda lived with us. We were wild boys, full of spirit, and she treated us hard. Looking back, she was trying to make ends meet, working all the time, but there was never any gentleness. That came from Granda. One time I ripped my school trousers on the wire fence at McGuigan's. I was heart scared of the beating I would get and so Granda got the sewing basket and I can remember him holding the needle and thread to the light, his hands shaking. Of course, she noticed and the usual followed, but what made the most impression was how he made such a good old stab at it, the sewing. Made such a good old stab at it.

Everyone is invited to congregate at the Levine house. Donal accompanies Bronagh. 'Yes, I know Barney might not advise it,' Bronagh says, as they drive towards Ladyhill, 'but let's be proactive, Donal. What's being suggested here isn't against the law.'

Donal's been in bad form recently. He's busy in work, plus he injured his back which means he can't go running – and, of course, there's this business involving Lyness. Donal keeps identifying factors that he thinks have had a negative influence on their son, from schools, to them as parents, to where they live. This last one has been a particular focus. Things would have been better had they lived in the country. He states this again in the car. 'Oh really, Donal,' she says, 'down in Ballygobackwards all the young men are paragons of virtue? Sitting down by the river watching the salmon leap and getting gooey over the sunset? Be sensible, please.'

'Well, what's your view then?' he says.

'That it all got out of hand. No one knew what was happening.'

Donal makes a feint of walking up the driveway with no sense of urgency. His most pressing concern is taking note of the choice of deciduous and evergreens in the beautiful garden. Come on! Bronagh says. When Frankie opens the door, without a hello or a smile, Bronagh notes how Donal straightens up a little, says very pleased to meet you. Oh, isn't that so incredibly, so pathetically predictable? That's men for you. Donal holds out his hand for Frankie to shake. She chews her gum as she says her name and then shows them into a dining room which has a long pale wood table and sixteen chairs. At its centre are three, well she doesn't know what they are, twisted metal works of art. On the wall is a huge painting that looks frenzied. Sitting there already is Miriam Abdel Salam and at the head of the table, Neil Levine. Of course that is where he is sitting. The seats are leather and when Bronagh sits, she feels it warm and supple. Always the sign of good leather, that it isn't cold to the touch.

'If only we were all meeting under more congenial circumstances,' Bronagh says.

'Neil Levine,' Neil Levine replies.

Despite not having been present or involved until now, Neil Levine has assumed the role of de facto leader of the group. Donal, by contrast, is leaning on the back legs of his chair as though he's a school boy with an inept cover teacher. Miriam is across the table from them.

'And I,' Donal says, 'am Lyness's dad, Donal Farrell.'

Miriam gives him a little nod.

Frankie comes in and, like some Bond concubine, takes a seat close to Neil Levine. Miriam hasn't got her husband, but she looks so self-sufficient, sitting there. When Frankie rearranges her legs, Bronagh sees Neil Levine glance over at his wife's thighs. So refreshing to meet Patrick, on the plane, someone with whom it was possible to have a meaningful non-sexual kinship. He probably needs to go for a check-up every year. She imagines him the days before, anxious but not mentioning it to anyone, low-key, stoic. She thinks about Neil Levine's balls, resting on the warm leather, cosy self-satisfied little spheres. Neil Levine is saying that a solution has come via a church connection. The transaction would potentially be very straightforward. Withdrawal at the station, then a payment would be made. There's no additional evidence other than the young woman's testimony.

'But I'm imagining,' Donal says, 'that we need to proceed with a major degree of caution here. No one is wanting to admit any—'

Neil Levine waves his hand.

'Don't worry. All taken care of. My legal will draft the agreement. No liability. Cash: might seem a bit wild west, but it's what they apparently want. That suits. Marion, you've got a connection in the church. They can hand it over.'

'No. No way. It's my mother and I don't want her involved. Haven't you got an office somewhere, an anonymous place, where it can be picked up? Surely that wouldn't be difficult? Actually, just to say, I'm Miriam. But couldn't you leave it in a secure locker somewhere, for it to be accessed by someone else who knows the code?'

'A straightforward physical handover in a designated spot seems sensible to me. Old-fashioned but easy enough. Why complicate things? It's what they asked for. Let's just go with it.'

'Well, I'll do it then,' Miriam answers. The sooner it was done, the quicker Rami might return to his old self. 'Give it to me and I'll hand it over. Presumably we're handing it over to the – great-grandmother? The one who made herself known to my mother? I've no problem doing it, passing it to the woman.'

'I'll go too,' says Frankie.

Neil says that isn't necessary.

'I'll go too,' she repeats.

'Well, in that case,' Bronagh says, 'if you are both going to do it, then I should be there as well.' Why should the two of them be there and not her? Is it not a type of solidarity?

Bronagh waits for there to be a discussion. The amount, when divided in three, is five thousand pounds each, obviously, but she has anticipated there might be a debate about this. Different actions, varying levels of culpability, it would seem, in the accusations at least. Lyness is not Chris and what Lyness did (or did not do) was not what Chris did (or did not do.) And that Rami boy, well that was something different again. The consideration of how to split the money is likely to be awkward, and one where she and Donal will be expected to pay the most. When Donal said that no doubt there would be talk of the money, she knew what he meant. She wonders if Lyness is autistic, if he has difficulty reading signs. Is there a link between autism and premature birth? She'll need to investigate that online. But, as it turns out, there is no mention of anything other than a three-way split. She presumes that Neil Levine, with his gold-plated balls, would think it demeaning to haggle over such a small sum.

On the way home, Bronagh turns to the subject of how Donal gawped at Frankie Levine. 'It was so obvious,' she says.

'Well, if that's your takeaway from the meeting that we've just had, then all I can say is that you have a very unusual outlook on life.'

Bronagh looks at his unsmiling profile, his hands on the wheel. There's a bottle of water sitting between them and she opens it. It's always curiously satisfying, when the plastic eventually gives, under your twist.

'To be honest, Bronagh, the more impressive person was Miriam. I thought she was smart. And nice. Those Ladyhill people, though, they're another breed.'

Bronagh takes a drink of the water, puts on the lid, places it back where it was.

'I mean, that KFC Bargain Bucket Steve Jobs. Just dreadful.'

Many, many years later, there was a contestant, a singer, on that TV talent show, that reminded me of her. Pretty but frazzled. She kept going on about her divorce. I knew she wouldn't make it to the final, or even beyond the second round. And I was right. But the woman I'm talking about was at Bristol airport.

We were coming home, Mum and me. The plane was delayed. Mum was reading a book whereas I was just looking about. I was about thirteen. I've never liked reading. I was watching people coming and going and one of them was this woman and what I would say is that she was in her thirties maybe, and wearing one of those dresses suitable for work, black, tight, but with bare arms. She looked a bit sad to me, like a business deal had gone wrong. She had a little chain on her ankle, very fine, you could hardly notice it, and when she got up to go to the bar, I saw the way she had little lines of blue and green at the back of her knees.

Two men started talking to her. They were much younger. They looked as though between them they had a suit: one was wearing blue trousers with a V-neck jumper and the other had the jacket with jeans. They were chatting to the woman and then they went to buy more drinks from the bar and they sat either side of her. She had a mini bottle of wine and one of them poured it into the glass for her when she was fumbling with it. I heard her laughing at something one of them said. At one point she got up to go to the toilets. They watched her and then looked at each other. I saw it. I decided to go to the toilet too. I went to a cubicle and when I heard a toilet flush, I came out. As I pretended to wash my hands I saw her run her fingers under her eyes and put on some lipstick. She put on some perfume. I could see it all in the mirror. When she came out, I was behind her. She tripped on a piece of carpet but managed to recover without falling. I watched them watch her do that. Do you want to go and see if we can get something to eat? my mum asked me. Nope, I said. I'm fine. I was just watching. Although they were talking to her they were looking more at each other. But she couldn't see that. I started to get kind of scared. It was weird. When we got on the plane, I saw that she was behind us, whereas they were in front. And I felt better then. But when we were leaving the airport, I saw her go out with them. One was carrying her bag and the other had his arm round her. Mum, I said. What is it? she replied. Nothing, I said.

When Boogie gave Misty a lift to the police station, she said for him not to wait around. She certainly didn't want him to come in. It was easier to do things alone. He had suggested she give him a ring when she'd finished so that he could take her to the fancy office where she would sign the papers. Why? she said. It's only a fifteen-minute walk. Don't be worrying. I'm fine.

In the station, Misty took a seat in the central area, near the pillar, where she'd waited before. Although she hadn't known of its existence prior to all of this happening, she now thought of it as her particular spot. She looked at the reassuring familiarity of the name Carlow scored into the plastic, the gouge in the plaster of the wall that someone had filled with a chewed-up piece of tissue. It couldn't just be this. What about places, things, feelings that she doesn't have a clue about yet? Maybe there's somebody in Belfast who'll actually fall in love with her, like in a song. She could already have walked past him in the street. Someone, at this exact minute might be thinking the same thing as her in Liverpool or Dublin or Manchester, in a forest or out at sea. Hi ya, she said to herself, Hello there. When Naomi McCrory, her special police person, came to take her upstairs, Misty followed one step behind. Naomi didn't make conversation.

In the room there were three of them, Naomi and two men. Naomi asked her if she understood what it meant to make a withdrawal statement. She said she did. Naomi asked, simply, why? Misty thought of the answers that she had gone through with Nan D. 'I just can't really remember,' she said. 'It's not straight in my head. I thought it was but it wasn't.'

Lying was like acting, but she hadn't taken drama to GCSE.

One of the men seemed bored already. He looked up at the ceiling and then down at the floor. Misty thought she should continue. 'Considering so many things,' she said, 'it maybe doesn't seem like a great, you know, case. Like conviction rates are so low aren't they and with this, with all the whole situation and the way I can't really remember too much or totally know that what I said was right, well, I just don't want to continue. It wouldn't be the right thing to do, would it?' When the man continued to stare at the floor, she added, 'Also, my mental health, plus the fact that I don't remember.'

'This is quite out of the blue,' Naomi McCrory said.

'For you but not for me,' Misty replied. 'It's what I've been thinking about since I first said.'

Naomi McCrory sighed at that point and rubbed her eyes with the tips of her fingers. She then inspected her fingernails as though her cuticles might hold the key to Misty's change of heart. The other man spoke then, and his voice was clean and gentle. 'Misty,' he said, 'we need to satisfy ourselves that you are doing this voluntarily. You understand?'

'Yeah. I understand. I get it.'

'We need to be sure that you are not doing this under duress.'

'I'm not.'

'Have any of the three alleged assailants been in contact with you? Has Christopher Levine?'

'No.'

'Lyness Farrell?'

'No.'

'Rami Abdel Salam?'

'No. None of them. It's nothing to do with them at all.'

'What's it to do with then?'

'It's to do with – it's to do with agency. It's to do with me having agency and saying that I don't want to go ahead because I can't remember and I'm not sure.'

He looked around to see if there was anything else Naomi wanted to ask. Misty, knowing that Naomi McCrory was looking at her, turned to meet the policewoman's gaze. Naomi McCrory tipped her head slightly to one side. She paused, as though she was going to say something important.

'Alright,' she said. 'If no one has any further questions, we won't detain you any longer.'

With another hour before she is due in the office where she needs to sign the papers, Misty heads to a café, a place well out of the way, so there's not much chance of her bumping into anyone she knows who knows what happened, or thinks they know, or wants to know. Let people say what they want, Boogie said. It doesn't matter. By next week they'll be on to something else. Life's short. Memories are short. It'll all be yesterday's knickers soon.

She's thought about maybe going back to college. She could do another course, maybe business studies. It's not too late. She doesn't want anything that requires a massive amount of concentration. If she had to describe her brain, it would be like that drawer in the kitchen that's jammed full of old leads and chargers, twisted round each other. The other day she walked past that place that she had applied to, the funeral parlour, to see what she could sense about the atmosphere. It actually didn't seem a downer. She didn't go in because you couldn't really, could you? You can't say, just browsing, just having a look. But through the window, Misty could see that the woman's outfit wasn't unlike the Elizabeth Barrett Browning one. She'd never heard again from Mike, after that night. She thought he might have hung around to see how it had gone with the police. But he didn't.

She picked this café as well because it's some distance from the police station. Maybe they have better things to do but she wondered if they would have followed her, if that guy was only pretending to be bored and had a whole team of people who were tailing her, hiding behind rails of clothing, standing in the shadows on street corners. She didn't think so, but in getting to the café, she'd doubled back on herself, gone down an alleyway as a short cut, visited the toilet in Castlecourt, sat in the cobbled square near the church, scanned the area for spies. She's pretty sure she isn't being tracked.

Even so, she still looks around as she goes up the stairs to a little first-floor office with vertical blinds and not so fancy after all. An old woman is there who looks as if she's just washed her face with soap and water. When she produces the agreement for a signature, Misty writes neatly, the way she did her name on the front of all her schoolbooks, a little circle on top of the i.

'Thank you,' Misty says.

'You have nothing whatsoever to thank me for,' the woman says, as she puts the document in a folder.

The bus home, full of people returning from work, has the bright automated voice that's thrilled by the names of the different stops it announces. They all seem great prospects. The places sound so beautiful, if you don't know where they are, if you don't know the actual specifics. Maybe that's true of anywhere: if you've got the real details, nowhere is that nice. Misty sighs and thinks of getting home: that short walk from the stop to her house, her hand trailing along the hedges, opening the front door, going upstairs, putting on her dressing gown.

But when she does turn her key in the door and step into the hall, Boogie appears to tell her that someone is there. 'Just to let you know,' he says, 'that somebody has arrived up.' The police must have pretended to be satisfied at the interview, with her reasons, but they weren't and now Naomi McCrory's here to rake it up all over again.

'Misty, it's your mum. She arrived up about an hour ago.'

Leigh is looking lean and tanned in a blue and white tracksuit. When she smiles it's clear she has had her teeth fixed. 'Baby!' she says. 'How is my baby? Come here on over to me, right this minute so I can give you the biggest hug.'

'She's doing fine,' Boogie says. 'As I've been telling you.'

'I came over as soon as I could after you contacted me. Sit down here right next to me and tell me everything that has been going on. I tried to message you but I couldn't get through. I messaged Geneva but she never replied.'

'The cops still have my phone but I'll get it back now before too long.'

'Oh Misty, oh my god. I mean, Jesus Christ. Gang raped. What a thing to have to endure.'

'Enough, Leigh,' says Boogie.

'Are you kidding? Enough? I need to hear everything that has happened. Right from the beginning.'

She takes Misty's hand.

'You've got your mummy with you now. As soon as I got that message from you, I was like, that's me, come hell or high water, I am going to get over there. Don't matter what I have to do.'

Boogie watches as Leigh smooths Misty's hair back from her face.

'Do you want a cup of tea?' Misty asks.

'Let me make it!' says Leigh.

'No, I'll do it.'

Leigh jumps up to sit on the worktop beside the kettle.

'You are looking in good shape,' Misty says.

'Oh yeah? You think? I've started playing football. Train four times a week.'

'How's Ewan?'

'He's with Farrah right now. Farrah got me into football.'

'Are you going to get down from there?' Boogie asks. 'Are you going to get down from my worktop?'

'Alright, Boogie, calm down for fuck sake.' She makes a leap to the ground. 'So, tell me all about it.'

'You got any photos of Ewan?' Misty says, as she pours the water. 'Oh wow! He's tall. And the wee glasses suit him.'

'I'm going to be a support to you,' Leigh says. 'Look, here's me and Farrah.'

There is the sound of a key in the door and Gen's shouts of goodbye to her friends. When she comes in and sees Leigh, she says a polite hello and then gets a glass of water.

'Well, aren't you just the young lady!' Leigh says, and she holds out her arms.

'What's for tea, Daddy?' Gen asks.

Yeah, I've always wanted to make a citizen's arrest. Since I first heard of it when I was a kid, I thought, that's gonna be me some day. There's things you got to do. It's actually called 24A. Basically, your threshold has to be that they're causing physical injury, damage or loss of property – indictable offences basically. That's what they call them. You got to inform the person what you are doing and why. You got to tell them what offence you think they have committed and then you have to use just reasonable force. Hard bit, you then got to get them to the police (or a magistrate). Imagine if there's two, or even three of them! Which there might well be. I think it would all be more straightforward if you had the threat of a weapon. I used to have an air gun that had been modified so it could do quite a bit of damage. Of course, it wasn't legal – that would've been a problem if I had performed a citizen's arrest because, technically, I could then have been arrested.

Time was I felt that the world was a fucked-up place. I wondered if soldiers like me, warriors of righteousness, I suppose you could say, should maybe take to the streets. I lay in my room for a day, two days, waiting for direction, and then it came, the message that I should go, at night, to a place of water in the north of the city. I told my mother that

I might never return. Why, where are you going? she asked. I don't like the sound of it. She had no idea of the evil forces at work in the world.

On the bus, my gun in my inside pocket, I looked at the other passengers. It was a hot night. From the window, I saw girls, cheap harlots, and the boys, muscular fineness put to corrupted ends. I wasn't seduced by the sound of the late evening birdsong, the damp grass, the lapping of the water, no, this park where I'd been led to, was a cesspit, an animal torn apart so the carcass presented itself in abominable glistening reds. I was an instrument of good. I touched the gun in my pocket. I thought about the sweetness of holding the metal to a temple, of the quaking heart of someone who knows that justice hovers above them, a fierce bird, a bird that is pitiless. Darkness fell on the park and I came across this guy by the closed-up toilets, the light of the phone illuminating his face. He said something to me, and then he reached for me, and no words would come from me when he laid his hand on my neck. When I came away from him, I ran back into the darkness. I fired the gun into the black and it resounded in the night.

Well, that was me back then. I thought the world was a fucked-up place and I was on a mission. I don't feel that way now, although I would still like to make a citizen's arrest: rapists, drug dealers, whatever. I mean, the world is still a fucked-up place. I was speaking to someone about this at my church. And they said, why don't you become one of those paedophile hunters, the ones that they made the documentary about? But I said no, those guys are strange.

It's a still, dull morning that, Boogie thinks, as he comes in from his two-hour early morning stint in the car, could just as easily burst into heat or a downpour. Nan D is already at the house, her freshly tinted hair set in precise waves. 'You know who's here?' he asks.

'Oh, I heard. Misty here filled me in.'

'Well, she's still in bed.'

'Don't tell me you slept on the sofa, did you?'

'No,' Misty says, 'he didn't. Gen slept in with me and Mum went in Gen's room.'

'What a waste of space, what a sorry excuse. The only person worse was your mother, Michael. Now there was the perfect example of someone who should have been taken out the back and shot.'

'Bit extreme,' he says.

'I don't really want to go, Nan D,' Misty says.

'What you mean? You need to go upstairs, put your cat clothes on, put your make-up on and pick up that money with a flick of your ponytail. Ta dah! Like that! There's no question of you not going. That's why I told them that I wanted it to be cash and that we would pick it up at the church. Because it is reparations. It's not some dirty deed. We're not skulking about!'

'Nan,' Boogie says, 'if she doesn't want to go, just do it by yourself. You're lucky Leigh's still asleep otherwise you'd have her along, wanting to get in on the act.'

'Waste of space. Alright, you don't even need to get out of the car, Misty. When we park at the church. You can just sit there.'

'There's no point in getting dressed up then.'

'So, you're going to come?'

'Let me put on a sweatshirt. But just as long as I don't have to get out of the car.'

'Are you wanting to be there, Boogie?'

'No. You kidding?'

As they're leaving, a figure appears around the corner, running in long, smooth strides. Leigh has just completed a ten-kilometre run. She wipes the sweat from her face as she asks them where they are off to.

'Can I come too?'

'No,' says Nan D.

'Oh yeah, and you get to decide, do you, Granny? It all comes down to you? Misty, so you want your mummy along?'

'Why not let her come?' Misty replies at last. 'If she really wants to.'

'Get in then,' Nan D says. 'No, we don't have time for you to get a shower.'

Misty sits in the passenger seat with her mother in the back. Everything here is so closed in, huddled together, the people and the buildings. What would it be like to work on a cruise ship, to look out and see nothing but sea in all directions and to look up and see the sky? As they go down the road, the traffic slow, she takes in the crumbling brick of the takeaways, the weeds sprouting from the gutters of the Chinese. The bus shelter has been tagged with some pink and red graffiti. The florist has got big plant pots out, a mess of colours, but someone has knocked one over and the soil's all over the kerb. On the cruise ship, for sure, you would have your work to do but you could go in your breaks and look at the nothing, nothing all around. She'll maybe look on a cruise ship website, to see if something like that is available.

'What's that smell?' Leigh asks, pointing at the air-freshener.

Misty takes a look. 'Tahiti Dreams.'

'Reminds me of a vape shop,' Leigh says.

There is no talk in the car until they get to the turn-off onto the motorway.

'I've been up since very early,' Leigh says. 'Most mornings I do strength and conditioning and if that's not what I'm up to, I go for a run. Being physical is so good for my mental health. I love going for a run just as it's becoming dawn. Have you ever heard the birds at dawn? What a racket. It's really some racket.'

'Dawn is not something that I got the time to do,' Nan D says.

Leigh sits back on her seat and looks out of the window. 'Well, I can certainly recommend it. Where's this place that we're going to?'

'The Shepherd Church,' Nan D says. 'The Shepherd Church car park.'

'Oh right. Are you religious, Misty?'

'No.'

'Neither am I. Although I believe in some stuff.'

'Like what?'

'Spirits. Energies. Tarot. Visions. Just shit like that.'

She leans her arms on the front seats. 'So, I hear you are religious now, D. What about the Holy Ghost? Is the Holy Ghost the opposite of the Grim Reaper, you know, same as the Grim Reaper outfit, except in white. And instead of holding a scythe, what could the Holy Ghost hold? Misty, what could the Holy Ghost hold?'

'Maybe a flower?' she suggests. 'On a long stem?'

'Yeah, that sounds good. A flower.' Leigh pauses. 'Does that mean, D,' she asks, 'that you have now become a nice, sweet person who tries to do good all of the time?'

'Just because you are born again doesn't mean you have to get on like a fucking cretin.'

'I'm just glad you've become a nice, sweet person.'

As they head out along the motorway, Leigh says, 'You alright, Misty?'

'Yeah. Fine.'

'Do you see that billboard we just passed? The one for suicide? Well, the guy in the photo who is pretending that he's close to topping himself, know what, he drank in a bar I used to go to. He was always really funny. Nothing like in that photo.'

'That's because in the photo he is acting,' Nan D says, murderously low. 'I don't believe you anyway.'

'Well yeah, but it's probably not what you think you are going to be doing. Big dreams of action movies or something, Jean-Claude Van Damme, and you're on a billboard pretending you are going to top yourself. I actually seen him in that same t-shirt he's wearing. He used to come into the bar in that exact same t-shirt.'

'Don't believe you,' Nan D says. 'But then, I believe very little of what you say.'

'What I don't understand,' Leigh says, 'is why Boogie just didn't do something to sort these guys out. You know, boom. Misty, your actual dad would have been knocking on a door within twenty minutes to get it sorted.'

'I'm sorry but Boogie *is* my actual dad.'

'Yeah, I know, doll. That's nice how you say that.'

'You slabber once more about Michael,' Nan D says, 'God help me, I'll make sure you don't ever speak again.'

There is a pause before Leigh says evenly, 'No worries, D. Chill. Just chill.'

They continue the journey in silence until Misty switches on the radio and it's a soul song, aching, yearning. Misty is briefly amazed when her mother begins to sing along, the car filled full with her voice, until Nan D switches off the radio. With the music gone, Leigh continues quietly, a final few notes dissolving into air.

The car park is fairly empty. A few old couples are making their way into the huge church hall. Nan D says that it is the senior citizens' tea this morning.

'Do you not go?' Leigh asks. 'Sorry.'

Misty stares up at the stained glass like smashed boiled sweets and then higher again is the triangle of gold that is the spire of the church. Other people get out of a car holding tartan rugs and a yoga mat.

'Stretch and relax,' Nan D says. 'On today too.'

'No sign yet of our people?' Leigh asks.

'That's absolutely not what they fucking are. They are not our people, no matter who they're sending. And they're late.'

The three of them sit in silence and watch more people get out of their cars and proceed towards the church buildings. There's a blue van that delivers supplies in cardboard boxes and then there is a taxi which lowers and then has a ramp to allow for the man using a wheelchair to exit. They look in silence at how, once the man has moved to the vestibule of the church, the ramp is folded back and the car slowly rises. And then, at long last, there is a certain car that enters the gates of the church and they all know that this is it. There is something in the way that it moves, slowly, almost insolently. They watch as it travels in a loop, before coming to a stop at the far corner of the car park, where thistles and nettles push through the metal fence.

Nan D lets out a long slow breath.

'Handy little spot to park,' Leigh says. 'Away over there.'

'I feel kind of frightened,' Misty says.

'There's no need,' says Nan D. 'They're the ones who should be frightened. We're not going to move here until we see who is going to get out. We are not shifting. No way. Let those cunts do the work.'

It seems to glow, the stained glass, when Misty looks at it. She thinks she can make out a face, a saint maybe, looking down at her, its halo tipping, the mouth a sad line. The windows of the Range Rover seem black in this light. The Tahiti smell is intensifying. Beyond the metal fence and the nettles and the briars is the water of Belfast lough and then further the sea. Imagine casting a message in a bottle into the sea. How long would it take before anyone would find it? Probably, with the tides, it might just stay in the same spot for years, moving this way and that, back and forward, but never reaching a shore. And even then, if it did, what were the chances of someone caring about your message? Next to zero? But someone might.

'Hold on,' Nan D says. 'I think I see something. Look.'

The door on the passenger side opens marginally, it seems, then closes again. Leigh moves to get out.

'No, stay,' Nan D says. 'Wait until we see who's there. Just bide your time.'

They watch as one person gets out from the passenger seat. She straightens her skirt and then tightens her scarf. Another emerges from the back. And then the one who is the driver opens the back right door and takes something out. It's the bag. The three women are all dressed in black.

'That's the bag?' Leigh says. 'I thought it would look more like a briefcase, you know the way you see in the films, that's more like a carry-on EasyJet—'

Nan D barks for her to shut the fuck up.

'What did you imagine, Misty?' Leigh says. 'Did you think it was going to be more like a briefcase?'

Nan D puts her hand on the door. 'Right, ladies, let's go.'

'I don't want to get out,' Misty says. 'I don't want them looking at me.'

'You are going to get out.'

'But you said before that I didn't have to. That's what you said.'

'Give her a break,' Leigh says. 'She's a ragbag. She would have put on something better than that if she was going to be getting out of the car.'

'She doesn't need to impress them!' Nan D hisses. 'They're not worth the smell of her shit. But I want them to see her. They should see her.'

A grey hooded sweatshirt and soft baggy shorts. Her hair is tied up with a stretchy belt that she found lying at the bottom of her wardrobe. On her feet are old Air Force 1s, that look more like clogs because of the way the leather is folded down at the heels. She slowly opens the door and gets out. So does Leigh, in her running gear, which consists of a football top and shorts. And then Nan D, with a little patent handbag over her arm, as though she is going to a Sunday service.

'OK, move,' says Nan D. 'But don't do anything else until I say.'

They walk slowly, together, in a line, Leigh, Misty and Nan D. The sky is the colour of concrete, not even a pale streak of sunlight. The three black figures advance with the one in the centre carrying the bag. For a sudden moment

Misty expects someone to pull a gun, maybe one of them, from a black blazer or maybe Nan D, a pistol from that handbag and then the first one falls and then the other two. They are coming into view now and she can see that it is Chris's stepmum who is carrying the bag, but then she passes it to another woman who comes forward to set it on the ground. And then, like they are laying a wreath on a grave, they all step back. It's as if they expect the three of them to come and fetch it.

Nan D hesitates. No one moves. Misty touches the belt in her hair as she feels those mothers looking at her, taking in her legs, her old pyjama shorts. The bag sits innocent on the tarmac, as if it contains a dress and a jumper, a plastic bag of toiletries ready for a city break. Nan D stares ahead, face impassive. Misty can see their faces now. Rami's mother is staring at her and she looks, does she? It seems she looks frightened. She wants to say to Rami's mother, I don't know why he did that, because he is a quiet boy, he's not a bad boy, but that bottle had hurt, and then there is Line-up's mum, she saw her on the TV one time, and she is smiling, sympathetic, as if she is saying, there now, once this is over it will all be alright, like the old pastoral year head. There now. And Chris's mum just stares without pity. Chris's mum stares at Nan D before her eyes slide to Misty's mum. She thinks they're trash. Grubbing for cash in a car park. Misty shouldn't have come, or agreed to take the payment, or gone to the police, had the examination, given the statement, met Naomi McCrory or the guy who pretended he was the woman with the red hair in the detective book. She stares at the bag, how tubby it is, full of the money. And then back to their faces. She opens her mouth, like a goldfish, as if to say something, but there is no noise, just empty air, and the silence, holding its breath, until suddenly song pours in around them, singing, ringing out sweetly and it is her mother's voice, what was on the radio, shapes of that old soul song, but sliding into something else and it is, yes it is, it's on the run and now it is

Jesus Loves Me
This I Know
for the
Bible
Tells
Me So

ringing out so sweetly, softening the concrete, releasing the colours of the stained glass and when Misty looks down she sees that they are holding hands, her, her mum, Nan D. The singing stretches and bends and Misty does not see the mothers for a moment, until suddenly, coming into the car park of the church, there is an ice-cream van, pink and white, two huge fake cones on the front like horns. And one of the women steps forward as the singing stops. She picks up the bag and hands it to Misty. It is Rami's mother. She looks sad and thin. When she walks back to where the others are standing, they all turn and walk back to the car. Chris's mum turns round to take one last look at her. Line-up's mum doesn't look back at all. She walks quickly as though she needs to get to an appointment.

When they get into the car, no one speaks. Misty realises that she is shaking. She pulls her sweatshirt down over her hands. Nan D starts the engine and they move slowly towards the gates of the church.

'We should've checked it,' Leigh says. 'To make sure that it's all legit. The notes.'

She unzips it now and takes out a bundle of cash.

'Leave that alone! That's nothing to do with you. It's Misty's.'

'I've never seen so much money in all of my life. I'd rather have the other notes, though. The paper ones. Not the plastic. I liked the smell of the paper notes.'

'Leave it alone. It's nothing to do with you.'

'What you going to spend it on, Misty?'

'I don't know. I haven't thought.'

'Why don't you just go and spend some of it right now? You deserve it.'

'Maybe just go home.'

'No seriously, Misty! You should!'

'I don't think so.'

'Go on! It'll be a giggle!'

'I'm not really up for it right now.'

'That's because it was so full on, meeting the three witches of Christmas past,' Leigh says. 'You need a drink or something. A cocktail. Because that was traumatic for you.'

'We're not far from the Abbey Centre,' says Nan D.

'If we are going to a shopping centre, why not that big place in the town? Where you can park the car underneath.'

'What do you reckon, Misty?' asks Nan D. 'We'd need to take the cash with us. We couldn't leave all of that in the car.'

When they return, Gen is delighted with the bag they bought her. She immediately transfers the books and files from her old one. She looks at the price tag. 'Wow,' she says. 'Unreal.' Boogie takes the tissue-wrapped jumper from the bag and slowly unfolds it. He holds it up.

'Hugo Boss. Thanks, sweetheart,' he says.

'You like it?'

'I do.'

'You not going to try it on?'

'I'll try it on in a bit.'

Later, when everyone else has gone to bed and Nan D has driven home, she sits beside him on the sofa.

'You don't like the Hugo Boss, do you?'

'It's a nice jumper. I do like it for sure.'

'You don't.'

'Well, Misty, you want me to be honest?'

'Yeah.'

'Times in the future, when I put that jumper on, I'm going to think, first off, yeah that's warm or that's comfy or that's made of good stuff but then second it'll be, oh yeah that's the jumper paid for with that cash. And that means I am probably going to want to take it off again.'

'Well, it doesn't seem to bother anyone else. Nan D got perfume and a cream. Mum got a necklace.'

'That's them. I'm me.'

Misty goes upstairs and comes down with the brown bag. She unzips it slowly and takes out a wad of money, fanning it carefully.

'Look at this then,' she says. 'This would be your depot rent for what, six months, eight months? Wouldn't it? Can you imagine? Wouldn't that help? You'd pay the depot rent and then you wouldn't need to think any more about it. You're always saying that the bosses are ripping you off. So, money from not nice people is being given to other not nice people.'

'You should keep it for yourself for the future.'

'Should I? Well, I can do that and give you this depot rent. Maybe I might get us a holiday. How would you feel about that?'

I know that she wanted to do all of the special effects make-up at one point, turn people into zombies and all of that kind of thing, night of the living dead, but Misty did my make-up for my son's graduation and it was so beautiful. I was nervous because I have actually let myself go recently, on account of a lot of things. I'd felt very down, to the point where, to the point where I wondered if I should continue. The right medication isn't the whole story, I know that, but I did get a really good doctor who got me sorted out a bit and I started to feel a lot better. But even so, I was very worried about the graduation because my son's dad, my ex, Tony, and his partner were going to be there. Even though it's years since we split up I've never stopped loving Tony. That's embarrassing, isn't it? You're meant to move on and all of that. But I would get back together right now if I could. I know that's never going to happen, though. On the graduation day, I just wanted to look presentable, not glamorous. I don't know what Misty did. It wasn't much. It didn't take long. But I looked like a lady.

Joanne, when she finished tidying, said that she wanted a word with Frankie. What she told her was that under Nina's bed she had found ten empty tubs of strawberry ice cream, maybe more. She thought that Frankie should know.

'Strawberry ice cream?' Frankie said.

'At least ten empty tubs.'

'Well sure, yeah, she should throw them in the bin. I'll tell her to do that.'

Joanne had paused and then spoken again. 'No, these are big tubs of ice cream.'

'I'll tell her to throw them in the bin,' Frankie repeated.

'OK, I'll leave it with you,' Joanne said. 'You'll know best how to approach it.'

It was only when Frankie was at the gym the next day, on the bench press, that she realised what Joanne was suggesting she should approach. When she returned home, she went up to Nina's bedroom, knocked on the door. 'Hi,' she said, when Nina told her to come in. She took a seat on her bed.

'What's up?' Nina asked.

'I don't know.'

'No?'

'I want to ask you a question.'

'About Misty Johnston? See. I know her name. I remember when she was here. They weren't that nice to her that day, Chris and Line-up and Lynchie. I listened and heard them talking.'

'It's nothing to do with her. Forget her. It's to do with tubs of ice cream.'

'Oh.'

'They were found under your bed.'

'OK.'

'Why are you eating all that ice cream?'

'I liked the flavour.'

'Why were you eating all that ice cream?'

'I felt like it.'

'Why were you eating all that ice cream?'

'It tasted the same when I puked it up.'

'That's a stupid thing to do.'

Nina didn't reply.

'You've got everything anyone could want,' Frankie said. 'So why you doing that?'

'You got no idea about me,' Nina said.

And so, Frankie thinks, maybe they should go somewhere together. Maybe they should spend time together. She asks Nina where she'd like to go and she says the folk museum.

'No,' says Frankie, remembering meeting that woman in the café. 'It's boring. It's full of kids and boy scouts.'

'The folk museum. It's massive. It's outside. It can't be full of anybody.'

'Oh,' says Frankie. 'That's a different place. And it's where you want to go?'

'Yeah. I like all of the little homes.'

Museums, museums, museums, why are they all so interested in them, Frankie wonders as they make the short drive to the folk park. All this old ass shit – peering at ancient bowls through thick glass, looking at some cottage from the 1800s that has been reassembled brick by brick – what was the point because, as Michelle said that time, long ago, it was all back story and who cared? It's boring. Boring to meander through parkland to a worker's cottage and then head down the road to a minister's house then walk into an old bank.

But here they now are, sitting in an old school house from 1905. There is only the sound of crickets and, just there, a neighing donkey.

'It is like you can feel,' Nina says, 'it's like you can feel what it would have been like to be one of the kids. If they wanted to sit up near the fire, they had to bring a piece of turf with them. And if they didn't have that, they had to sit at the back in the cold. They told us that when we came here with the school.'

Frankie looks at the tattered old map of the world on the wall, the British Empire coloured in red. Nina never hid those strawberry ice-cream boxes. If she had wanted, she could have kept it all secret.

'And then, in one of the other houses, we'll get to that one, people slept with the animals. There wasn't anywhere separate for the animals. But that kept them warm, the heat of the animals.'

'Why don't we go to the coffee shop?'

'They had no lights either, just tallow candles. Mustn't they have loved the summer, Frankie? When it was warm and light.'

'I don't know anything about these people and what they thought.'

In one of the houses, across from a church, it is possible to get photographs taken in period costume. 'Let's do it!' Nina says. 'It'll be a laugh!' There are rails of clothes, or rather half-clothes from Regency and Victorian periods, the front of outfits that tie at the back. They look through them before Frankie picks one, black with a high neck, a gathered, full skirt. Nina puts on a white Regency dress with a sash. The scoop neck gapes so she stuffs two pairs of kids' tights down the front. The photographer tells them not to smile because, back in the day, people didn't grin. They wait around until the photo is produced and put into a paper frame that looks like fake wood.

'What do you think of it?' Nina asks. 'I hate what I look like.'

'You got great boobs for sure in that picture,' Frankie says.

They go to another cottage, smoky, dark, where a woman is doing embroidery. And then there is a weaver's, the loom vast, the suspended threads catching in the light. On the way back to the car, they go to one other place. It's a church, plain and austere. It's just a white rectangle. There is a bench along one wall and when they take a seat the whitewashed wall is cool against Frankie's back.

'They haven't done much with this place,' Frankie says.

Nina is looking up at the roof and so Frankie does the same. White, white wood.

'This place is boring,' Nina says. 'This is the most boring place we've been to.'

So much whiteness everywhere you look. When Frankie glances out of the window, that sky is bleached too.

'Georgia Heydock was scouted for a model agency in London. I mean, she is only in the year above me, so she is still too young, but there you are, London. She's really pretty, so it's not a massive surprise.'

'Yeah?'

'Yeah.'

Frankie stares at the ceiling.

'They say that she is exactly what they are looking for and that she could do it all. Shows, magazines. She can go to New York and Paris. Georgia Heydock,' she says again.

Frankie's voice is low. 'You can go to any of those places if you want. Your dad could get that sorted at any time. And you've been to them anyway. We went to New York last year. We ice-skated on that tiny ass rink.'

Nina shrugs. There is the sound of a bird outside.

'We should paint more things white in the house,' Frankie says. 'Just white.'

'I think we should paint more things black,' says Nina.

Nina lies back on the wooden pew and stares at the ceiling as she asks, 'When did you come to live in our house, Frankie?'

'A few years ago,' she replies.

'Did you meet my dad after my mum died? Is that the way it worked?'

'Yeah,' she says. 'Alright, Nina, no. No I didn't. I met him when your mum was sick.'

'Oh,' replies Nina. 'That's what I thought. Well, that wasn't very nice.'

'No, it wasn't very nice.'

'What was the girl like? The girl, Misty?'

'You know what she's like. You said that you saw her.'

'No, the other day. When you went to give her the money. Yes of course I know. I've heard you talking. What was her hair like?'

Frankie thinks. 'Just in a ponytail,' she says.

'She has a Bennyz.'

'So they say.'

'I would never do a Bennyz. Not because it's slutty but because I would feel so bad if no one wanted to be my benefactor. Like if I got zero sign-ups.'

'You don't need a benefactor. What are you talking about? Bennyz is for people looking for money.'

'What if Chris murdered someone? Do you think that we would still pay to get him off?'

'Chris was basically a bystander. He more or less was just at the party,' Frankie says.

'Uh huh,' she replies. 'Imagine Dad doing that when his wife was lying there dying.'

'It wasn't planned.'

'Doesn't matter whether it was planned or not. Don't think it would have mattered to my mum, whether it was planned or not, do you? My mum used to read me a story every night. She would sit on the edge of my bed and do that.'

'Sure,' Frankie says.

'So, when you came to live in our house were you just so in love with Dad?'

'I don't want to talk about this with you. Let's go.'

The car park. That woman singing. She wanted to join them, pass over to the other side and stand with the kid, the granny and the mother. Let's get in the car and drive away. Where we going to? A café where they all drink tea, tired, laughing, sharing chips, or all piled on a bed heaped with dirty clothes, empty perfume bottles along the windowsill. That mother. Hers, with her arm hanging off the bed. She painted her mother's nails one time when she was waiting for her to wake up, rubbed a little lipstick on her mouth, a coral smudge. And then one time she didn't wake up.

'So, what do you think, Frankie? Do you think that I would get any benefactors?'

'I don't know. I haven't a clue. As I said, you don't need them.'

'I bet you, if you went on, you'd get loads.'

'Doubt it. Let's go.'

'You don't think I would get any. I know you don't.'

A couple wearing rucksacks and hiking boots have appeared in the old mission hall church. They look around and nod at each other, speak in German, say the word Zwingli.

'I think you are just mean, Frankie,' Nina says. 'Just really mean. You are saying that I couldn't get any guys to look at me on Bennyz, unlike the girl that my brother and his friends are accused of raping and who are you anyway? Who are you? You are somebody who was having sex with my dad when my mummy was dying!'

The German woman looks at her in surprise.

'Let's go,' Frankie says.

They are making their way down the path, high on each side with flowers, when the German man comes running after them. He is waving something. It's the photograph.

They show it to Chris when they get home. He is there with his new girlfriend, Charlotte, and they are going into Belfast for him to make the final booking for his year abroad. He is going to Bali for a month to surf, before going to Brisbane where he has a placement in a hospital. Then he is going on to Sydney where he's staying for another couple of months. Charlotte is saying about how much she is going to miss him. After the flights get sorted, they are going for a meal. Charlotte's skin is glowing. She does a face that changes from consternation into a beam. She says that the photo is adorable. 'You really look like you are from the olden times!' she says, consternation then beam.

'I'm sure you are going to miss your big brother when he goes away, Nina?' Charlotte says.

'Not really.'

The consternation and then the beam. 'I know you are only kidding!' she says.

When they leave, Frankie tells Nina that she is going for a run, but Nina ignores her, just as she did for the journey back from the folk park, when she studiously watched a video on her phone.

'Do you want something to eat?' Frankie asks.

Nina doesn't turn her head.

'You've been spoilt,' Frankie says.

'So have you.'

'My mum died too. But I lived in children's homes. I haven't been spoilt.'

'I didn't know that,' Nina says. 'That's something you have never said before.'

'You don't know anything.'

'Well,' she says, 'if I had been in the children's homes, I would have liked you. I would have been your friend. I would have been your good friend.'

'I'm going for a run,' Frankie says.

Frankie's pace is quicker than usual, along the shore, but her breathing stays slow and controlled, as she passes a man who says hello to her, and is ignored, as is the dog that chases her, barking, an owner calling its name. She runs without her headphones but she hears nothing of the seagulls or the police car's siren, as it goes to some emergency. It is only when she almost trips on a stone on the path, is propelled forward before she catches her balance, that she slows down and starts to walk. There's a bench, looking out across the water and she sits down on it, folds her knees up towards her chest, hugs them. Like many of these benches, there is a little plaque, for someone she supposes has died: P. Reavie. She does the calculation and P.

Reavie was nineteen years old. Boy, girl, who knew, but P. Reavie, according to the bench, was in the hands of the Lord. It's got colder and the sky is grubby. What are those three doing now? She looks at the waves. Maybe the girl is sitting in a fluffy dressing gown, fluffy slippers. Maybe she has spent some of the money already. Was P. Reavie a girl? Was P. Reavie ill? Killed in a car crash? Had P. Reavie had enough, even at nineteen? Fuck it. P. Reavie was dead. P. Reavie. P. Reavie was dead and gone. She gets to her feet and starts running again.

When she eventually gets back to the house, Neil is there, in the clothes he likes to wear in the evening: polo shirt, baggy shorts and deck shoes.

'Wow,' he says, when he sees her. 'I love you in Lycra.'

'Let's go out for dinner tonight,' she says.

'Why not just order something in?'

'I want to go out, babes.'

'Alright, if that's what you want to do.'

'I've got something new I want to wear. Why not book La Ferme?'

'Sure.'

The water of the shower is hot and the scented oil, orange and neroli, is heavy in the steam, and the towel, when she dries herself, is huge and soft. She inspects her face under the unforgiving light of the dressing room. Her skin is flushed after the run. All she needs is a tinted moisturiser and that beautiful peony lipstick. She smooths body lotion over her breasts, on the inside of her thighs where the skin already, in its smoothness, feels almost damp. In the big white box is a dress that was couriered last week. It clings as though it's wet.

When she goes downstairs, she pours herself a glass of wine, the one that Neil says is so good. It tastes just like any other. Michelle, when she drinks white wine, always put an ice cube in it. Frankie rubs her finger along a tiny stain on the marble top. She hasn't been in touch with Michelle since that last trip. Nina comes into the kitchen.

'You look nice,' she says.

'We're going out.'

'Well, you look nice.'

Frankie thinks of the four of them around the table in the kitchen. But no, Chris will not be back this evening. Well then, the three of them, Nina loving talking about the history of the houses at that boring ass place. Frankie takes a sip of the wine.

'You can use my card. To order yourself a pizza.'

'Sure. Thanks, Frankie.'

'Wow,' Neil says, when she walks into the big living room. 'Let's go. The car is waiting outside.' She lifts her kid jacket, her woven handbag with the lacquered bamboo handles. 'Bye, Nina!' Neil calls, as they close the front door.

'See you later, Nina!' Frankie calls.

'You look so hot, Frankie,' Neil says, when they get into the taxi. He runs his hand along the firm flesh of her leg. As the car pulls away, Frankie thinks of Nina, with a pizza, with ice cream, a woman singing. There is a button loose on Neil's denim shirt, the one most particularly on his stomach. It hangs by just a couple of threads. She takes his hand. Frankie sees Nina, watching their car drive off, her face small and pale.

'Hope we get our usual table,' she says.

'Why would we not?'

'Babes,' she says. Because why would they not?

Yeah, the future is hers.

It's a bit ironic. Because I am married to a firefighter, and firefighters are considered by a lot of people to be hot, you know, all those charity calendars with them stripped off and holding the hoses in strategic places, so yes a bit ironic when all of my friends couldn't get down the Titanic Quarter quick enough when the World Police and Fire Games were on a few years ago, a bit crazy that what I really find attractive are guys in business suits. Let me be more precise: suit, black, really nicely tailored but a bit slouchy, white shirt, maybe the tie just a bit undone. I suppose what I'm saying is that I like the idea of a guy being a bit wealthy. Or even very wealthy. Which again is funny because I'm actually a welfare rights officer. My days are spent advocating on behalf of people who are being screwed over in terms of their benefits. Years and years ago I used to work in a hotel, cleaning the rooms after guests. And I used to have this kind of fantasy that I would go in to do a room and then while I was involved in, say, cleaning the sink or making the bed, this rich guy, wearing the suit, would have sex with me. And of course it would be brilliant. Shifts, other bedrooms, time itself, all gloriously suspended. Sometimes I would develop it out a bit and we would go for a meal in a top restaurant and we would have sex in the toilets. Or like a laundry cupboard because that's where Boris Becker did it, yeah? But mainly it stayed in the hotel room. But then there was that guy, Dominique Strauss-Kahn, can you remember? The French guy. The politician. He was accused of sexually assaulting a maid in a hotel in New York. It was whenever I was working in the hotel. The woman received a settlement I think. I can't remember her name, but in the pictures, she had her hair tied back in a scarf, well, more like a wrap. I didn't find him attractive at all, Dominique Strauss-Kahn. I thought he was a creep. We all did. I don't think anyone, me included, found anyone who came to that hotel attractive, even though some of them did wear those kinds of suits, were those sorts of people. I've never been unfaithful to my husband. I wouldn't dream of it.

Leigh had left that morning. She'd given Misty a journal, with a dog on the front of it, to write down how she was feeling. 'I think you'll find it really good,' she said. She also offered to make her out a programme, for the gym. 'It's incredible, I'm not kidding, how different you might feel, if you did some exercise!' She couldn't stay any longer. There was just so much going on and the little kid was missing her.

'Thanks for coming,' Misty said. Her mother was wearing the necklace Misty got her.

'No worries!'

'Here.' Misty gave her an envelope with some cash in it. 'You're a good singer,' she said.

'Oh, get to fuck!' her mother said, immediately opening the envelope. 'Misty! Thank you thank you thank you, baby!'

Then two interviews in the one day! The first was the sales and marketing one and it took place online. She had changed the position of her laptop from the one she had always used for Bennyz. This time she sat at her dressing table, sitting on one of the chairs that she had brought up from the kitchen. She wore a blue jumper and sat with her hands in her lap. The man who was interviewing her kept looking off to the left as though he had his script taped up there. He said that, initially at least, it would be commission only, but the person who was one below the managing director only started as a trainee six months ago. So, quite obviously, the sky was the limit.

'How would you sell yourself?' he asked.

'Well,' said Misty. 'I suppose I would say that I'm pretty hardworking.'

'That's good and I am glad to hear it. But you know, many, many people are hardworking. So, what else?'

Misty cast her eye around her room for some inspiration. The Makeup Revolution Forever Flawless Affinity Eyeshadow palette was on the floor, the pale colour called Moments missing because it fell out in her bag one day.

'I have an affinity with lots of different people,' she said.

'A what?'

'An affinity. I can get on with different people. Lots of different sorts of people.'

She didn't know if that was true. To be fair, it probably wasn't.

'Can you evidence this ability to get on with different people?'

'Well,' she said, gaining confidence. 'It's on my CV that I worked in a restaurant. And all different types of people came into the restaurant.'

'Social skillset,' he said.

'Yeah, that.'

At the end of the interview, she asked what she would be selling. He said it would just depend on who the clients were, but the principles were the same whatever the product. He leaned into the screen confidentially. I shouldn't really tell you this, he said, but I am actually going to reveal to you who our latest client is. G.E.E. Gamma Energy Efficiency.'

'Oh, right.'

'Commission only, but that suits the people who work for us. Because they are hungry. Last person to the field, last person to make money.'

The funeral home's sign has gold lettering in the same font as her old maths textbook. Inside, a painting of a waterfall seems to have flowing water. Misty thinks at first she is imagining it but it's an effect, like one of those fires with fake flames and glowing embers. She is watching it, when the woman appears, small, plump.

'Are you here for the interview?' she says. 'Because if you are, you're late.'

'Yes I know,' Misty replies. 'I'm sorry. And there's no excuse because I only live up the road!'

She can see the woman taking in what she's wearing. Two men appear, dressed in the same black as the woman. They look like they're extras from a film about the Victorians. They're even wearing top hats. Misty saw one time in the park where they were filming some drama and the medieval people were on their break and all eating tacos from a van. The guys in top hats will be vaping round the back. The woman's photo is in the brochure below where it says A Personal Message from Ann McCullough. You can see that same waterfall behind her.

'Well, you're here now,' Mrs McCullough says. 'Come on through.'

She takes her to another room, which is very different. There's a big box of chocolates with no lid, a bag of popcorn, loads of arch files and a calendar with a guy wearing a cowboy hat. Mrs McCullough asks Misty why she applied for the job and why she thinks she is suitable. She says the same thing, about being hardworking and having an affinity, but Mrs McCullough doesn't write it down. She simply looks at her.

'This is a job,' Mrs McCullough says, 'that requires a lot of maturity. Do you know what I mean? People say, about this and that, oh don't worry about it, it's not a matter of life and death. But here's the thing. Get this. Here, it is a matter of life and death.'

'Well, that's true,' says Misty.

'I wouldn't be saying it if it wasn't true, love. And what it means is, the very best way we can be of assistance to people is by being organised and efficient and competent. So that, no matter what else is chaos, this part is taken care of and under control. Do you see?'

Misty nods.

'I don't need divas. People focused on their own problems. Last thing you want when someone is waiting to bury their child is everybody hanging around for some cretin who can't get themselves out of bed with the good-looking fella they met the night before. Anyways, says here you can do make-up?'

'I can. I did it at the college.'

'Have you ever been in the presence of the deceased before?'

'No.'

Mrs McCullough looks at her CV.

'Why did you leave the job in the restaurant or the hotel or whatever on earth the place was? That's your last place of employment, yeah?'

'I just didn't want to work there anymore.'

'And that's it?'

'Yes.'

'No reason other than you just didn't want to work there anymore?'

'No.'

'Why did you not want to work there anymore? What did you not like?'

'Nothing in particular.'

Mrs McCullough looks again at the CV.

'Just didn't want to work there anymore, that's what you're saying.'

'Yeah.'

'Alright,' says Mrs McCullough. 'I'm just trying to build a picture here, of who you are.'

'Sure,' Misty says.

Mrs McCullough asks a few other questions, jotting down a few points. She asks Misty if there is anything that she wants to say, before the interview finishes.

She hesitates and then says, 'That other job, well, I was assaulted at a party. You know, assaulted – assaulted in a, a sexual way. And the people who worked there knew some of the ones involved. And I went back to work in the hotel again but then I decided that I couldn't really do it. I couldn't go back. Like, one of the people kind of involved used to work there. I tried but it didn't work. So that's it, really.'

'Alright,' Mrs McCullough replies. 'Don't say any more.'

'Sure.'

Mrs McCullough looks at her with pale, calm, unblinking eyes. Then she gets to her feet, her gaze shifting to the cowboy on the calendar. 'Alright, well, thank you very much, Misty. As you can imagine, we have multiple candidates to see and it'll be a while before we'll be able to make our decision.'

'Sure,' Misty says. 'Thanks for seeing me.'

As she is leaving, she says goodbye to the two men in top hats. Mrs McCullough, coming out of the back room, says, 'Misty? Can I just check that we've got your right phone number?'

'Yes, that's it.'

'Alright, love,' Mrs McCullough says. 'Thank you.'

* * *

When she finds herself walking past the travel agent's, she goes in. The heavy guy at the desk is doing a lottery scratch card.

'Yup?' he says without looking up. 'What can I do for you?'

'Did you win?'

'Nope.'

'I'm wanting to go anywhere that's a good deal.'

He makes a face, as though that's an unreasonably tall order.

'I got cash,' Misty says.

He slowly raises his eyes from the unlucky card. 'What you done? Robbed a bank? You on the run?'

'If I was on the run I wouldn't just have had an interview for a job in an undertakers.'

'How did it go?'

'Don't know. Might've gone better if I'd seen a dead body at some point in my life.'

'If only you'd made more of an effort to see a dead body on the off chance you might have to go for a job in an undertakers.'

'Well, we'll see if I get it. I quite liked the woman.'

'To the matter in hand. Where do you want to go, and when, and who is coming?'

'Me, my dad, Gen, Nan D, my mum, my mum's kid, maybe this woman my mum is friendly with. So seven. And I want to go dead soon.'

'You aren't making it easy.'

'I got cash.'

'Cancellation. Bulgaria.'

It was a shit party. I had just read Bataille and there I was, listening to two guys talk about air-fryers. I had noticed some days before that my hair was starting to recede. Those things galvanised me to apply for a term abroad in Utrecht.

For Christmas, a friend got me a series of mindfulness classes. The place was above a fried chicken takeaway. It didn't get off to a wonderful start, as far as I was concerned. We all sat in a circle while the woman ticked our names off her print-out. When she came to one participant, she said that his name wasn't on the list. The guy said that his girlfriend had got it online. The mindfulness woman got quite agitated about him possibly not having paid because he wasn't on the list which to me didn't seem terribly mindful. Then the young man said, Jesus Christ, do I look like the kinda guy who would want to scam a mindfulness class? Most of the circle gave a little laugh at this, because he didn't – well, who would? – and I watched the mindfulness woman clench her fists. So no, I was hardly sold on it. When she started on the breathing exercises, all I could smell was fried chicken. However, in the middle of the session, the woman told a story, a homily really, about a table. It was the idea that a simple table's being was predicated on the existence of a multiplicity of other elements such as the forest, while the wood grew, the rain and the sun necessary for such growth, the factory where the table was made, possibly the workers' hands, their sweat, the machines and tools made by other workers in other factories, and then the transportation and distribution that had brought the table to this spot, the shops, the shop workers who had placed it in a box, their parents, their ancestors. Obviously the story was to reinforce a pleasant sense of connectivity with the earth and its inhabitants and to suggest the multiplicity of even the most straightforward of things, to suggest how all is contingent. But the effect it had on me was quite negative. The simplest action, like getting a glass of water, became so mind-blowingly complex and dizzying in all of the avenues that could be pursued – the filtration, the plumbing, the ancestors of the glass makers, the installation of the taps, the molecular structure of the water – as to be paralysing. It was like a monster with multiplying tentacles. There can be just too many perspectives. It made me crave single source elements. Single source only.

As well as the message to say that a sizeable sum had been secured for the centre by the US donors, there was a little note from Mary Donovan-Leitner to say that, should she be interested, Bronagh was welcome to stay at the Leitner residence in upstate New York. She insisted it was a very modest little place and, were she to go in the fall, she should pack plenty of warm layers. (The Leitners were intending to stay with friends in Umbria for a month.) Mary detailed the dates when the house was free. There was a store that would deliver whatever provisions might be required. Bronagh had told Donal about it over breakfast this morning. He wasn't enthused. A freezing cold house in the middle of nowhere? No thanks. No problem if she wanted them to head to Manhattan, but some place in the sticks? What would they even do?

'Talk to each other, Donal?' she had said.

'Sorry, but you're not selling it to me,' he replied. 'Only joking.'

When she gets to the centre, the police are there owing to reports of intruders on the roof. They find one window cracked and some smashed bottles, but nothing more than that. The police ask if they can have a look around inside. They are particularly interested in talking about Finn Anderson. They look at the photos of him outside the Johnny Anderson gym. 'You seen the new film?'

'No,' Bronagh says.

'Oh, he's great in it. The accent. You wouldn't think he was from here. Unbelievable.'

'His brother,' Bronagh says, 'that's who the gym is named after. He was a lovely boy, a good boy.'

Once the policeman has taken a photo of the photo of Finn Anderson, he shows Bronagh a photo, saying, 'That's me with Casey-Ann O'Brien and Dee Irwin.'

'I don't know who they are,' Bronagh says.

'Seriously? They do the drive time on Cool FM.'

'How do you feel about the number of Early Intervention Projects in this area?' Bronagh asks. 'I've worked in an advisory capacity in that area.'

'I'm not sure. I'd need to ask someone about that. Does Finn Anderson do his own stunts?' the policeman asks.

When she goes to her office she passes a few kids who are in for the breakfast club. There are no whispers. She didn't think there would be. It all passes quickly. She has seen it so many times before. Something else comes along and attention moves to that. She has rationalised it quite successfully to herself. There was bad behaviour for sure, fandango, brouhaha, fracas, and yes, Donal is probably right when he says that Lyness has been over-indulged. It was always going to be that way with an only child. An only, much-longed-for child. When he heard what had happened with the money, he hugged them both. They stood in the kitchen, the three of them, in an embrace that lasted for ever. 'Guys, thank you,' he said. 'Although I don't think there was any chance it was ever going to go to court.' He shook his head, incredulous at the notion. Donal went to say something, but Bronagh put up her hand. It said, leave it. But yes, she has reconciled herself to it, because as Lyness said, it would never have gone to court and that girl, who could have been any of the crowd at the centre, that girl would have been put through something pretty unpleasant. And so, in a way, it has worked out well for her, that she has this sum of money. It's not so much that it's going to change, radically, her life in any way, but it would certainly help her, well, get on with things. And it's non-disclosure, as a pre-condition, but also, no admittance of culpability. So yes, all fine.

When she sits at her desk, Bronagh searches for Finn Anderson, for news. There is a photo of him in a restaurant with Brodie Shaq and a baby in a highchair. The text says that he is about to start filming soon on a period film set in 1950s Hollywood about a sixteen-year-old from Dakota who comes to seek fame and fortune. He plays the boyfriend from back home who takes revenge on the Hollywood bosses who chew up and spit out his beloved. *As soon as I heard about it I knew it was the kind of project I wanted to be involved in. Exploitation, it's just wrong.* Bronagh clicks off the page. She imagines he has maximum solidarity with that LA waitress on the minimum wage who has just brought over that organic puréed whatever the baby is eating. She looks to see how Erica from the band is doing. Just fine. She remembers that time after they had been at that festival in France she got the news that the guy had left her and then she said that she wanted to kill herself. Funny the way she was in the café next day, where there was a big mirror, her eyes sliding to it periodically to check what she looked like when she was a person threatening to kill herself. Oh well, still hanging on to life after all these years.

Later she sees how someone has spilt something in the corridor that leads to the main hall. It's sticky and has resulted in footprints the length of it. Bronagh goes to the janitor's room to get the mop and bucket. 'I'll do it, Mrs Farrell,' he says.

'No, let me. It's fine.'

As she mops, she looks at the speckles of the floor, the way they become bluer with the swipe of the wet mop, and with the wetness how there is even silver there, little chips that only present themselves with the water. A house in Donegal had a terrazzo floor like that, a house they stayed in long before they bought their own holiday home. By the sea, and Donal was reading a book about space at the time and he kept stopping to tell her things about it. She didn't understand or care about it at all, but his sense of wonder was so noticeable. At night Lyness was upstairs in the travel cot in that little square room and they sat, outside, blankets around them, drinking whiskey. She dips the mop into the bucket, twists it round, presses it against the plastic. They had gone to the beach every day, whatever the weather. She had made bread a couple of times when she was there. She had used a packet mix, but that doesn't really matter because what's important is simplicity. She realises that now. There are so many clouds of complication and confusion really, insecurities and petty, ugly little motives. Who said that about life being like the flight of a sparrow through the baronial hall? She doesn't know. It's brief, though, that's for sure. She thinks again of Johnny. He shouldn't have died like that, in a room by himself. The terrazzo comes alive again with the water. He hugged her.

'What happened?' one of the kids says, as they walk by. 'Did somebody shite themselves?'

'Nothing so dramatic.' And she carries on with the mopping.

When it comes to lunch time, she thinks that she will do something that she hasn't done in years. She will go to visit Donal in work, surprise him. It doesn't matter if he is busy. She can wait around and they can get a coffee. She wants to talk to him, across a table, in a way that is sincere and open. She thinks about the first time she ever met Donal, at his friend's wedding. She was there because she used to go to school with the bride. They stayed up talking in the residents' bar and when they looked at the time it was three in the morning. When Mick comes to speak to her about an issue with two of the counsellors she says that she's going to work from home this afternoon. 'What's up with the counsellors?'

'They've fallen out.'

'Over what? Well, I'll let you deal with it,' she says. 'Bang their heads together.'

She parks her car in the multi-storey, which is only a short walk to the office where he works, housed in an old insurance building converted into multiple units. In the foyer, there is a centrepiece which looks like light sabres piled up like logs. The woman behind the desk asks her where she needs to go, and Bronagh says lightly, oh don't worry, I know my way. But it turns out that she doesn't because the lift only goes up one floor to a huge and pristine aesthetics clinic. When she comes down again she says she is looking for Taggart McCann.

'Oh, they have their own door. Around the corner. Next to Heaney Wealth Management.'

She says Heaney Wealth Management in the same matter of fact tone she might have used for B&M Bargains.

Taggart McCann has a logo like the Giant's Causeway, and in echo of this, the flooring in the reception is hexagonal. There are stylised pictures of some of their projects: an airport, a pipeline, a tunnel. Where was the pipeline? Slovenia? She remembers his trips there. He brought back one time a jar of honey which had, predictably, oozed out; they'd had to throw away the suitcase afterwards. Bronagh takes a seat because there is no one in reception. She arranges herself neatly. She notices that her shoes, pale suede, have a waterline round them from the mopping. Oh well. She can buy another pair. A man and woman appear, laughing about something. 'Takes one to know one!' the woman says. When they notice Bronagh, she says that she is here to speak to Donal Farrell.

'Oh, Donny's not here,' the man says, who Bronagh notices is wearing a suit that is much too tight. 'Donny's always in the other office out at Ballyclare on a Friday afternoon.'

'Oh yeah always,' the woman says. 'That's where Donny is on a Friday.'

When she goes back to the car park, she wonders if she wasn't listening when Donal told her about these afternoons in Ballyclare. But what did it matter really? Donal has never been office-bound; he has always been off at various sites. There's nothing strange about that. However, Bronagh thinks as she pays for the less than an hour she has been there, what is strange is Donny. That is the issue. That is very much the issue. She's never called him that and she cannot recall, past or present, anyone else who has. He was always Donal to his parents. Donny sounds young. Donny sounds like a pop star. Donny sounds like someone getting up off his high stool on the key change. She has never known this Donny. Donny Osmond. Donny Hathaway. Donny Farrell.

She decides to go to the big supermarket to get something for the tea. They usually have a takeaway on a Friday night, but tonight she thinks it should be something simple and wholesome. Possibly an Irish stew, but with excellent ingredients. Irish Stew Luxe. The three of them will sit down and yes, Lyness might head out afterwards to some bar, but they would sit and talk about their day. They will be serene and relaxed. She had been taken to the Irish Club in London once. She had thought it was going to be like a GAA club, but it was in Connaught Square and they served the Irish stew with pearl barley, which was a nice touch. Which aisle held the pearl barley?

Donny. What's with the Donny?

When it comes to the checkout, there are people in splashy yellow and red t-shirts doing a bag pack. They pounce on her items. 'Hello, Bronagh!' someone says. It's the mother of one of the boys who was in the car when they all had that crash. And there isn't the boy himself standing beside his mother and right this minute putting Bronagh's bottle of wine into the bag.

'Nathan is part of a team,' the mother says. 'They're going to Tanzania. They're building a school. This is our second fundraiser. We were at Tesco last week. Made a few hundred pounds.'

'That's wonderful,' Bronagh says. 'Well done to you.'

This is where there is the space for her, in time-honoured quid pro quo, to say a sentence about Lyness. It could be trivial and it would not even matter particularly if it wasn't true. All that is necessary is to say something, anything, with a deprecating or earnest or slightly peeved tone. But nothing – she opens her mouth and closes it again, knowing that there is nothing she wants to articulate. Bronagh looks at the coins in the bucket, the dullness of them, the few crumpled notes. She cannot find her card wallet in her bag and the girl at the checkout smiles kindly when she says that she will have it in just a minute. She hasn't got any coins, only a five-pound note, and she gives it to Nathan's mother, who gives it to Nathan, who puts it in the bucket.

When she gets to the car, she sees that she has a text message from an unfamiliar number and immediately she thinks, Patrick from the plane. He has managed to find her! Now that was a true conversation. And he has found her. But when she clicks on it, there is a message from a TV production company who need to interview some kids for a documentary. Ethnically diverse, if poss. She doesn't reply.

Sitting in the car park, she wonders why she hadn't told Patrick on the plane about Johnny Anderson. He would have said something sensible, if there was anything sensible to be said about a boy dying alone. She starts the engine and then switches it off. She calls Donal but after a couple of rings it goes to voicemail. She pauses at the end of his voice, affable, apologetic, saying he'll get back to you soon. 'Donny,' she says, trying to make a joke of it. And then Donny. Donny, her voice unexpectedly breaking. Donny. Donal Donny Donal. And then she presses end call.

Brown the meat, first of all, she thinks, on the journey home. Just consider methodically what you are going to do. Brown the meat and then put it aside, or should she have started with the barley? Alright, begin with the barley and then brown the meat, but what should the vegetables be doing at this point? So maybe chop the vegetables, then do the barley and then brown the meat. She will have a shower when she gets in, before she starts to cook. She will have a shower and change into something comfortable and sit, looking at something utterly and beautifully banal like the Boden catalogue. She will look at those smiling, healthy faces and lithe bodies and she will order a stripy jumper, like a superannuated member of the Velvet Underground. And she will sit down at the table with a glass of wine, knowing that, cooking on the stove, there is a sublime version of stew and that, winging its way, is a cashmere black and white sweater, worn by wholesome people who know what they are doing. In fact, she will order it right now. She will pull over and go on the website and buy one. She purchases a Catriona Cotton Crew, in black and white. The woman is fresh-faced with a chin-length bob, her nose wrinkling prettily as she smiles at some joke. OK, so OK.

When Bronagh opens the front door she can tell immediately that Lyness is playing one of his games. 'Lift the rifle!' he is shouting. 'Ah I told you to lift the rifle, you absolute useless cunt, you fucking dick, you should have lifted the rifle!' The late sunlight cuts into the kitchen, showing the smears on the windows from where they had been cleaned. She puts the bag of stew ingredients on the table and moves the milk that has been sitting in sunlight to the fridge. There's a brown paper bag with a receipt stapled to it. Lyness's lunch, it would seem. The takeaway box is on the worktop beside a poetry book. It's Rainer Maria Rilke. A particularly vibrant person at a party once recommended it and so she had duly bought it. She lifts it up and puts it down. Its shininess had obviously made it good for rolling a joint.

Eventually Lyness comes down the stairs in jogging bottoms and no top. She looks at his skin, still like a child's, a little flabby around his middle.

'What's for tea, Mum?' he asks.

She points to the bag on the table.

'You should have put all that in the bin,' she says, indicating the bags from the takeaway delivery.

'Alright, chill,' he says.

He gets the orange juice from the fridge and drinks it from the bottle.

'So, what time will we be eating tea because I want to meet the guys at nine.'

'I don't know,' she says. 'Put that stuff in the bin please.'
'We're going to a party in Ladyhill. Andy Bryson's gaff.'
'Oh, are you?'
'Yeah, that is the plan.'
'Put that stuff in the bin.'

Lyness crumples up the brown paper bag and, playfully, throws it at her.

'Good shot!' he laughs when it hits her squarely in the middle of the forehead.

She picks it up and throws it back at him.

'Missed!' he says, when it falls at his feet. 'Andy Bryson's gaff in Ladyhill, so what time is tea, Mother dear?'

She sees the vase then. Bronagh throws it, the flowers flying out in a spectacle of pink. The glass just misses his head before shattering on the wall tiles. Incredulous, he doesn't move to avoid her clenched fist hitting him full in the face, Bronagh's knuckles splitting with the impact.

'Mum!' he says, doubled over.

'Mum, stop it!' he says as she hits him again and again. He doesn't fight back.

'Mum! Stop it!' He doesn't try to catch her wrists but curls into a ball on the floor, crying, 'Stop, Mum! Please! I'm sorry!'

His blood is on her hands and when she kicks him she curses the softness of those suede pumps. Her baby, so longed for, that tiny scrap in an incubator, fighting for life, Bronagh, praying, willing the tiny soul to have courage because he was so loved. She kicks again and again in his face. He has his hands over his eyes. 'Mum, please!'

There used to be a guy worked here who talked everything up big time. Loved a bit of drama. He used to call this place Dante's Inferno. When it got to the busiest part of the night he would shout, Prepare to enter the ninth circle of hell! People are five, six deep at the bar, trying to get our attention, mouthing their orders. I ignore some people if they're rude, like the one the other night who stuck his hand in the air and repeatedly snapped his fingers. I looked it up one time, the ninth circle of hell, and turns out it is for those who have committed the crimes of treachery and betrayal. The ninth circle of hell is in fact a frozen lake with a crumbling ice bridge. Even Satan himself is stuck waist deep in ice. So wasn't that guy full of shit when it came to fourteenth-century poetic references because all of that is nothing like a hot, packed bar playing techno.

There is a new café near Miriam and the boys. She liked their page online. It's run by a young man whose father was one of the first people Kahlil supplied. She has suggested to Rami that they go to it, maybe for breakfast. It's early days. There won't be too many people there because they are still trying to establish themselves, she tells him. Miriam shares a little message online wishing the young man and the café good luck. It is liked by the café and someone with the profile picture of a castle. Miriam a day later shares a post about cuts in library services. Again, it is liked by the castle. Next comes a message request. And then the message, Hi, I hope you don't mind me getting in touch but I thought you might like to speak to me. Miriam ignores it. The castle comes back the next day with I think it would be really good to speak to you.

Well, Miriam doesn't want to speak. It would not be *really good*.

It isn't that she doesn't feel sorry for her. That day in the car park, she looked such a tiny little thing, embarrassed, younger than she had thought. But time, now the money has been paid, for everyone to draw a line, move on, have closure and one hundred other clichés. Things have been improving. She is going to go back to work. She has had a conversation with her boss about it. And Rami seems to be in better form – almost cheerful. Unexpected! She makes a list each day for what he needs to do: get up, get breakfast, have a shower, go for a walk, go to the gym, help Haady with maths for half an hour, see friends. In the last few days, she has heard him playing FIFA. His curtains are open. There is the reassuring smell of Tom Ford. He has started to put on some of his favourite clothes again, that white sweatshirt that he got with his first pay check at the shop. She has never imagined Rami with a girlfriend. She supposes she has always thought of him with another young man. Kahlil could have adjusted to that, if it had been the case. She recalls when they were in Italy and those two guys checked him out. He was pleased. What can I say, Miriam? You got yourself a good-looking guy.

A message comes from the castle yet again to say that they would really like to meet. I don't think, Miriam replies, it would be a good idea. Best wishes sounds too upbeat so she signs off, wishing you well, Miriam. It comes back, I just want to explain what happened. Miriam has no desire for more details about what happened. I'm sorry, she types, but at this stage and with everything that has happened it might be best not to. She wonders if the girl is contacting the other two, Bronagh and Frankie, as well. Surely she isn't just focusing on her. It was bizarre when that woman started singing. That lone voice. On the way back she and the other mothers didn't speak, having nothing to say. She hopes she never has to encounter them again. Glamorous, sad Frankie. Castle wants to meet in a place called the Movie Café. I just wanted to explain about why I was in the car that night.

Miriam sits on a red velvet cinema seat below a picture of Humphrey Bogart and Lauren Bacall. The waiter says they don't have a drinks licence yet, so she has a cup of tea as she stares at Bogart and Bacall's drinks. Her hands are shaking. The person is late. The person who has asked for this meeting in the midst of this shabby memorabilia has decided not to turn up. Miriam stares at the picture of Jayne Mansfield, oozing out of a satin dress. Everyone can look like a movie star nowadays, if they want. Call into a pound shop and you'll be served by someone who could be a B-movie star with the false eyelashes and the pout. 'I think you should go,' Martha had said when she told her. 'Because I think you will find that there was never anything to worry about.' She's not so sure. And it is still an option to leave. Miriam looks at the door, swagged with velvet.

'Hi, sorry I'm late,' a girl says, sitting down. She's dressed in baggy overalls, the sleeves rolled up, her arms covered in whimsical tattoos. The waiter comes over and she orders an apple juice.

'Sorry I'm late,' she says again.

Miriam loves what this girl looks like. She loves it.

'Don't worry,' Miriam says. 'But I don't know your name.'

'Holly,' she says. 'I'm Holly.'

'Holly,' says Miriam. 'Well, thank you for getting in touch.'

'I don't live with my mum and dad anymore,' Holly says. 'Like, we haven't fallen out or anything but I live now with Lou. She said it was a good idea to contact you, which is kinda funny because my mum and dad always said that I shouldn't. That I should keep out of it.'

'I see,' Miriam says.

'Do you like true crime?'

'Not particularly.'

'Well, me and Lou watch true crime a lot, read it too, although we debate the ethics of it. You know, looking forward to sitting down with a biscuit and a cup of tea to watch a programme about a woman being raped and murdered.'

'Sure thing. I get the concept of ethics.'

'Well, there was this one that we watched and it was about these two guys that were killed. Two of them. They were shot in the woods and then the killer departed. It was the 1980s. But there was this little kid who came along. Oh, merci beaucoup!' she says to the waiter who has brought the apple juice.

Miriam wonders how Kahlil could have tolerated this person in his car for even five minutes.

'But there was this little kid who came along. One guy was dead but the other one wasn't and his dying words were delivered to this little kid. But the kid was mute and so he couldn't tell anyone. Like, he couldn't verbalise it! But what he did was draw pictures of what the guy said. These really detailed pictures. Anyway, it was eventually all discovered and these drawings became, like, sacred texts for the family, and revealed important things to them.'

She takes a gulp of the apple juice. Miriam looks down at Holly's canvas tote bag which has an approximation of a woman's body on it.

'So, what have you got for me in there then? Some drawings you've done?'

'No, what happened was that after we watched the programme about this case, Lou said, my god, this is actually really like what happened with you and that guy and the car crash and so you must, you really must get in contact with the family.'

Miriam leans forward. 'What did he say? Tell me.'

'Well, the thing is, he didn't really say anything. Here's what happened. I'd not been working there that long and so I was kind of useless, shit at it all. I'd made loads of mistakes with orders that night and so I thought I am going to get the sack but I really needed it as a part-time job. At the end of the night there was a flood. Don't know how it happened, but the thing was that I offered to help clean up to try to get into the good books because I thought I would be able to get a lift home with Kev Gilmore. But anyway, the manager ended up ringing Kahlil, because he didn't know what to do, and then well there was just water everywhere and your husband was there and the manager. Kev Gilmore had had to go and so I thought I would get a taxi, it was real late, the last bus had gone, and when I rang for a taxi they said it was going to be half an hour. And so Kahlil said, your husband said, I'll give you a lift. Where is it that you need to go? And I just thought, oh brilliant, because I didn't even have the money for a taxi. I would have had to run in and woken my mum and dad up to try to get the money from them.'

I'll give you a lift. Where is it that you need to go? She can hear him say that.

'So,' Holly says, 'I got into the car with him and I'd never actually been in a car with a man other than my dad before. So it felt a bit strange but not creepy. He didn't really talk because he seemed kind of tired. And that was fine because I didn't know what to say. I had already said thank you a few times. And I didn't know whether to call him Kahlil or Mr Abdel Salam or what. He just seemed tired. And then there was a really bright light and I felt the car turn upside down. I don't remember from then until I was in the ambulance. I still have a bad shoulder,' she adds. 'I have to get physio.'

I'll give you a lift. Where is it that you need to go?

Holly scratches her arm and sighs. 'The thing is,' she says, 'I wondered if I should have come here and told you all kinds of things like that wee boy's pictures, you know that he was saying, at the final moments, how he loved you and how amazing and incredible you were and then, when I said that to Lou, she said, no just tell the truth.'

'Good advice.'

'But I'm sure he loved you and thought you were amazing and incredible.'

'We thought that about each other.'

'I was wondering,' Holly says carefully, 'I was wondering if you thought I should write about this. I have been doing a course in non-fiction. Although obviously the two genres, fiction and non-fiction are often porous.'

Holly pauses, as though waiting for a challenge on this matter.

'That's what the tutor says,' she adds.

'Potentially nothing anyone says of their own experience is objectively true.'

'So,' Holly continues, 'could I have your permission to write about this? Hopefully for publication in a literary journal. The car journey and the hospital and meeting you. Would you have a photo of you and Mr Abdel Salam that I could use? Like a hi-res image. It would be good if it was a hi-res image.'

Miriam looks through her photos on her phone: the two of them having a meal somewhere, them on a beach, Kahlil and the boys in their new blazers, the shoulders so square. There's Kahlil in that expensive tracksuit he liked so much.

'I'll need to choose one,' Miriam says. 'But I'll find you something.'

'So do I have your permission?'

'You do. I'm grateful to have met you.'

'Oh, right cool, well let's get a photo of you and me together,' Holly says. She inclines her head towards Miriam, extends her arm. 'Smile!' she says.

I'll give you a lift. Where do you need to go?

It's hard to hear anything other than that, even in this bar with its tables of laughing, shouting people, music booming from the speakers even in the middle of the afternoon. I'll give you a lift. Where do you need to go? She hadn't ever doubted Kahlil, not really. What he must have thought of that dopey girl. Although she also thanks god for Holly. He was tired and quiet. He just wanted to get home. He wanted to turn on that shower full blast, the way he did, full heat. The room was always so steamy after he had been in. He just wanted to have his shower and then tumble into bed after he had said goodnight to the boys. He went into each of their rooms and kissed them, even when they were asleep. He never stopped doing that even when they were older. Miriam would be warm in the bed and even when she was half asleep she would be reaching out and wrapping herself around him. It's so sad. She looks at a couple, sitting at a table under a big screen showing a silent movie. Don't start crying. I'll give you a lift. Where do you need to go?

At JPX, when she goes up the escalator, she sees that there is now a great pyramid of footballs in rainbow colours. It was a grand love; there was nothing tawdry or petty about it. It was epic. The mannequins have been moved towards the back. She is standing in front of one that is wearing a black tracksuit. The angle of the hips, the way the hands are resting. The other two are in pale blue and black. Her hand rests lightly on the arm in black nylon and then she touches the leg, just gently. She looks up at the smooth and eyeless face that seems to be saying, Miriam, you fool, you total fool. How could you ever have thought?! I'm just going to have a shower here. Can you kiss the boys for me?

'Can I help?' a young assistant says.

'No.' She moves away from the mannequin.

'Anything you're looking for would be over there,' he says, pointing at the rails of blue and black tracksuits. 'All the sizes should be there.'

'No problem. Thank you.'
She buys two tracksuits, one for each of the boys.

When Miriam gets back to the house, she calls her mother to ask if they would like to come around for something to eat. Short notice, so just a few things thrown together, but it would be lovely to see them. Her mother sounds pleased at the invitation but she says that it'll just be her. Miriam's dad is tired. A haircut. A colour. That's what Miriam will book. She'll go to that very efficient place where they can do it all in an hour and a half. When Haady comes downstairs he asks if she can give him ten pounds because he wants to go into town with friends. 'Sure,' she says, 'but don't be too late because we have Granny coming round. Shout up to Rami and see if he wants a cup of coffee, would you?'

'Rami's not in,' he says. 'He went out a while ago.'

'Oh,' she says. 'Well, good! Where's he away to?'

'Don't know. Didn't ask.'

When Miriam goes to his room, the bed is neatly made and the window open. She puts the tracksuit on his bed. Sitting on the desk is his phone, his headphones and his bank cards in that strange little wallet that cost him so much. She looks around to see if there is a plate or a cup that needs to be taken downstairs, but there is nothing. All is pristine.

When Miriam's mother arrives, she comes with a pavlova. 'I know you did say to bring nothing, but this is just a little something! There's also some soup if you want it.' She puts a plastic tub in the fridge.

'Rami's not here, Mum,' she says.

'No? Out with friends I suppose.'

'I don't know. I'm wondering if I should be worried.'

'No, why should you be? He's eighteen. He should be out and about. I mean, even allowing for all of that business. Now, what do you need me to do? Peel potatoes? Chop something?'

'He's left his phone. And his wallet.'

'Miriam, stop. Let me tell you all about Martha's new house. She sent me some photographs. Look. What a beautiful place.'

When Haady has returned from the cinema, they sit down to have the meal. There are two empty seats. Her mother says grace. Miriam doesn't bow her head and Haady does a gang sign at her. She smiles back.

'I wish Rami had taken his phone,' Miriam says, as they eat.

'People can survive without them,' her mother replies.

'I think it's weird he didn't take his phone. Or his bank cards.'

She stays up most of the night, waiting. She sends Holly two photos of Kahlil. He is in the back garden in one. In the other, he and she are in a restaurant, where someone came round with a polaroid camera and a bucket of roses. It was extortionate. Kahlil is beaming at the camera whereas Miriam is looking off to the left, as though the whole affair is silly. The rose is on the table. There's a noise at two in the morning and she jumps up, thinking it is him, but it is a taxi, stopping at the wrong house. He is still not there by the next afternoon. She sits on his bed, staring at the bank cards and the phone.

I really like my work. Psychiatric nursing. Got a lot to do with the fact that I rate Gemma big time. I'd never worked with someone like her in charge. She made it clear from the beginning about how she expected us to operate: no bitching, no back-stabbing. When she gave her first unit briefing, she said at the end that we got to carry each other. Under my breath I went, oh for God's sake, because at that point I wasn't yet convinced by Gemma, and this was how she was getting on, coming out with a line from a U2 song. It just seemed cringey as fuck. But we do got to carry each other, in the end, really.

I was in a bar with Martine. She doesn't get out all of that much because of the responsibilities she happens to have at home, so we were having cocktails. Anyway, some guys at the next table got up to leave and I saw that one of them was Daniel, somebody I was seeing a couple of years ago. Who you looking at, Jonathan? Martine said. Oh, just one of those guys just leaving. I used to know one of them, Well actually, I said, we went out for a few months. We went on a trip to Rome together.

He was quite a nice guy, although a bit too serious for my liking. He'd done a degree as a mature student – is twenty-five considered mature? – and then he'd done some kind of further study. Did he not want to party in Rome in the Via San Giovanni? Martine asked. Well, I said, not really. It wasn't his thing. We actually ended up going to an old graveyard, believe it or not. The place was crawling with cats. It was all very intense. He wanted to see where somebody he had studied for the last few years was buried. I mean, this was some old guy from centuries ago, some little old man who was a hunchback and who was thrown in a prison. And Daniel picked a flower and put it on the grave. He knelt down in front of it. Which was kind of sweet. He knelt down, just looking at the grave. But it wasn't ever going to work out between us. We didn't have much in common. Sounds like Antonio Gramsci, Martine said. Sounds like you were actually at the grave of Antonio Gramsci. Well, whatever, I said. Who's for another drink?

I didn't want another of those rum-based ones.

They fly to Burgas airport. At Hotel Thracia Palace, they'll have three adjoining Lagoon suites, Gen and Misty; Nan D and Boogie; and then Leigh, little Ewan and Farrah. The transfer takes one hour from the airport and it's evening by the time they get to the hotel. They're the only people on the connecting coach to get off at this hotel; the rest must journey onward to less impressive locations. 'Wow,' Gen says. 'It looks like a massive puzzle. So many bits.' And so it does, with its series of pristine oblong blocks placed in irregular formation, its azure pools.

'Misty, what a place,' Boogie marvels. 'I didn't think it was going to be this kind of set-up! I thought it was going to be some poky wee two-star.'

'Cancellation,' Misty says.

They're greeted by smiling receptionists who give them a welcome drink and then they go to look at the rooms: Gen and Misty have the best view because it is at the corner of a cube and so has two sets of windows. Nan D and Boogie have a double bed with a canopy. When Leigh, Farrah and Ewan arrive, later, from Glasgow, Ewan manages to open the connecting doors between the suites and begins running through them, until Nan D locks everything down and puts the keys in a drawer. In the late evening, the hotel glows golden with all of the lights.

In the morning, doesn't the universe seem bright and fresh? The hotel is large enough that they don't need to see each other all of the time. The next day everyone goes down for breakfast at different times. Later, Farrah and Leigh take turns going to the gym and for a run along the beach. Nan D reads a magazine on the terrace, Boogie sits on a sun lounger beside the pool. Geneva and Misty go for a swim and then sunbathe on the beach. They all agree to meet in the evening for a meal in the grand restaurant. Everyone is varying degrees of pink. Boogie thinks, when all the drinks are poured, that there should be a toast of thank you to Misty. But then he thinks, maybe not.

The next day after breakfast, Gen says to Boogie that she wants to go on a tour of a Thracian tomb. It's leaving at twelve noon. She picked up a leaflet about it at the reception desk. 'You go down a corridor,' she says, 'and then you go into the main chamber. The main chamber is a place,' she says, 'where light and darkness meet. There's a wee minibus that takes you to it.'

'What do you actually get to see?' Misty asks. 'Mummies and embalmed people?'

'Leaflet says absolutely nothing about that. Leaflet just says it's a tomb.'

'I'll give it a miss.'

'There's this other thing as well. A Byzantine tour of the area.'

'Gonna give that a miss too.'

Gen goes to the Thracian tomb with Farrah, the only person who is interested. As they walk round the ruins, Farrah asks gently if her sister is alright.

'Yeah, she's fine. I was the one who went to the police station with her, originally.'

'You're a good person to have around.'

'Look at that stone,' Gen says. 'Look at the carving on it.'

* * *

Over dinner, Leigh is sulky because she was left on her own with Ewan most of the day when Farrah and Geneva were at the tomb.

'And?' Nan D says. 'He is your son. I don't think anyone should feel they are being short-changed because they have to look after their own fucking kid.'

'I'd appreciate it,' Leigh says, 'if you didn't use language like that around Ewan.' She covered his ears with her hands. 'He's not used to that kind of thing.'

'Oh, shut your face, you complete numpty.'

'Ladies, please,' says Boogie. 'Could we all chill?'

In the hotel complex there are two nightclubs called Plazma and Horizon. Horizon is where Farrah and Leigh go, with Gen babysitting. They get talking to a Turkish couple who are Galatasaray supporters and they start spending time with them. Plazma is for younger people and goes on into the early hours of the morning. There are some young people around the hotel, a group of German girls and three brothers from Limerick who are there with their parents. These guys are always showing off in the pool, doing somersaults. One keeps on his t-shirt because he is now so sunburnt, his neck the colour of his hair. In the couple of evenings that they have been in the restaurant, they have all dressed in the same white shirts and black shorts. Misty has noticed how the boys are always polite to everyone in the restaurant. Misty looks around the tables and sees the guy who is a bit like she used to be, running around and doing the things that no one else wanted to do. And so, when the one who always wears the t-shirt asks her if she would like to go the club, The Plazma, he calls it, she doesn't immediately say no. There's a group of us, he says, and then he lists names, people that are probably his brothers and the German girls. She wonders if she should, but she decides, with a sad shake of her head, no. 'But thanks,' she says.

'Another night then?'

'Maybe another night.'

She looks at this boy with the tattoo of a horse's head on his arm, the silver necklace on the sunburnt skin.

'Thanks anyway. Thanks for asking.'

Misty's lying on her bed when a message comes up on her phone. It's from Mrs McCullough. Just to let you know, it says, that you are the successful candidate.

'I got a job!' she says to Gen, who is tonging her hair.

'Doing what?'

And then there is another message. When are you available to start? Well done, Misty. We are so pleased you are going to come and work with us.

Mrs McCullough has signed it Mrs McC x.

'Funeral parlour.'

'The what?'

'The funeral place. I want to go and tell Boogie.'

'I need to go home,' Misty says.

Boogie's on the balcony, eyes closed, feet up on the white railings, a beer in one hand.

'The end of the week isn't too far off. Unfortunately.'

'No, I want to go home. I'm not saying that anyone else needs to. You guys stay on. But I've actually got a job I need to start.'

'What you on about?' He puts down his beer, looks at her.

'The woman's just contacted. From McCullough's. The funeral place.'

'You're on a holiday. Nobody is ever going to expect someone to cut short their fucking trip so that they can start a job. That's plain ridiculous. Just tell them you're in another country at present and you'll start when you get back! Anyway, jeez, is that not going to be a bit depressing? Working in a funeral place? Are you sure?'

'Not really. You live. You die. That's life.'

'Yes for sure, but I just don't want to be reminded of it every hour of the working day. And anyway, you're not just going to be involved with a bunch of old timers, had a good innings, etcetera etcetera, par for the course, it'll be loads of tragedies and little kids and suicides.'

'I like the woman. I've had enough of it here.'

'But she won't care if you wait till the end of the week!'

'I just want to go home. I want to get started.'

He said that if she was going home then he was too. Nan D and Gen were sorry they were going, but pleased to get the rooms to themselves for a few days. Charter flights were only on Fridays, so they had to speak to the representative from the travel company, a young man called Dylan who was very proud of his belt. He kept touching it as he talked about the possibility of getting a taxi and bus to another airport where there would be a flight before Friday. Eventually, he came up with a plan to travel to Varna and then London, where they would then get the connecting flight to Belfast. Dylan was keen to have more information. Why was it all so urgent? Had something awful happened?

'Like your belt,' Misty said.

'It's Hermès,' he replied. 'People think it's a fake but it's not.'

Farrah, Leigh and the couple from Turkey had organised a football match involving lots of kids in the hotel. Leigh was sorry that Misty was going to miss it. She gave her a hug and said that it was the best holiday she had ever been on in her life. As the taxi pulled away from the hotel, Farrah had her hand on Ewan's shoulder as the two of them waved Boogie and Misty off.

The house, when they get home, seems cramped and dark. Shabby. Since when was there that smell of damp? Funny how easy it is to become accustomed to shiny floors and huge rooms, to triangular flower arrangements and fresh towels. All here is tired. There seems to be piles of stuff everywhere: a soft tower of unfolded washing on the sofa. And so many textures of cushions and rugs and wallpaper.

'I'll go to the shop and get us a loaf,' Boogie says. 'You hungry?'

'A bit.'

'Maybe we should just get a takeaway. So, what's your outfit? Do they give you a uniform?'

'I think maybe the woman is going to have an outfit for me tomorrow. But I've got something that I can wear.'

'Well, give it to me and I'll wash it for you, give it an iron. Get it decent looking.'

'Would you? Thanks, Boogie.'

'You should get to bed real early. It's tiring, all of this jet-setting.'

'I know. Funny to think,' Misty says, 'that we were sitting in the sun only this morning.'

Later, Misty is having a bath and Boogie shouts up to her, 'What shoes are you wanting to wear?'

'Black ones. With little heels. Do you know the ones I mean? They're under the stairs. Think that's where they are, Boogie. The ones with the little heels.'

He goes to look and finds them, eventually, at the back of the cupboard, behind a jumble of old towels and a fluorescent swimming bag. There's also, rammed in the small space, three bags of coats, too small, that he had intended to drop off at the charity shop. They're on top of an old portable TV, its back bulbous. He will give them a polish, the ones that she wants. Bit of a clean and they'll look fine.

Boogie presses the skirt, placing a tea towel over it so there's not an over-ironed sheen. Never looks good that. Nan D had shown him that tea towel trick at some point, or his own mother, maybe. The blouse he irons at a hotter temperature, manoeuvring the shoulder over the soft point of the ironing board. Boogie stares at the weave, its cross-hatching. Then he takes the little ribbon, lays it straight, runs the iron up and down it. All ready for tomorrow.

Misty, out of the bath, is in her pyjamas and the dressing gown that Boogie brought back from the supermarket. She's wondering, as she sits on her bed, about who she might meet tomorrow – maybe some sad person, dreading, right this minute, opening the door of the funeral place. But, know what, she'll be sitting there, wearing that blouse and her voice, when she speaks, will be calm. They'll know to trust her. Misty sets the alarm for half past seven, but then changes it to twenty minutes earlier. She doesn't want to be late for Mrs McCullough.

Acknowledgements

I'd like to thank everyone at Sceptre, particularly Ansa Khan Khattak and Nico Parfitt. It's been such an utter pleasure to work with you. I'm also so grateful to Lucy Luck, Katie Kennaway and Saida Azizova, plus everyone at Hachette Ireland. I'd like to acknowledge the support of the Arts Council of Northern Ireland, and also Queen's University Belfast, where I was Seamus Heaney Fellow in 2021/2022. Glenn Patterson deserves particular thanks.

If I've not written *The Benefactors* sitting at my kitchen table, it's been in one of these beloved spots: Belfast Central Library, the Linen Hall Library, Woodstock Library, Zentralbibliothek Zürich, the Mitchell Library, Glasgow, the Central Library, Liverpool and Central Library, Dublin. Thank you. Nowhere finer than a public library.

I want to register the helpfulness of the MSD manual relating to medical examination and sexual assault. And I'd like to thank the following people who, whether we were having a drink, coffee or email conversation, wittingly – or unwittingly – clarified something or made me think: Latifa Akay, Will Ashon, Joan Atkinson, Kate Briggs, Liam Cagney, Lucy Caldwell, Kevin Curran, Nikki Ditty, Adrian Duncan, Martin Durkan, Joy Gibson, Sonya Gildea, Jacqueline Gray, Chris Heaney, Judith Kimber, Tim MacGabhann, Paul McVeigh, Caroline Norris, Ben Pester, Niamh Reid, Kate Ross, Irvine Tait, Susan Tomaselli, David Torrans and Emma Warren.

I'd like to thank some wonderful pals who read, with enormous insight and generosity, early versions of the novel: John McBride, Jill Crawford, Emily Haire, David Keenan and Declan Meade. Thank you.

Two more groups of people are due my gratitude: all my work colleagues, especially Debbie, Andrew, Erin and Hannah. And then, the taxi drivers I use practically every day, particularly the old Cregagh Cabs/ East Belfast people.

Finally, here's to the brilliant Paul and Bobby Reid for putting up with me.